Praise for *Time Will Break the World*

"In *Time Will Break the World*, Aaron Jacobs presents a dynamic, kaleidoscopic portrait of a historic school bus kidnapping of nineteen children and its lasting effects on all the players, victims and perpetrators alike. This is an electric polyvocal novel, expertly told."
–Sara Lippmann, author of *LECH* and *Jerks*

"*Time Will Break the World* nails that sweet spot between page turner and page gripper. You get swept up in the harrowing story of the Brookwood bus children, their captors, and their community. But the sentences also stun you into not wanting to read on too quickly, so you can say them under your breath. Bear witness to how Jacobs makes fiction out of the absurd and the hurt of the real world."
–Gene Kwak, author of *Go Home, Ricky!*

"Aaron Jacobs' *Time Will Break the World*, inspired by a true story, will draw readers into a tense, well-written page turner. Break out the candles, you'll be up all night!"
–Rodman Philbrick, author of *Freak, the Mighty*

"Jacobs deftly weaves multiple characters and decades-apart settings. 1984 is brought vividly back from the present day but this is no nostalgia trip. This is a compelling, often disturbing story about young lives interrupted and never truly restarted, and how memory can be chosen or imposed, the bemusement of being both a child and an adult who has forgotten they ever were, let alone that ten-year-old victim of a life-defining trauma."
–Tom McCulloch, author of *The Accidental Recluse*

Editor: Krysta Winsheimer of Muse Retrospect

Book Design: Gary Anderson

Cover Photograph: Aaron Jacobs

Cover Design: Gary Anderson

ISBN: 979-8-9869930-2-7
Run Amok Crime, 2023
First Edition

Printed in the USA

TIME will BREAK the WORLd

AaRon JaCoBs

For Katie

ROBERTA

Even before my uncle lost his legs, I wanted nothing to do with our granite quarry. I thought the place was evil. Don't ask me where this feeling came from. Maybe the image of an immense, dark pit that men crawled in and out of just spooked me, or maybe the word quarry sounded too much like quarrel, which I knew was bad from my parents' *conversations*. This was at a time when being caught on the wrong side of the good-bad divide carried social, if not eternal, consequences, and it hurt more than my dad's pride to have his life's work rejected by his only daughter. Most of all, it confused him. Extracting stone from the earth was what Reillys did. Evil? The idea made no sense to him. I made no sense to him. When he came home at night, I would hide from him until he scrubbed his hands and face. No one told me he spent most days in an office on Fifth Avenue. On his desk at home he kept a framed photograph of himself, sporting denim coveralls and an apron, proudly dwarfed by a twelve-foot cutting saw blade. I was unaware the photo was taken when he was just nineteen, when he worked for my grandfather, a summer manning a sand blaster. I thought that was still his job. He played along, though, making a big dramatic production of rolling up his cuffs and removing his watch and wedding ring and lathering his hairy hands and forearms in the kitchen sink, as if he were a surgeon, while I peeked out of the accordion doors of the hall closet.

Uncle Fred was beer drunk when he piloted a dump truck overladen with rich, yellowish-brown granite off the road. That he survived the crash should have had me thinking positive thoughts about the quarry. This, at least, was my dad's opinion. I can admit now that he had a point. Then again, perhaps he shouldn't have saved the human bones he found on-site and exhibited them in a glass cabinet in the second-floor study like a collection of antique coins. It was obvious that displaying a fully intact mandible on a shelf eye level to my height at age six helped contribute to the chilly sense of doom I associated with his work. The bones belonged to the Indians who gave our business its name: Munsee Granite Company Inc.

I was eleven when Uncle Fred came to live with us. He had no wife and no children and now he had no legs from just above his knees down. He refused prosthetics, so my mother had his pants tailored to match his reduced inseam. It was 1944 and Fred regretted not enlisting after Pearl Harbor. If he'd left his legs in the Pacific, he said, he would have lived out his days as a hero. But there was no glory in his disfigurement. I thought my dad was the sweetest man in the world to let my uncle keep his job once he could no longer do it, but later I learned Fred had inherited an even share of the company when my grandfather died, and my dad had no say in his employment. They were equals on paper, and while my dad had always portrayed the intellect, and Fred the muscle, their roles were more complicated than that. A decade earlier, as my dad attended to the lingering death of their father, it was Fred who oversaw the delivery of 50,000 cu. ft. of granite for the ongoing construction of the Cathedral of St. John the Divine.

Like my dad, Fred did nothing to ease my fear of the quarry but, as I got older, only said that my feelings were wrong, and I had no basis for feeling them, and I needed to get ahold of whatever was bothering me because one day the business would be mine. I was about fourteen when he said this. We were in the living room and I was standing in front of where he sat on the davenport. I told him I didn't want the business. I would give it away. He said that was the stupidest thing he'd ever heard. If that were the case, I said, blinking back hot tears, my arms hugging my elbows, I would take all the black powder the company owned and blow up the quarry so there was nothing left. Fred reclined into the couch cushion, crossed one stump over the other, and considered my proposal. He was smiling when he said that was the stupidest thing he'd ever heard but wished he could be there to see it.

The Munsee people, whose bones my dad collected and kept in a glass cabinet, settled the Hudson Valley, along with the Mohican and Lenape, after migrating north and east during the melt of Ice Age glaciers. They cultivated the region for a thousand years before ever stumbling upon a European. They are gone now. So is our business that was named after them. I didn't need to blow it up. I just needed to wait long enough for my sons to come around.

THURSDAY, AUGUST 2, 1984

The kids—they were in a good mood, even the weirdos and rubberheads. A great mood, thrumming with joy and hope and fearlessness.

It was terrible.

Pat Earl was especially in tune with the frequency of their moods. Experience dictated that the happier they were, the worse his day would be. A great mood meant it took them forever to do anything, the supposedly bright kids no exception. Behind him, they squirmed on the scorching vinyl, while he wore out that old International diesel, barreling over the shadows of dogwood and beech lying wavy across Overland Avenue, trying to get through his route and make the first pitch of Eddie's travel league game and worrying he'd miss it due to these unquestioningly happy kids dicking around in the schoolyard after dismissal, delaying pickup.

Over the last few days he'd watched the emotional temperature of the school bus rise to combustible levels as they approached the end of summer school, making operating on anything close to a regular schedule simply out of the question. Pat Earl was approaching an end as well, that of his grandson's travel league baseball season. All week he'd witnessed the slow-moving collision of the undisciplined students with the one event he cared about, and now the impact was upon him—their happiness was making him late to Eddie's championship game.

He glanced up into the wide rearview mirror, from which he saw clear to the back of the bus. Nineteen on board that afternoon and everywhere he looked was mayhem.

Brenda and Emily Mashburn, the twins, ten, pushed their noses out the window for a breeze like a pair of sunburnt Labrador retrievers, waving to get the attention of other cars, and then aping monster faces at them. Seven-year-old Andy Kraven was in the aisle, doing a full-body reenactment of some movie he'd seen, something about ghosts, for the benefit of Kaito Watanabe, who watched Andy's spastic, spittle-flecked retelling with a captivated grin and wiped a sweat moustache from his upper lip with the sleeve of his Izod shirt. Toward the back of the bus, Jodie Hoffman and Lindsey Robinson were in an ear-shattering dispute over which of them would marry Matt Dillon. And, there in the last row, Martin Mendoza—at thirteen, one of the oldest passengers and the lone student not vibrating with uncontrollable glee—suffered like he did every day, as Lance "Doodoo" Viscuso hovered over him, feigning spitting on him, and running through a litany of nicknames.

"Fartin' Martin," Doodoo sang. "Hey Martian, hey, Marcia."

He cocked his fist and let it fly but reined it in just short of Martin's jaw. Martin stared straight ahead, simply living with the abuse as though he never considered an alternative.

"That's right, Fish Fucker. You little Fish Faggot."

Pat didn't know where the aquatic-centric slurs originated. He only wished Martin would crack Lance in the nose. Just once. He waited for it to happen, having decided he would look the other way, say he was minding the road and didn't see a thing.

"Linds, you might marry Matt Dillon or whatever, but Fish Faggot's going to marry Shamu," Doodoo said.

"Shamu is an orca. Orcas aren't fish," Martin said, merely expressing a fact.

"What the hell did you just say to me?" Doodoo said.

"Butts in the seats," Pat yelled, glaring into the mirror in a way that made it seem as if he was looking directly at each passenger and the reprimand was personal. Brenda and Emily dropped down at once, giggling nervously. Pat always pretended he couldn't tell them apart, but he knew Emily's face was longer than Brenda's, and that Brenda flashed a small scar on her chin, that Emily wore their light, thin hair in a braid held with a plastic clip, while Brenda's hair hung like cotton candy around her shoulders. They were still young enough to believe he possessed authority to punish them on par with their parents, teachers, police, and that made him like them. The older kids knew better. They knew his uniform retained only the faintest whiff of power, his threats were largely empty, and he was, ultimately, in *their* service.

He pushed the bus harder but backed off at the first sound of whining from the engine, riding the breeze through the open windows. The radiator fan belt, he assumed, was once again pin-holed and cracked. The last time the belt went on him was a late-January morning, still dark out, four blocks from Melanie Anderson's house, the first pickup of the day. Rather than calling in to dispatch for a tow truck, he unlooped his pants belt and fed it through the pulleys to restart the engine and finish his route. Bus #8, known by drivers and students alike as "Burnt Velveeta," was the oldest in the district fleet and Jeff, the dispatcher, assigned it to Pat because no one else would touch it. Jeff said it was impressive how he finessed Burnt V's salty temperament, her whims, her idiosyncrasies. But Jeff was a bullshitting fraud, thought Pat, terrified of confrontation with the other drivers. Pat told the students the 2x4 he carried was for beating the wild and rude, but it was for long uphill stretches, when the transmission popped out of gear. Whenever he reached the base of an ascent, he downshifted and wedged the block of wood between the floor and gearshift, pinning it in place.

"Please," he said, begging the fan belt to hold on, like it was a loved one in intensive care. If he broke down, he would never make the game. He let the bus coast downhill on Overland Avenue, positive that showing up even half an inning late could affect the outcome. If, however, he was on time, if he found his customary spot just off to the left of the backstop, still donning his uniform, chomping an unlit Garcia y Vega, and jawing with the home plate ump, whose job made him a captive audience ("Come on, Blue. Let's keep that strike zone true."), then whatever transpired on the field wouldn't be his fault. He would have done his part to support Eddie.

He leaned toward the window, listening for the fan belt. No whining sound came from under the hood, just the sweet odor of oil burning on the engine manifold, yet still he heard it. Turned out to be coming from inside his head. More than a whining, it was a melody, a slow stirring of strings and piano. Then he realized—the commercial, the campaign ad. *It's morning in America,* the narrator said over this tune Pat kept hearing. The commercial had been the last thing he saw before turning off the TV and joining Sally in bed. He was relieved it wasn't a faulty fan belt but also annoyed that the ad had burrowed its way into his subconscious. That it played throughout the broadcast of the Olympics probably had something to do with it. Simply too much red, white, and blue for one man to digest on a school night.

They rode over the bridge spanning Beavertail River. Pat turned right on Cherry Road, feeling some slight progress, with his first drop-off a half mile away. But he braked immediately. A Dodge cargo van, the color of pistachio ice cream, blocked the lane, hazards flashing. Pat stopped behind it. To their right was the gravel parking lot of Butler Reservoir. Would've made more sense for the van to coast into the lot than stall out in the middle of the street, the bus driver thought, and he marveled at the idiocy of the general population.

"Our feet are the same, Mr. Pat," Andy Kraven said, his curly brown hair always in his eyes and always looking a little damp. He had come to the front of the bus, his hand on the dashboard.

"Back behind the line. Go sit with Watanabe."

"His name is Switchblade. I'm Stingray. We're in a gang," Andy said.

"What is wrong with you, Kraven?"

Pat didn't know what to make of him. Normally, he would have felt an urge to protect a boy like that, so small, so vulnerable. But this kid was insensible. Depending on the day, he announced he was the world wrestling heavyweight champion, or a break dancer, or a Jedi knight, whatever that was. Today he was in a gang.

"Our feet are the same," he said again.

"*What?*" Pat said.

"That's how you say goodbye in Germany."

"You mean auf wiedersehen."

"That's what I just said."

"Are you a rubberhead? Get behind the line!"

A man's arm emerged from the van's window, sleeveless, hairless, sleek with sweat, a watch on its wrist. The arm made a swimming motion, as if encouraging the bus to go around. Pat turned the wheel and watched for oncoming traffic, but then realized the driver was calling him over, beckoning him. He could have fallen back on protocol, on regulation, if he wanted to. Never leave the students unattended. He might not have had the authority to punish them but he sure as shit was responsible if, God forbid, one of them got hurt on his watch.

The driver's arm swam faster in the glassy afternoon light. Pat couldn't just leave the guy sitting there. He checked the time and mentally measured the distance and traffic of his route against the scheduled first pitch of Eddie's game. It didn't look good that he would make it. He held on to his failsafe if he cut it too close—driving the bus straight to the game and returning it to the lot later. That wasn't protocol either, but what could Jeff do about it?

"Stay in your seats and keep it quiet," he said to the students, pulling the handle on the door and lumbering down the steps.

He wheezed into his fist, the humid, still air hard to breathe. He heard bedlam from inside the bus but ignored it.

"Hey, guy," he called, walking up to the van. "What's the problem?"

He noticed the gun before he saw the driver, the barrel resting on the open window. It was the same service pistol he carried in the war, Smith & Wesson M&P. He was too close to turn and run away, so he stood there, waiting, the gun a dark, toxic blur hanging at the bottom of his vision. He declined to acknowledge it, the way he might have politely avoided gawking at a physical deformity, a mangled or missing appendage, or third-degree burn scars.

"Hi," the driver said, a black pantyhose stocking on his head.

The stocking distorted the man's features, and Pat averted his eyes. He looked to a picture frame dangling from the rearview mirror. Empty of photographs, the rectangular piece of plastic twisted on its string when the driver shifted in the seat.

The driver told Pat to get in.

Pat said no.

"Sorry, but yes," the driver said.

"There are little kids. On the bus," Pat said.

"I hear you. Get in."

"Take my wallet."

"What for?"

"Who are you?"

"Just a Steel Town girl on a Saturday night looking for the fight of her life," the driver said.

"What?"

"You like that song?"

"I'm just a bus driver."

"You are. Get in."

"Just children. Don't."

"In the van, sir."

"Sir?"

"In."

He told him to get in on the passenger side. At the front of the van, Pat eyed the license plate, whispered the number, trying to memorize it, but he was nervous and started transposing digits and letters. He took in more details: the grill was laced with rust, the headlight covers were cloudy, the tires sat on white rims with black lug nuts, a crack in the windshield spiderwebbed along the glass, a long CB antenna was magneted to the roof. Pat was lifting the door handle when the cargo doors at the rear of the van squeaked open on dry hinges and another pantyhosed man jumped out carrying a shotgun, sprinting for the school bus.

"Children. Please," Pat said.

"In," the driver said, and cocked his pistol.

Pat got in.

Later that afternoon, Eddie Earl would trot from the Indian's bench to the pitcher's mound and hurl a complete game shutout, with seven strikeouts. Pat would see none of the game, nor watch his grandson be the first on his team to hoist the championship trophy over his head.

The driver started the van and shouted, "Citius, Altius, Fortius," revving the engine.

Burnt Velveeta flashed in the side mirror, rolling into the reservoir parking lot, down the hiking trail into the woods, and out of sight.

When I was twelve, our mother, Roberta—Bertie—one day removed the locks on the bedroom doors. "Schotts keep no secrets," she said. She really said that, said those words as if they were true or as if saying them could make them true, as if they weren't just the strange boast of a strange woman. With the locks gone, Jason and I on occasion interrupted each other strumming an energetic rhythm on our pink cocks. I could never defer to him after that, sweaty perv that he was, and vice versa, so there was never a clear leader between us. I pulled rank when needed because I was twenty months older and could kick his doughy ass.

Then we grew up. High school a half-decade in the rearview and not one higher degree earned between us, though our names were known to the bursars at a smattering of private East Coast colleges. The time had come to go into business for ourselves, we decided. Jobs awaited us at Munsee Granite, but we took after our mom in our refusal to work the quarry. Our father, George, had come to the family business through marriage, so he never saw our legacy as anything but the great opportunity it was for him. He wanted it for us. We had no time for what he wanted. We dreamed of real estate and we dreamed of movies. We dreamed of moguldom. Jason and I believed in inevitability. The world would give itself over to us like an open bank vault. We were positive of this. I can't say if our father loved us, but I know he didn't like us. He had a great reason for not liking us. We were total shitheads. Our expected success would deodorize our bad personalities when the time came, we thought. Whenever we were together, George asked how in the name of our skinny, bearded Lord could we be his sons.

"Arrogant failures," he said, describing us.

"I wouldn't call us failures, per se. That would imply we tried at something," I said, egging him on.

"He's got you there, Father," Jay said, pronouncing it *fah-thah*, like we were blue bloods.

"You know, talking to you two is like talking to potatoes. But with potatoes I can always melt cheese on them and eat them," he said, and skulked off to fetch Bertie, the two of them huddled over the kitchen sink, guzzling jug wine out of Steuben stemware.

He could have called us pouty mediocrities and been on the money. At any rate, we rarely saw him, or our mom, and ignored their sniping when we did. We slept days and passed long, twitchy nights in my Cutlass, driving for hours, sometimes passing the quarry twenty miles away, with its imposing front gate and tall surrounding fences, pondering the only question of significance: where to start our empire.

The answer to that naïve question put us in a bad situation, and trying to get out of the bad situation was what got us into the school bus thing, insofar as actions have consequences. Thirty years later, I'm still not so sure. Inevitability was what my brother and I believed in, to an almost religious degree, and perhaps there was something unavoidable about these events for us. But, as I've learned in various offender rehabilitation programs, what they keep drilling into me, is it's not about *us*, me and Jay, or the Schotts and Reillys and the quarry, but the *victims*. Start with the victims, twenty of them, not a small number to begin with, then add their families, and their friends, the school district and the rest of the community, the neighboring communities, the police department and the FBI, and even Vice President George Bush, and pretty soon you start to see the incredible magnitude one vanished school bus had on so many lives.

Vanished was what they called it in town, as in without a trace, but that word came hours later, retrofitted onto the event during a time when they were still without answers but at last too impatient to wait and see. Even if giving it a name didn't explain what happened, or why, it was a step in the right direction, for how could anyone hope to get to the bottom of a situation so mystifying or rare as to be nameless? But again, vanished came later. In the absence of an earth-splitting cataclysm, like a natural disaster, where it was obvious from the start it would take a long time, if ever, to get back to normal, here on a cloudless August afternoon, on the second to last day of summer school, a bus carrying nineteen students, with Pat Earl behind the wheel, went missing. And for a few hours, nobody realized what was going on.

THURSDAY, AUGUST 2, 1984

Jason crouched in the back of the van against the carpeted wall, pantyhose bunched up on his forehead, shotgun in his lap. The shells were in his pocket. He wouldn't bring a loaded gun on the bus, and he didn't give one-and-one-half shits what Calvin had to say about it. They had blacked out the rear windows with Krylon, and a thin line of daylight peeking between the cargo doors was the only illumination. His AC/DC T-shirt was translucent with sweat, his jeans gummed to his legs, his fingertips wrinkled under latex painting gloves. He could smell himself—ass, feet, armpits, breath. His mouth felt gluey, his tongue enflamed, and he spat dryly on the floor. He waited for the sound of the bus driver getting in. That was the signal to move. He heard the guy and Cal talking, both calm sounding, like they were exchanging directions to the nearest gas station. Then he heard the door open. He yanked the stocking down over his face and busted out of the van without thinking, sunlight washing out all color and stinging his eyes until they adjusted. One hand carrying his weapon, the other forming a visor over his brow, he sprinted for the school bus, jumped its steps, and was on board, legs splayed wide across the aisle, shotgun pointing at the faces of children. Why was he surprised they were children? The whole point was to take children. Whenever he'd thought of this moment, he pictured a *group* of kids, a generic collection, sort of abstract in their assemblage. He never envisioned separate individuals, each in possession of a unique life. He'd imagined they would react to him jointly, all screaming in terror, or all shrinking mutely in fear. He couldn't anticipate different responses from different kids, and the variety of what he encountered threw him.

Some screamed, of course—how could they not? But a couple scurried under their seats, and one boy recited the Lord's Prayer in a quavering falsetto. A pair of girls, maybe sisters they looked so much alike but maybe just best friends, hugged each other and hid behind their backpacks. More than a few stared at him in disbelief. They looked worried, but also waited for him to explain himself, to get to the point, as if the gun and pantyhose raised more questions than they answered.

A girl, one of the older ones, chubby with long straight hair, crept out of her seat, snaked on her belly in the aisle to the emergency exit at the rear of the bus, and tried the lever.

"Don't do it, you little bitch," he yelled, training the shotgun on her.

The girl crawled—sobbing, flinching—back to her seat.

Jason mumbled "shit" under his breath. He shouldn't have called her a bitch. He shouldn't have had to say anything. What was more fearsome than a silent man? These kids weren't the only ones falling short of expectations.

"Shut up. Got it? Your mouths, keep them closed. All of you. Shut up your mouths." What was he saying? He sounded moronic.

He took a head count. Nineteen. Fewer than there should have been. He and Calvin regularly counted twenty-three. He wasn't sure how this would affect the plan.

A skinny kid in the front row stood up. He had shaggy hair and pink crescent moons of sunburn under his eyes, wide clusters of freckles across his face. His teeth were too big for his head. He didn't say anything but was standing in a way to catch Jason's attention.

"Sit down," Jason said.

"Why are you so mad, Bunny Man?"

"Sit your little ass down."

"Come on, Bunny Man, chill out," the boy said. "I want you to meet my righthand man, Switchblade," he said, and pointed at a Japanese boy staring blankly out the window, hoping not to be noticed.

Jason's jaw burned where the pantyhose rubbed his stubble. He gulped air through the fabric, the part around his mouth wet from breathing. He wanted to know why the boy wasn't afraid of him and then he got to the bottom of it himself: because he wasn't scary. For a big guy, he found few people treaded lightly in his presence. A prime example was the other night, when Vicky the bartender, a woman older than Bertie, bounced him and Calvin out of The Knight Spot. He'd torn down the dart board in defeat and Calvin broke his beer bottle against the blank space on the wall in celebration. Vicky hadn't waited a moment weighing likely outcomes before coming out around the bar and shoving them to the exit. How could she have known they wouldn't turn their violence on her? That the fight would drain from them once they stopped fighting inanimate objects? From his core, Jason must have radiated softness, he thought. What else could Bunny Man even mean?

He wished he were in the van with the bus driver. So much easier dealing with one old guy and not nineteen kids. He could only blame himself. He and his brother were in this trouble because of him and he was ashamed of it being his fault. When they were deciding who would handle the driver and who would ambush the bus, he threw down scissors, knowing Calvin would pick rock over and over. It seemed the least he could do. He turned from the boy and sat in the driver's seat, shifted into first, and rolled the bus into the gravel parking lot of Butler Reservoir, down to the clearing that led to the trails.

"He's going to drown us," Emily Mashburn yelled, hugging her twin sister.

That got the students shrieking and Jason whispered to himself, "There is a God," thankful the danger he represented was finally sinking in.

The only students who didn't shriek were Emily and Brenda— Emily, because she'd said it, and Brenda, younger than Emily by twenty-four minutes, who felt calmed by her sister's prediction.

Until then her stomach had been full of dry clay, shoving against her insides, making it hard to breathe. When the masked man entered the bus, she guessed he was going to kill them, but wasn't sure how. Now that she knew he was going to drown them in the reservoir, she stopped wondering. It was no surprise that Emily figured it out. That was how they worked. One of them would get the beginning of a thought, or part of a feeling, and the other would pick it up without being asked, flesh it out, and fill in the missing pieces. Brenda had guessed they were going to die, and Emily, without prompting, recognized how it would happen.

She felt Emily trembling against her and knew it was because they were going to die in cold water. They hated cold water, hated goosebumps and blue lips and chattering teeth. Last week their mother left three ceramic pots on the concrete patio in the backyard that filled with thunderstorm rain and spent two days heating in the sun. The twins loved dipping their feet in the warm, silty water that collected in the pots and then running inside when they had the urge to pee. They loved everything warm and hated everything cold.

The man in the mask drove into the woods, the bus bumping along on the trail, tree branches scraping the sides. Through the trees the reservoir sparkled white as ice.

"It's okay, it's alright," Brenda said in her sister's ear. "We'll swim away."

She opened her lunchbox and unscrewed the cap of the thermos of orange juice, which emitted a slightly fermented odor. She fished out the plastic straw.

"Look, look." Brenda put the straw in her mouth. "Like a snorkel. We'll hide under the water and swim away when he's not looking."

The bus came to a section of the trail that widened, a meeting place for nature groups. The man in the pantyhose mask turned off the engine. Everything was quiet but for his heavy breathing and a noisy starling roost close by.

Emily rummaged through her lunchbox but came up empty-handed.

"You swim away," she said, smiling. "I'll stay and die."

Brenda gnawed her straw in half, gave one piece to Emily. "I hate your pig face," she said.

"I hate yours more."

They hugged each other, lips clamped tight around the straws, and closed their eyes.

Brenda called Emily in search of guidance, or sympathy, or a simple string of words, maybe, to make the moment feel less colossal. She was forty years old and her career was over.

"I turned down an assignment," she said.

"That's it?"

"What do you mean, that's it?"

"What was it?"

"A standoff between cattle ranchers and the FBI."

"Why?"

"Something to do with cows grazing on federal land."

"No, why did you turn it down?"

"Because I'm afraid."

"You?"

"I know."

"Afraid of what?"

Of what, Brenda couldn't say. Existential doubts abounded. Howling jackals on the outskirts of the campfire. Marauding hordes. Dark machinations. At all times, beneath whatever else she was feeling, churned apprehension and foreboding, an awareness that her sense of safety was just that, a sense, and nothing certifiably true.

"Is this what it feels like to be you?" she said.

"Maybe that tear gas canister knocked something loose."

"Maybe."

"Or maybe you're actually human."

"What a nightmare," Brenda said.

Three months earlier she'd woken to find people asking her questions. There had been two of them, or four maybe, men or women or both, and they were asking her questions while rolling her onto a stretcher.

"What is your name?" they said. "What day is it? What is the president's name?"

"I'm the one that asks questions," she said. Was that true? It might have been. She didn't know why she'd said it unless it was true. This was true: she was on her back, and she knew this because behind the faces asking her questions pulsed the luminous blue sky of—where? Anaheim! She was on her back in Anaheim. Beyond that, she wasn't sure of much.

They asked more questions in the ambulance. She answered them, or at least thought she did. Again, it was hard to tell. The throbbing in her head—*in* her head, from inside her skull— subjugated. Wait, was that the right word? Subjugated? Whatever, close enough. The throbbing subjugated. And her vision was blurry too. She couldn't remember what she'd been doing before the throbbing and blurry vision started, or what she was doing in Anaheim.

She didn't know how much time had passed before she found herself in a hospital bed. A nurse said she was lucky to be alive. If the tear gas canister hadn't caromed off the building before striking Brenda's head, if she had taken the blunt force of it, she would be dead.

The nurse was small with cropped blonde hair and moved around the bed quickly. Too quickly to watch, in fact, as her speedy movements made Brenda nauseated.

"Tear gas?" Brenda said, and leaned over the bed rail and threw up on the floor.

A fractured skull in Anaheim. The humor wasn't lost on her. She was the Catastrophe Queen, after all, a nickname bestowed upon her by an associate producer in Colorado Springs because if she showed up anywhere near you with a camera, something terrible had happened to your life. She was still interning at WETM-TV her senior year at Ithaca, logging tapes and coordinating scripts—if she wasn't filling lunch orders—when she got the opportunity to assist on a video shoot at a valve factory where a malfunctioning industrial oven killed a worker. She was on-air at WJHG when Hurricane Earl dropped sixteen inches of rain on northern Florida and killed two people. She won a Society of Professional Journalists Award for her work covering the tornado outbreak of 2001 in the Southeast that killed thirteen people and caused more than fifty million dollars in damage. Her work on the Texas City Refinery explosion resulted in an Edward R. Murrow Award. As she advanced her career by changing jobs and working at stations across the country, she'd covered all manner of disasters, natural and man-made, so of course she almost died at a simple police protest in the shadow of Sleeping Beauty Castle. And what was funny, what was incredibly hilarious—again, the humor wasn't lost—was that she wasn't even working, but visiting an old sorority sister who lived in California. Classic story: wrong time, wrong... you know.

Dr. Singh said brain injuries were unpredictable. Recovery time differed from patient to patient. Some people snapped back almost immediately; some dealt with symptoms for years. Years? thought Brenda. *Fuck. That.* She was just ten months into her job as a contributing correspondent to the news division of a major network, the kind of job she'd been working toward since that first internship, the job that let her come back to New York and brought her close to Emily and her parents but allowed her to travel for stories. She didn't have years to wait out a prolonged recovery. Still, when she came home from California, she reluctantly followed the doctor's advice to take it slowly and, over the weeks, the staples were removed from her head, the nausea and the sensitivity to light and sound subsided, and her equilibrium returned. She was on the mend but not whole. Mind-bending headaches and crushing fatigue would come on out of nowhere and disable her for hours. Most frightening, it seemed as if she were undergoing alterations to herself as a person. She confined her travels to familiar places—the office on W 66th, Café Lalo on W 83rd, Westside Market on Broadway, home on

W 84th—because the unknown and unexpected disoriented her, *her*, who made a living on the unknown and unexpected. She took cars because the subway was loud, crowded, stifling. Dr. Singh said that she could expect mood changes, that patients often reported depression and anxiety. Of the many possible symptoms, she dismissed these out of hand, even after researching the subject and finding the same information. Maybe *other* patients reported depression and anxiety but not Brenda Mashburn. If her mood didn't change after what took place when she was ten, nothing could make her mood change.

This was what she had believed. And she was totally wrong.

After the other symptoms abated, she was left with one that she couldn't shake. A low-grade nervousness shaded every moment with certain, imminent doom. She'd been afraid before, at work and in her personal life—she wasn't a psychopath and knew what real fear was—but this was different. She'd always believed she had the skills, the intelligence, the temperament, the goddamned good fucking luck, to circumvent disaster. She'd had faith that, for whatever reason, the Catastrophe Queen was an observer of the worst life could offer, not a recipient. Maybe it went back to the abduction when they were ten. Maybe she got the worst thing out of the way early. At any rate, she no longer had faith. She was as vulnerable as anyone else, and that meant continuing to do the type of work that inspired her was impossible.

So, she called Emily, the one person she could call to say that her career was over. She was lying on a yoga mat on her bedroom floor, studying a collection of dust under her bed that looked a lot like dead mice.

Emily said this sounded like a temporary setback, not the end of a career, but if it turned out Brenda's feeling, or whatever this was, was permanent, there were plenty of things she could do. Emily listed some of them like the fierce advocate of her sister that she was: producing, teaching J-school, writing a memoir.

Brenda supposed she could land a book deal or a visiting

faculty position somewhere. But that was hardly the point. She didn't want to do something else. How could she explain the odd emptiness of having pursued one thing her entire life and now lacking the ability to do it? This must have been what professional athletes went through when they got too old to play. She still remembered the first time she saw the camera and lights and the beautiful reporter with wavy, honey-colored hair, holding out a microphone. On that occasion, Brenda was the interviewee. Emily too. Their parents still had the VHS tape in the attic, probably in the same box with the old VCR. The girls were wearing hospital scrubs that were way too big, the short sleeves hanging down nearly to their wrists. They and the other students had been given new clothes at the hospital, where they overran the emergency room, their own filthy outfits kept as evidence by the FBI. Pat Earl was the only one whose scrubs fit, though in his interview he kept glancing down, crossing and uncrossing his thick arms, as if he were an imposter surgeon on the verge of getting caught, or perhaps it was the sudden mantle of hero he found difficult to step into.

"I've wanted to be a reporter since the night at the quarry," she said, and rolled to her feet. She walked to the fridge and got a can of Diet Coke. She held the chilled aluminum to the back of her neck.

"Since you mentioned it," Emily said. She said that Calvin Schott was up for parole again. "I didn't know if you were ready to hear about it," she added.

"I'm fine," Brenda said, pressing the can to her forehead.

"You are. Totally fine. So totally fine you can't do your job."

"Bitch," she said, and cracked open the Coke. She found her purse and the bottle of Ativan inside it. She washed down a pill and sneezed from the carbonation.

"So, now you know," Emily said.

"Now I know."

It was always Emily who spearheaded the opposition to their

abductor's parole. Brenda remembered when Jason Schott was released over Thanksgiving week in 2002, for the insane reason that since he pleaded guilty, while Calvin was found guilty at trial, he was sentenced to twenty-five years instead of life. She hurled a pumpkin pie onto her parents' front lawn and Emily had to pull her aside. They drove to the liquor store for more wine. For Emily there were no tears, no shouting, no outward signs of anger or sadness or disappointment. No pumpkin pie throwing, that was for sure. Just a weird, detached calm that settled over her. They sat in the parking lot of Brookwood Wine & Spirits and she swore to Brenda, and more likely to herself, that Calvin Schott would die in prison. By now she had mastered the usual tactics whenever he came up for parole: starting a petition of concerned citizens to present to the parole board, relentless posting on various community-related Facebook pages about the danger a free Schott would pose, badgering local politicians and business leaders into voicing their opposition, hounding the hometown paper, the *Daily Times*, to keep the story alive, and writing yet another victim impact statement and encouraging others to do the same. And it had worked. It didn't hurt that Calvin Schott was less than a model inmate and refused to take responsibility for his crimes.

"I think he's getting out this time," Emily said.

Brenda looked for an ice pack in the freezer but found only a bunch of frozen-brown bananas, a bag of edamame, and an iced-over box of Dr. Praeger's California Veggie Burgers.

"You know I've never asked you to use your position to help," Emily said.

Brenda had to sit down. She sensed where this was going and regretted having called.

"The longer Schott's been in, the more people forget why," Emily said, "and this time I'd appreciate it if you stepped it up."

"Step it up? What does that mean?"

"Nothing specific."

　　　　　　　　　　TIME WILL BREAK THE WORLD

Yeah, sure. What it meant was that Emily wanted Brenda to produce a video, something short, a couple of minutes, describing their efforts to keep Calvin Schott in prison. If the parole board knew a journalist, who was also a victim, was shining a light on the situation, they might not be so quick to release him. Brenda's influence could make it a big deal. Then, Emily hoped, the pressure would be too strong and the state would have to do the right thing, whether it wanted to or not.

"I called to tell you I can't do my job. You're asking me to help you by doing my job. See the problem?"

"Just think about it."

Brenda left the Diet Coke on top of the fridge and found her way back to the yoga mat. She said she would think about it. She said it to get off the phone. She had no way of thinking about it right then. Anything more demanding than contemplating dust mice under her bed was too overwhelming. Soon the Ativan kicked in and she began stretching.

THURSDAY, AUGUST 2, 1984

Martin Mendoza didn't think the gunman was going to drown them in the reservoir, but he screamed with everyone else when the twin girl said it because he agreed something bad was going to happen to them. He wouldn't rule out death, but it seemed like they would be shot if that were the case. He pictured the man in the pantyhose mask marching them into the woods, forcing them to dig their own graves, shoving them to their knees. He imagined the last thing they would ever feel in this life was the rocky soil on their legs and the shotgun barrel to the backs of their skulls. If Martin struggled or fought back, the man would bash the bridge of his nose with the burnished walnut gun stock, or bury an elbow in his gut, doubling him over, before ridding him of the crown of his head and kicking his corpse into the shallow pit.

His gaze ranged around the bus. No one was making eye contact. They had retreated into their own fear, they couldn't handle taking on anyone else's. Robert Avery sat with his bootleg Jackson Victory Tour concert tee over his face and Jodie Hoffman had her head between her knees like the safety illustration Martin saw the only time he was on an airplane to visit his grandparents in Buffalo. Lindsey Robinson had been practically hyperventilating since she tried to escape out the back door and the gunman called her a bitch. Martin felt like throwing up, the bile in his stomach spilling back up into his throat. He unwrapped a piece of grape Hubba Bubba, the gum flattened from all day in his pocket, hot and gooey. He popped it in his mouth to wash away the sour taste.

"Give me a piece, Fish Fucker," whispered Doodoo, who pressed into the seat. He held his palm up and Martin could see it glistening with sweat. Belying his nickname, Lance Viscuso didn't smell like shit. He stank of bologna. He was absolutely revolting.

Martin dropped a piece of gum in Doodoo's hand, the last in the pack, another shameful act of surrender. It was fitting in a sad way that he would be bullied right up to the end, and he only hoped he'd be lucky enough to watch Doodoo get shot before it was his turn. He pushed the wrapper out the window, wishing he could somehow fit through the narrow gap, the school bus bouncing and rocking deeper into the woods. He thought about his only friends, Scott and Brian, who got to go to Camp Wanaksink because their parents weren't divorced like his and could afford it. What were Scott and Brian up to right then? Probably canoeing or doing archery or Frenching girls and touching their titties, four things he had never done and that were kind of the whole point of sleepaway camp as he understood it. Whatever they were up to, Martin had to believe they weren't being held hostage. He was already jealous of them and the inside jokes they would return to school with, but maybe he would be dead by then and not have to feel left out.

The bus shuddered to a complete stop at an opening in the trees not far from a van painted primer grey. He wondered if there was another man inside, or several men.

The gunman twisted out of the driver's seat, stepped into the aisle, and looked out the back window, drumming the tops of the seats on either side of him like he was impatient. The green Dodge van that had stopped them on the street came into view, bumping down the same trail. In the clearing, it turned and backed up so it was end to end with the bus, its cargo doors even with the emergency exit. The masked man stormed down the aisle with the shotgun. Doodoo wedged himself hard against Martin, his arm greasing all over Martin's.

The man with the shotgun threw open the back exit, the alarm buzzing. Martin saw the driver slide out of the green van. This one wore black pantyhose on his head and a black T-shirt with the sleeves cut off. He tucked a handgun into the waist of his jeans. He pounded the side of the van with his fist and opened the doors.

Pat Earl was inside, squinting and blinking in the daylight.

"Mr. Pat," Lindsey Robinson yelled.

"It's okay. I'm fine," he called back.

The one with the black pantyhose climbed onto the school bus. "Let's go. The clock is ticking."

"You take him," said the one with the shotgun, pointing up front at Andy Kraven.

"The little guy?"

"He called me Bunny Man."

"Why?"

"Who knows, but it freaked me out."

"Probably a metaphor," the one with the black pantyhose said.

"Do you even know what you're talking about?"

"The clock is ticking."

"So, take him."

The one with the shotgun got Andy and steered him by the shoulder. "Get going."

"Yes, sir, Mr. Bunny Man."

Andy jumped from the school bus into the green van and threw his arms around Pat Earl.

"Is this a game, Mr. Pat?" he said.

"No," said the bus driver.

The gunmen worked fast, breaking the students into two groups. One group was put in the green van; the other remained on the bus. From what Martin could tell, there wasn't any logic to how they got separated. He decided they probably wouldn't be murdered, at least not right away. They might be sold into slavery, or given away to couples who couldn't have their own kids but were evil so they weren't allowed to adopt. Or the gunmen were child molesters, and they belonged to a club or organization of molesters, and they were going to have a giant molester party, an orgy, and do nasty things to him and the others, stick all kinds of things up their butts. The gum had lost its flavor and Martin really thought he might throw up. He wanted to go in the green van with Mr. Pat because it might be safer around him, but he changed his mind when Doodoo got pulled out of the seat and told to join Andy and Pat. Martin would rather take his chances on the bus than be anywhere with Doodoo.

The one with the shotgun stood over the twin girls. "Go with him," he said.

They scooted out of the seat, wearing their backpacks, a piece of plastic drinking straw sticking out of their mouths.

"Not you," he said to Brenda.

The girls froze.

"Go on," he said to Emily.

The girls didn't move. They wrapped their arms around each other.

"I don't want to leave my sister, sir. I want to stay with her, please," Brenda said.

The girl was so composed, so civil and polite in her request, that Jason reeled from a lack of equilibrium. He had nothing to say back to her but knew he couldn't give in to her simple, reasonable appeal.

When he yanked them apart, they started crying and fought to stay together, saying, "Please, please," and then, "No. No. No," their faces red, the thin cords in their necks straining. They made a sound unlike any Martin had ever heard, an unceasing ferine wailing that made his stomach clench. He wanted to help them, if only to stop that sound, but instead he stared out the window, the reservoir gleaming through the trees. He put himself, mentally, out there, in the middle of the water, in a rowboat, away from the gunmen and the sound of the twins. It was what he did when Doodoo really laid into him, removed himself from the situation to a place where he was safe and in control.

The one with the shotgun wedged his body between the twins

and forced Emily down the aisle, holding Brenda back, one hand encircling her skinny bicep. Brenda slapped at him with her free hand and tried to bite him. Emily dropped to her knees, still crying "*nonononono*," now cough-sobbing. The one with the black pantyhose picked her up and slung her over his shoulder.

"You don't have to do that," Pat Earl said, standing at the cargo doors of the green van.

"Take her," the gunman said, and threw her off the bus.

When half the kids were in the green van, the one with the black pantyhose locked them in and leaned back into the bus with his gun drawn while the one with the shotgun bounded out of the front door. Martin heard the engine of the dull-grey van turn over and stall, turn over and stall, before catching and being revved to a high whine. A cloud of exhaust drifted through the windows.

The one with the shotgun was out of breath when he returned, sweating so much you could almost see his face under the pantyhose, though Martin didn't dare look at him.

"Come on," he said, and waved everyone to him.

Martin and nine others fell into the aisle.

"Faster," the one with the black pantyhose said.

There was something in his tone, beyond the presence of the gun, that made Martin think that if he wasn't fast enough, the man would put a bullet in his back.

MONDAY, APRIL 7, 2014

It was such a Bertie thing to do. Just when it was time to go see Stern, she sprung on Jason this haircut request, acting like it was something they had scheduled weeks ago.

She stood in front of him in her red windbreaker, leaning sagely on her cane. She combed her fingers through hair the color of copper at daybreak and tugged at the ends resting just below her long earlobes. "No, this won't do."

"You look fine, Mom."

He watched her take another pass over her skull. Her hair looked no longer than it had last month. Her hair always looked the same.

"You can drop me off at the salon on the way," she said.

"I can take you after."

"On the way."

"I can take that cane out of your hand and crack you in the noggin with it."

"Try it and I guarantee you'll never make me a grandmother."

"How about I cut your hair? That'll save money."

She squinted behind her glasses. Jason couldn't tell if it was the macular degeneration or just her habit of narrowing her eyes at him in skeptical appraisal. She unzipped her windbreaker and pivoted on her cane.

"The good scissors are in the utility drawer in the kitchen," she said, and padded away.

He prayed she was bluffing. He checked his phone for the time. It wasn't yet noon and he was already exhausted. Calvin's parole hearing, his eleventh, was scheduled for the end of June. His lawyer, Jon Stern, wanted to talk strategy. He said he also had a bit of good news that was worth delivering in person. Jason had canceled a job chipping a fallen birch tree in the Barlettas' yard to make the meeting.

"You coming?" Bertie called from the bathroom.

He stuffed his phone in his pocket and made a mental note not to blame the inevitable fallout on a lack of foresight. He knew going in that trying to cut her hair was bad business. Success in life was about identifying possible missteps before you made them, in order to choose a wiser course of action. And in cases where a course correction wasn't accessible or easy to navigate, as were most things related to Bertie, then you had to step up and own your mistake. He learned that at Auburn, the prison not the college, in the class for long-term offenders.

He got the good scissors out of the utility drawer, thought about testing their sharpness on a major artery, and followed his mother.

In a show of brinkmanship, she'd arranged herself on a folding chair and draped a towel over her slender shoulders. Her cane was hooked over the sink vanity, and she held a hand mirror. Jason blinked hard and cracked his neck. He brandished the scissors, taking quick short jabs in her direction.

"Who's ready for Dr. Weedwacker? Or would you rather go see Mr. Stern and then I can hand you over to a professional?"

"You offered. I accepted. Get on with it." She examined herself in the mirror. "My hair grows faster than moonflower."

He stood behind her and saw their faces in the mirror, hers with the parchment skin and his with the mournful pouches under his eyes that he'd inherited from his father, the thinning hair too. He and Bertie had the same nose, narrow bridge and bulbous tip, and the zealous Reilly chin, and he shared her habit of grinding her teeth when anxious, which he noticed they were both now doing.

"There are no flowers on the moon, Mom," he said, and looped his fingers into the scissors. He got to work. Don't think, he told himself, just cut. He started on the back, taking her coarse, dry hair between his fingers and grazing the ends with the blades. An eighth of an inch, a sixteenth. The trimmings fell on the towel. Bertie's nose whistled raggedly as her breathing increased, and her shoulders squirmed up and down. She was in pain. Her lumbar discs were crumbling like Stilton. There was a list of stretching and strengthening exercises under a magnet on the refrigerator door that she hadn't looked at since the day the physical therapist handed it to her. She was in too much pain to do the exercises, she said, but her lack of mobility exacerbated her pain, which prevented her from exercising, and that only intensified her agony, and the wheel spun, round and round. And yet, miraculously, she hefted gallon jugs of Carlo Rossi Chablis up the basement stairs like a pack mule.

He put a hand on her shoulder. "Hang on. Almost done," he said, and moved to her front to cut her bangs.

She exhaled and looked up at him. "Moonflower is a vine," she said.

"I just covered a fence at the Smiths' with it. I know what it is."

"Handyman," she muttered.

"I own my own business. Just like Dad."

"My father *gave* your father his business. Don't ever forget that."

"Close your eyes."

He combed down her bangs and worked right to left. It was a rare chance to see her up close, his eighty-one-year-old mother. How could he have an eighty-one-year-old mother? How could she have a fifty-three-year-old son? Her eyelids looked like walnut shells rendered in crepe paper, surrounded by a wild tessellation of cracks and creases. Jason had it on good authority—Bertie herself—that a superficial study of the lines on her face revealed the names Calvin and Jason. Sometimes, depending on her mood and whether or not she'd dallied with Signor Rossi, she would bitterly and gleefully add the names George, their father, Dan, her father, and her legless Uncle Fred to the list of men who had aged her beyond what she deserved.

If he hadn't been so rushed, this would have been a nice moment. Jason was the first to admit that life with Bertie wasn't a misery. She was independent and didn't mind being alone, so he was free to spend several nights a week at his girlfriend Angie's. And Bertie could be funny as hell. She harbored a bawdy crush on LL Cool J and demanded to know why he always wore a hat. "He needs to show off that big round head of his more often," she liked to say.

He moved the scissors levelly across her forehead, but she flinched. Her head jerked forward, her eyes snapped open wide, as if startled out of a nap. There was now an isosceles notch missing from the center her bangs. Jason didn't have the poker face to keep it from her. She took the hand mirror out of her lap to inspect the damage.

"Look what you did to me. Shit for brains." She lurched to her feet and tried yanking the towel off her shoulders but froze with a spasm in her back. Hobbled, and holding herself up with the folding chair, she shouted, "Help me, you dumb, stupid retard."

He whisked the towel off her shoulders and brushed the back of her neck with his fingertips.

She leaned over the bathroom sink and stared in the mirror in horror, her hand up near her bangs, hovering there, seemingly afraid that touching it would cause physical pain.

"We can get it fixed. It's not the end of the world. Let's go see Stern and then I'll take you to get it fixed," Jason said.

"Stern? Stern? I can't see anyone looking the way I do. Stupid shit-for-brains."

"You can't see anyone because you're blind." He held up two fingers. "How many, Mom, how many?"

"Cheap shot," she said, and she was right.

But shit-for-brains? It wasn't that Bertie had said it, but the *way* she said it, so caustic, so unnecessary, that compelled Jason to lash out, to return some of the hate, for he didn't have space inside of him to absorb it all.

"Get your fucking jacket and get in the car," he said.

"I'm not going," Bertie said, still examining her hair in the mirror. "Waste of time, that guy."

"What are you talking about?"

Once again, she narrowed her eyes at him. "Cal's never getting out. He's gone, okay?"

And that, finally, was what this haircut was all about: a stalling tactic to miss the meeting. Her oldest son had been in prison for thirty years and, at this point, the only thing more painful than his never coming home was the prospect of his imminent release. When Calvin and Jason went away, she and their father had needed to devise methods of coping. George Schott managed the loss by watching Munsee Granite collapse under the weight of a thousand lawsuits and dying before the reunification of Germany. Bertie had survived by writing her sons off. She liked to pretend they were astronauts selected for the first manned mission to Mars. They were never returning. Jason's release in 2002 required her to reformulate her strategy. Though relieved he was home, she was frosty and forbidding during the beginning of his lengthy parole, terrified he would screw up and be taken from her again. By now she'd spent too long abstaining from hope for Calvin, and she was incapable of handling their lawyer's shy, optimistic manner with anything other than total scorn.

What else could Jason do but drop her off at the salon and proceed to the lawyer alone?

Jon Stern was rangy and could have pulled off youthful were it not for a look of constitutional fatigue. His office suite was claustrophobic with file cabinets and bookcases, the air perfumed with stale coffee.

Jason sat across from his lawyer, the leather seat spiderwebbed with cracks, the wooden arms shiny from elbows. "Hey, Jon," was all he could think to say.

"Where's Roberta?" Stern said.

"Couldn't make it."

"I thought she'd be thrilled to hear the good news." He picked at eczema flakes on the back of his hand with a paperclip.

"The only thing that thrills my mom is *NCIS: Los Angeles.*"

"The TV show?"

"And the Mets," Jason said.

"Two and four start to the season."

"Plenty of time to turn it around."

"Isn't that what we say every year? Are we delusional or just faithful? Is there a difference?" He flicked the paperclip on the desk and frowned, troubled by his insuperable questions. He then brightened and told Jason that state senator Dana Carvalho had taken an interest in Calvin's parole hearing.

"For or against?" Jason said.

"Good news, remember?"

Prison reform was part of Carvalho's reelection platform, Stern said, and she viewed Calvin's life sentence as excessive. Though not a model inmate, he'd served three decades, an eternity for a first offender who hadn't committed murder. Plus, his crime was so unique that he was an unlikely candidate to reoffend. His continued incarceration was of no service to him, the state, or the public. He was a middle-aged taxpayer burden. Time to send him home to his family.

Stern was convinced that Senator Carvalho's letter to the Board of Parole in support of Calvin would weigh heavily at the hearing.

"Cal is in really good spirits lately," the lawyer reported.

"He was in good spirits last time. Time before that too," Jason said.

"There were circumstances, you know that."

"My brother is a fuckup. I guess that's a circumstance."

A year and a half earlier, Calvin got busted for possession of pornography just prior to his hearing. Two years before that, they denied him due to a physical altercation with another inmate. The parole board agreed he acted in self-defense, but the report indicated that he'd provoked the argument that led to his ass-kicking. Every time he got close to getting out, he did something to botch it.

"I'd like to give him something to look forward to. How about taking him to a Mets game? He's never seen Citi Field," Stern said.

"Cal was never into baseball. Too bad the Olympics aren't this summer."

"I didn't know he likes the Olympics."

"He doesn't like them, he has an obsession. The next time you talk to him say, 'Citius, Altius, Fortius.'"

"Is that Latin?"

"Faster, Higher, Stronger. The Olympic motto. He used to say it like a catchphrase."

"That's good. Remind him of that. Remind him of things you used to do."

"Maybe not all the things we used to do," Jason said.

"All I'm saying is a positive attitude helps at the interview. You're still going to offer him a job? Employment is important."

Jason snatched a rubber band off the desk and began stretching it. He thought about Calvin coming to work with him. *With* him, not *for* him. The Schott brothers teaming up and running their own business, the way their grandfather and great-uncle helmed Munsee Granite back in its heyday. That had always been their dream, partners ruling the world.

"The job is his if he wants it."

"It's crucial to show that Cal has a support network waiting for him, to ease his transition."

The rubber band slipped out of Jason's hand and flew into a sickly potted weeping fig plant. He smiled an apology at Stern.

"Everything is lining up," Stern said. He drew an imaginary line in the air to illustrate his point. "You and Roberta need to start believing that Cal is coming home."

Which was what Jason wanted, right? That was what he tried

to resolve on the drive back to the salon. And the answer was yes. He wanted Calvin home. For one thing, it would soothe his conscience. The kidnapping had been his idea, and before that, it had been his idea for the real estate business that got them in trouble. He was responsible. And he blamed himself for failing to convince Calvin to plead guilty to first-degree kidnapping and not go to trial, where he stood no chance of an acquittal, and where the state brought additional charges of attempted murder and bodily harm. His inability to change his brother's mind was why he got twenty-five years and Calvin got life.

There was also the matter of Bertie. Jason and Angie wanted to get married. It might be too late to start a family, but he could still be a husband. He could give the Schott name to someone who wanted it. They lay in Angie's bed and built an elaborate fantasy life that had but one obstacle: the care of Roberta Schott. Calvin could be her caretaker. It was his turn.

But there was a part of Jason already troubled by the attention Cal's parole would bring his way. He and Bertie no longer lived in Brookwood proper, his childhood home sold off when the civil suits against his family began clogging the court system, but in Brookwood Heights, an abutting, shabbier community. There he'd been able to piece together a tiny but independent life, a landscaping and minor construction business. Most of his customers were younger couples and families who hadn't lived in the area in the summer of 1984. They knew Jason from his work, not that he'd caused the town its greatest historical horror. Every couple of years, though, when Calvin went before the parole board, there was an uptick in awareness, a brief flurry of articles in the *Daily Times*, afternoon petition signings outside Stop N Shop by the Survivors of the Brookwood Bus Kidnapping, a victims' group fronted by Emily Mashburn-Bauer, the concurrent social media postings, and a rash of phone calls, where anonymous neighbors invited physical and sexual violence upon Jason and Calvin and Bertie, after which, upon their deaths, they were free

　　　　　TIME WILL BREAK THE WORLD

to fulfill an eternity in hell. He would lose jobs and scramble to replace them farther up county, until the attention waned after each parole denial. What Jason was nervous about now was the reaction if Calvin actually got out.

Bertie waited on the sidewalk, leaning on her cane. Her hair was blown out, especially in the front, and made her look like she was wearing a helmet.

"Looking glamorous," he said, and helped fasten her seatbelt.

"Everyone was laughing at what a dummy you are."

"I'm glad I could be a source of amusement."

"What did Stern have to say for himself?"

Jason drove a few blocks without answering, but at a red light, Bertie asked again.

"Come on, what was the good news?" she said.

"A state senator says Cal's done enough time."

"Does Senator Obvious have the power to get the job done?"

Jason lowered the window, his hand swimming in the air current. He couldn't decide what to say. No matter what he told her, she would blame him if the information turned out to be wrong.

"Mr. Stern is optimistic."

Bertie grumbled and shifted in her seat.

At home, as he was getting out of the car, she jabbed him in the ribs with her cane.

"I have one son. That's more than some people have. It's you and me, got it?" she said.

"Got it."

My mom, Frances, nearly hemorrhaged to death giving birth to me and couldn't have more children after that. I don't think she ever forgave me, but since I was all she had, she chose not to hold a grudge against me for destroying her body. This doesn't mean she was an affectionate woman. She rapped my collarbone with a wooden spoon to point out I was too skinny. She used the same spoon to feed me the daily fish oil that was supposed to stave off polio, her chapped, red fingers clamped to my chin as I twisted away from her. My dad, though, Dan Reilly, loved me without really understanding me or having much of an interest in trying to understand me.

He was a legendary figure in the granite world, himself the son of a legendary figure, who was respected and rich, who chewed tobacco and drank red wine and bow hunted deer. In 1952 he was named Man of the Year by the National Building Granite Quarries Association. And while I might have been ignorant of his hefty position in the world, I couldn't mistake that he was an outsized person at home—raucous, laughing, boyish.

Why was I so scared of him then? Because he was also angry and violent, not consistently so or even semi-regularly, but the unpredictability of his moods left me expecting the worst, or else falling for a devastating bait and switch. One of my earliest memories was bringing him a bowl of ice water to soak his busted knuckles in after an altercation—a *conversation* he called it—with our neighbor, whom my dad held responsible for the wind that kept blowing maple leaves onto our property. My dad had *conversations* with many people: our gardener (whom he also blamed for the leaf situation), employees he suspected of disloyalty, hunting buddies, the town's tax assessor, Uncle Fred (though never after his accident), and even my mom.

Of his abuse toward my mom, I didn't want to think too badly of him. Instead, I blamed the quarry, having developed a theory that the inherent malevolence of the stone pit had altered his personality, in the way that mercury poisoning can affect behavior. How else could I square the man who gave me horsey rides and sat for tea parties in my room, with the ogre who dragged my mom down the hall by her hair for slights so small no one could ever figure out what they were, including my dad. Nearly every item in my mom's jewelry box was a morning-after act of contrition. She was no passive victim, though, and her revenge was a feat of emotional savagery so vicious that my dad never recovered. Had she sprung her trap earlier, this whole trouble with Calvin and Jason and the school bus might have been prevented. But by then, my husband, George, was an executive at Munsee Granite, meaning my dad could have his breakdown without hurting the business.

Martin still wasn't home, and Jackie was primed to kill him. She'd told him she wasn't picking him up again, that there was nothing wrong with riding the bus with the other kids. He wasn't special. She had her own responsibilities, one of which definitely wasn't a taxi service. She'd explained that today it was nonnegotiable that he got home to watch his brother Ben because she was having an ingrown toenail removed, a minor but painful surgery she was already cranky about, and she would be absolutely stunned to goddamn silence if Martin could just, please, get his butt home on time without acting like some kind of oppressed dissident.

Of course, that had been too much to ask, hadn't it? She looked at the kitchen clock. Even if Martin waltzed through the door right now, she would be late for Dr. Hannah's office. She ran her hands through her hair in frustration. From the living room, she heard the television booming.

"Turn it down, Benji," she said.

She went to Martin's room. Yesterday he'd overslept on purpose to miss the bus, so today she woke him up with a glass of water on his head—a joke, God, it was just a joke to break the tension.

"I can't believe you did that," he wailed, holding his wet face in his hands as if she'd tossed sulfuric acid on him.

She'd laughed, not to mock him but to make the point that it was a joke, and asked if he wasn't being a little dramatic. Martin stomped out of the house without breakfast. On his way, Jackie reminded him that it was okay if he was mad, but he still had to come home after school and watch his brother. She knew he heard her because he shouted back, "I hope they amputate your foot."

Now she looked around his room, dim from perpetually drawn curtains and smelling eternally of feet. The walls were papered with drawings of whales, mostly in pencil and charcoal, some tacked up next to the photograph or encyclopedia illustration he'd copied, and some creations of his own. Martin was obsessed with killer whales and drew elaborate, detailed pictures of them from all angles: pages of pectoral fins and dorsal fins with differing sizes to denote sex (the male's nearly twice as large as the female's); pages of them breaching the ocean surface, hanging curved in the air, and obscured in waves of their own making from slapping the water with their tails.

In a way, his drawings were why she'd enrolled him in summer school. It seemed unhealthy, unwholesome, to be so withdrawn at his age, to want nothing more than to barricade himself inside and draw the same thing over and over.

"You're not going to spend eight weeks stinking up your bedroom," she'd said.

"You can always send me to Camp Wanaksink with Scott and Brian," he'd said.

Jackie sighed and felt a stab of guilt. She would have loved nothing more than to send Martin away with his friends, but where was the money going to come from? She didn't have it, and neither did Tony, her ex. Martin knew they couldn't afford it, so she said nothing to that point. She said, "It's summer. You need to be outside."

He fought her on that too. "Why? Who am I hurting in here?"

Himself, she wanted to say, but he wouldn't get it. She said that he was thirteen and needed to act like a kid, with other kids. She said that she wanted him to have *fun*. The way it was explained to her back in May, when Mr. Weed, guidance counselor at Brookwood Middle School, proposed the program, summer school was more like day camp. For most of the schedule the children were engaged in extracurriculars—dodgeball, tetherball, softball, swimming, arts and crafts, something he vaguely called

"Nature"—interrupted by forty-minute blocks, before and after lunch, to reinforce academic skills, retention of previous instruction he called it, so that come September, Martin would hit the new school year running. It wasn't sleepaway camp, but it was something, wasn't it? What was the harm in sending him, if it got him out of the house and gave him a leg up in the classroom?

But they had spent the last month of school battling. If Martin couldn't be with his friends, he just wanted to be left alone. Jackie wanted him tan, laughing, exhausted. She suggested he would make new friends. He rolled his eyes so hard she thought he was having a seizure. He finally relented because what else could he do? He was the kid and she was the mom. Still, from the very first day, he begged her not to make him ride the bus, and since then he'd done everything he could to avoid it. When she asked him why he didn't want to take the bus, he answered, "Cuz it sucks."

And when she told him that wasn't a real reason, he said, "I hate it, okay? I just hate it."

But it wasn't okay to *hate* riding the bus. What was the big deal?

Jackie left his room and returned to the kitchen. She called her ex and asked if Martin had said anything about staying with him.

"Not that I remember," Tony said.

"Well, have you seen him?"

"Even when he's here, I don't see him. That boy is a ghost."

Tony's path rarely crossed with Martin's unless he initiated it, choreographed chance encounters outside the bathroom or in the kitchen while Martin poured a bowl of cereal, where Tony tried, no one could say he didn't take a stab at it, to understand this son of his who receded deeper inside of himself every single day, becoming less knowable the older he got, sharing none of Tony's interests—that was fine with him, he wasn't looking for a clone or a buddy. The whole relationship had become, he didn't know, sad or something, the two of them living together part time

 Time Will Break the World

and having nothing in common. Like the whale drawings. What was that all about?

"Orcinus orca," Martin muttered without lifting his head from his sketch whenever Tony asked about them.

"Trying to be a marine biologist?"

Martin would aspirate a nearly mute "no, thank you," hair in his eyes, and keep drawing, not rude or even dismissive of his father, but rather uninterested. What Martin's parents didn't know, or couldn't understand, was that Martin liked what he liked and didn't feel the need to help anyone else come to terms with it, not his mother and father, and especially not the Asshole Brigade of Idiots, as he called them, boys like Doodoo Viscuso and Eddie Earl and their friends, who were so, so stupid, total morons, who didn't know that orcas weren't even fish but members of the dolphin family, and who reveled in their stupidity, calling him a Fish Fucker and thinking they were hilarious. Why bother trying to make sense to guys like that?

"The little shit didn't come home this afternoon," Jackie said on the phone.

"I'll let you know if I hear from him," Tony said.

"Do me a favor and call the school."

Tony was at work and didn't see why it was a big deal that Martin wasn't home, but he heard the strain in Jackie's voice and realized it was easier to give in. He found the number in the phone book. The line was busy. He called again. Busy again. He was about to quit but thought of Jackie's reaction if he told her he didn't get through. It took five tries before someone picked up. The woman explained that bus trouble was the culprit for the delay in the afternoon drop-off.

"Burnt Velveeta must have broken down. Raymond from D&J Auto Repair is out in the tow truck looking for it right now."

"Burnt what?" Tony said.

"I'm sorry, that's just what we call Bus #8. Because it's so old."

"Is that a joke? I can't tell if you're joking."

"It might've gotten a flat tire or overheated."

"That's not what I mean."

"Pardon?"

"You think it's acceptable to put my child on a bus so old you have a nickname for it?"

"I'm not in charge of dispatch, sir."

"I don't mean you personally. I'm talking about what the school district thinks is okay. Aren't there regulations?"

"Sir, I'm not going to sit here and argue with you. Good afternoon."

He couldn't believe she hung up on him. When he called back, he was confronted by the busy signal again. This time he gave up, not knowing that one of the other callers trying to get through to the school was Andy Kraven's mom, Jean. First, she'd called Mei Watanabe, to see if Andy had gone home with Kaito. But Mrs. Watanabe said she thought Kaito had gone home with Andy. So Jean tried the school, worried that Andy had landed in trouble again, and for another bullshit reason. Bucking common consensus, Jean thought Andy was smart, curious, and creative. Where the school saw hyperactivity and lapses in concentration, she saw independence and a lack of challenge. Ms. Gordon, his teacher, could choke on shit with her pedagogically-cruel end of year recommendation that without summer school he should repeat the grade, as if a mulligan would overcome his "motivation issues," unless maybe—here was a thought—motivating students was the teacher's job, in which case any issues in that department belonged to Gordon.

After several tries, Jean got an answer at the school. The bus had stalled out and a repair truck was already en route to replace the faulty battery. Alright, good, she thought, that was a relief; he wasn't in trouble or hadn't missed the bus, still at the playground absorbed in some game he made up, or decided to walk home alone, calling it a quest or crusade.

Both she and Andy had been percolating with excitement on

that first day of summer school. She had been excited because he was excited.

"It's going to be so rad," he'd said when he was leaving, and Jean wished Ms. Gordon could have seen his positive attitude, his eagerness to try new things. He slipped past the driveway to the bus stop on the corner and Jean felt a nervous hopefulness in her chest that made her cry a little. Then, not two hours later, he was almost expelled for disappearing from the group during Nature. "Elopement," Dr. Watters, summer school director, called it. Jean took issue with that word, as if Andy had run off to Atlantic City to get married. At any rate, Watters said, the school couldn't assume the liability.

"If we left the other students unattended while looking for Andy out on that trail, if something had happened..." He let the implications hang in the crackle of the phone line, and then he said, "Could you please pick him up?"

Jean exhaled audibly but said nothing.

"You still there? Mrs. Kraven? We need someone to get Andy."

"No," she said.

"If you're indisposed, then maybe your husband or a neighbor. The important thing is—"

"When my son is with me, he's my problem. When he's with you, he's yours."

"Excuse me?"

She was exhausted by the chickenshittedness of the punks who ran the school district, who treated her son like the Tasmanian Devil. Since kindergarten it had been obvious that Andy wasn't welcomed, that the school only wanted quiet, passive, and, quite frankly, boring children.

She said, "While we're on the subject of liability, you want to explain how you lost my son? I want to know who's in charge over there. You?"

"He's not lost," Watters answered. "He just wandered off for a moment and now he's back, safe and sound."

"Then why are you bothering me?"

That was the last time she heard from the director. Subsequent reports about Andy had been stellar. He was thriving and gaining confidence. His counselors and teachers said they would miss him when the program was over.

He would miss it too. He cried the night before, knowing there were only two days left.

"It's so much better than regular school," he sobbed. "I'm in a gang."

"I know," she said, though she was clueless about what he meant regarding the gang.

Jean got off the phone with the district office. She worried about the school bus, and the kids in it. It was getting later in the day and she hoped Andy wouldn't be scared; he was seven, after all (a fact that was sometimes easy to forget), and small for his age. Knowing him, though, he would probably think the whole thing was an adventure, and if she should worry about anyone it was the bus driver who had to deal with him.

By five thirty, only Doodoo Viscuso's parents hadn't noticed he was missing. By five thirty, they were the only parents not doubting the story about a mechanical problem with Burnt Velveeta, the only parents not asking where the bus had broken down so that they could pick him up. They weren't worrying because Lance was the youngest of nine and they were old and tired and let his siblings raise him, his sister Mary in particular. They didn't keep tabs on him. To Leon and Carol Viscuso, it was just Thursday evening. And that was the funny thing about worrying. The eighteen other families agonizing and stewing over where their kids were had no advantage over the oblivious Viscusos. Worrying couldn't change what was coming for them.

Let's talk sports. While the whole town freaked out over the news that their kids had disappeared, the Games of the XXIII Olympiad were underway, "The quadrennial festival of eternal youth," to quote Baron Pierre de Coubertin, founder of the modern games. Maybe you don't remember, but we were the host country. The games were on our turf, taking expectations to vertiginous heights. There was the controversy of the Soviet boycott, whose national committee claimed anti-Soviet mania created hazardous conditions for their athletes, but rational people understood their snub was a tit-for-tat retaliation to our boycott of the Moscow games in 1980. Our embargo wasn't built upon the flimsy pretext of athlete safety either. The Russkies invaded Afghanistan. It would have been tacit approval of communist aggression to have sent American athletes to Moscow, "an unsuitable site for a festival meant to celebrate peace and goodwill," according to Jimmy Carter.

I was first enchanted by the Olympics in 1968 when the summer games were held in Mexico City, which was a misnomer since they took place in October. There was a darkness to this competition I wouldn't know about until later. I commandeered the TV every night to watch the ABC primetime broadcast, acting like an orchestra conductor whenever I heard the opening refrain of "Bugler's Dream," the drums and cymbals introducing the rousing, triumphant horns. Everyone knows George Foreman was a two-time heavyweight boxing world champion, electric grill entrepreneur, and father of five sons also named George, but at the time of his gold medal match against Ionas Chepulis, he was just a nineteen-year-old kid from Pleasanton, California, with eighteen bouts under his belt. This was the first Olympics broadcast in color, so in round one, as blood streamed from Chepulis's nose and ran into his mouth, I could tell it was a darker red than his Soviet tank top. When the referee stopped the fight in the second round, I jumped up from the floor where I was sitting, hands over my head as if I had won. Foreman raised an American flag and bowed to the crowd at all four corners of the ring.

My cheering drew my dad into the living room. I told him the good news.

"George Foreman knocked out the Russian!"

"That's great, Cal, but George Schott is going to knock you out if you don't go to bed."

Jason and I reenacted the fight constantly, despite his hating having to play Chepulis each time, hating hearing me mimic the announcer while I whaled on him, "Foreman throwing bombs in there . . . Ripping punches by George Foreman . . . He's all over the Russia . . . Chepulis looks all through . . . George pouring it on." The fights usually ended with both of us crying—Jay from the beating I gave him, and me from the spanking Bertie gave me.

In the morning, I scoured the sports page for results. USA women's swimming won eleven of fourteen events. Mexico City was also the games of the Fosbury Flop and "The Leap," Bob Beamon's superhuman long jump of twenty-nine feet, two and a half inches, a mark almost twenty-one inches farther than the previous record. It was the games of John Carlos and Tommie Smith's Black Power salute, a gesture that to me, at eight years old, meant nothing. Try to picture my disappointment when I learned that the Olympics were not a regular TV show like *Bonanza*, that they lasted only a couple of weeks, and then were gone—for four years! Practically the distant future.

Fifteen years later, Jay and I were in financial ruins, the fallout

     TIME WILL BREAK THE WORLD

of our failure surrounding us and the worst consequences yet to be faced. This was the first time in our lives that our self-perception had been challenged and it set off a dark and searching season for us where we dove wildly into distractions. As 1984 began, I treated the upcoming games as more than games. I put upon them a disproportionately deeper meaning than their actual value, comparing the trials of the athletes to my own problems. I looked to their persistence for examples of a way forward for myself.

My brother was a casual sports fan. He never cared the way I did. He became hung up on politics, the local and national elections. Reagan vs. Mondale. I believe he was seeking proof of a broad downward trajectory for the country that paralleled ours. If society at large was taking it in the chops, maybe he could go easier on himself. People remember the landslide election result, but the race was competitive for a while, if not a nail biter. Goddamn Ronald Reagan. There were plenty of reasons to hate the president, and not even facile critiques were considered controversial. Almost half the country hated him. Part of the reason to have a president, any president, was to hate him, and this guy sitting in the Oval Office with a dopey solemn expression on his face fit the bill. I'd learned from my father that only former presidents were good, and that they didn't become good until leaving office. The signature achievement of any administration was going away. I'd intended to vote for the Republican ticket, if only to say I was on the winning team. I never got the chance to cast my ballot.

I know it doesn't seem like the Olympics or Ronald Reagan have much to do with a missing school bus and, in terms of a direct link, I guess it looks like I'm trying to avoid or misdirect from the truth. But the point here is that we'd been following our respective interests in the news, and it was Jay who spotted an article in the *Post* that reported New York State had passed a $35.6 billion dollar budget. What did the state budget have to do with a missing school bus? Quite a lot, it turned out.

THURSDAY, AUGUST 2, 1984

"You sure this isn't a game, Mr. Pat? I won't tell if it is."

"It's real, Andy."

Pat Earl could feel the bony scrap of the boy pressed against him in the crowded van, the engine droning, tires humming on asphalt, the almost numbing sensation of forward progress. For the first few minutes they were moving, he focused on the turns—a left out of what he assumed was the reservoir parking lot onto Cherry Road, a right onto Overland Avenue—trying to position them on the intricate road map he kept in his head, wanting to predict where they were going, but he soon became distracted.

The heat was too much. It was the kind of day that grew hotter as the hours dragged on, where the air was a wet stew even after sundown. You would be arrested for keeping a dog in a car in this weather.

He flicked his eyes around the darkness and assumed the denser shades of black were people. They bumped into him when the van changed speeds. The transmission was worn and jerked and jumped as it went through the gears, shaking them around. He heard their crying, coughing, sniffling, their whispers, prayers, questions. After the man with the black pantyhose closed them up in the van, Pat had done his best to comfort them, but it wasn't in his nature to tell them they were safe, and everything would be alright. Pretty sure they weren't going to be alright. He was wise not to say that either. He fell back on Army wisdom about bravery not being the absence of fear but harnessing the fortitude to endure it. He said that it was fine to be scared, it would be unnatural if they weren't. The important thing to remember was that they couldn't give in to the fear, because the fear thrived on the unknown and right now none of them could predict the future.

He came off gruff and hard, which he often did, and which wasn't his intention, but it was the best he could do considering who he was.

"Is part of the game that you tell me it's not a game?" Andy said.

Pat didn't answer. The van had come to a stop and he listened to the uneven chug of the idling engine, waiting for the driver to turn the key and get out, open the doors and take them to the next phase of whatever this situation could be called. It must have been a red light because they started moving again.

Wherever their destination was, he hoped they reached it soon. He labored to breathe, as if through a wet washcloth. Sweat covered him and dripped down his neck, off his forearms, from the tip of his nose onto his shirt. He felt his socks gummy inside his boots and when he wiggled his toes, his right foot cramped. He drew a breath against the sharp pain and smelled their collective reek. He always joked that the kids were nothing more than wild animals, but the scent he caught in his nose was distinctly human. He'd encountered few analogs of it outside of war and understood he was smelling the physical response to an anticipation of death.

He wondered about Eddie and how the boy was doing, if his fastball was live today. The thought was supposed to calm him but never took shape in his mind the right way. It was dismantled by a question: Why? Why had he climbed out of the bus? Why had he been so stupid? He was so preoccupied with rushing to his grandson's baseball game that he'd misplaced his common sense. He was now answerable for the fate of these children. If the worst came to one of them, he thought, he would have to kill himself, if the masked driver didn't do it for him, and beg Sally from beyond the grave for forgiveness. It was the only honorable thing to do.

He pushed himself up, his foot cramp releasing, the bodies around him complaining. He banged his head on the low roof.

Maybe they should try to escape. At the next red light, he could put his weight into the doors and see if they would bust open. Tell the kids to run into the daylight, to run and run and not stop running until they were safe. Then he remembered the other van. Even if he and these kids got away, he was still responsible for the others. More shameful than getting them into this mess would be to abandon them.

He slammed his palm several times on the partition at the front of the cargo area.

"You got to let us out. It's too hot. Someone's going to get hurt," he said.

Did the driver not hear him, or did he ignore him? Pat pounded with the side of his fist and yelled, "Let them go and keep me."

He must have imagined the laughter. He couldn't have heard it. No one would really laugh. He punched the roof and said, "This is wrong."

"This *is* wrong," a voice echoed. This time Pat wasn't imagining it.

The voice came from the floor. He stared down with widened eyes and saw only the dark, but the voice spoke again.

"This is a mistake," she said.

His knees cracked as he squatted. "Brenda?"

She was quiet, maybe nodding in the dark.

"You need to speak up. I can't see you," he said.

"I'm here," she said.

He felt her breath on his face and he leaned back, uncomfortable with the closeness.

"What are you saying? What's a mistake?" He needed to know what she knew.

"The other man was supposed to drown us."

"He said that?"

"No, Emily did. Emily said so. She said he was going to drown us in the reservoir." Brenda sounded disappointed that her sister was wrong.

At the mention of being killed, the other kids chimed in with their own theories, fueled by the worst they could imagine. Pat told them not to get worked up. They needed to rest, to preserve their strength, he said, but really any of their speculations might have been spot-on and he couldn't listen to them. They wanted to go home, they said. They wanted their parents.

"I know, I know," he said.

"I'm starting to get the feeling this isn't a game, Mr. Pat," Andy said.

"No shit, Sherlock," said Doodoo.

"Get some rest, everybody," Pat said.

He slid down to the floor, his back against the partition. The van took a hard turn to the left and Brenda fell against him. She stayed snug at his side.

"Emily said so," she said.

"I know," Pat said. "Get some rest."

Following his own advice, he closed his eyes.

In the driveway, the boys were playing "Piñata," the game where they took turns beating each other with a foam bat. Emily kept an eye on them from the front door, the day outside raw and damp. Twins run in families, but Ryder and Sonny were separated by two years and looked more like cousins than brothers. As she sometimes did when she knew they weren't paying attention to her, she searched and failed to see herself in them, finding no trace of attached earlobes, or thin eyebrows, or sharp shoulders, or a gathering of lips into a pucker when concentrating. They took after their father Roger, lumpen and earthy, russet-potato people.

She checked the sky, as if consulting the sun for the time, but only found woolly clouds low to the ground. Brenda wouldn't tell her when her train was getting in, even after Emily offered to pick her up at the station. *Specifically* after Emily offered to pick her up. A pointless power move on Brenda's part. The important thing, though, was that she was coming. And staying for the weekend, maybe a few days, maybe a week. *Maybe*—it was Brenda's go-to answer to a lot of questions lately.

A taxi pulled up at the curb in front of the house. Brenda climbed out of the backseat. The driver retrieved her roller bag from the trunk.

Emily called the boys inside, but Ryder and Sonny were too fast. They closed in on Brenda wielding their foam-rubber bludgeons.

"Look at these cute little pieces of shit," she half sang, as if it were a line from a nursery rhyme.

"Jesus, don't say that about my kids," Emily said, crossing the lawn and shooing the boys from their aunt.

"I said they were cute." Brenda grabbed her sister and hugged her. "You're a cute little piece of shit too."

In the clench of their hug, Emily smelled her sister's unwashed hair.

Inside they stood on opposite sides of the kitchen island, huddled around coffee mugs, the damp day finally giving itself over to hard spring rain. Roger had corralled the boys into the living room, where they were watching *Wreck-It Ralph* again, the sound of 8-bit video games filling the house.

Every collaboration begins in discussion. Emily couldn't remember where she first came upon this nugget of insight, grad school or perhaps she had made it up, but she believed it was true, in business and personal matters. What she had in mind with Brenda was both business and personal. She wanted to talk about her video proposal, the one she couldn't stop thinking about. The moment Brenda had *maybe* agreed to *maybe* bring to the project her almost two decades of experience, something happened to Emily. Inspired wasn't the word. More like inflamed. She'd waited all week to tell Brenda face-to-face that what had started as a maneuver to keep Calvin Schott in prison, a two-or-three-minute video to send to the parole board, had evolved in her mind, becoming grander and far more complex, which was why she needed her sister's expertise.

But she didn't want to rush it. Brenda looked thin, wan, her lips chapped, the rims of her nostrils red. It occurred to Emily that perhaps she hadn't come here to help but was looking for help herself.

Brenda watched Emily stir Splenda into her coffee. "That stuff causes cancer."

"That's a myth."

"Lab rats got leukemia."

Emily tapped her spoon stiffly on the rim of the mug, and then let out a puff of breath and just blurted it. She felt it was impossible to resist. "I want to make a documentary."

"A what?"

"This is our chance to get it on record, as adults, the Mashburn twins reminding the world—"

"Whoa, the world?"

"Stop rolling your eyes! Calvin and Jason Schott are responsible for so much more than hijacking a bus."

"Isn't that enough?"

"We can track down the others, Martin and Lindsey and all of them." Emily had another idea that was so dangerous it made her lightheaded. This she knew not to say aloud.

Brenda couldn't understand what she was hearing. Make a movie about their kidnapping? What was the point? Calvin Schott was up for parole every couple of years. Why this time? Where did the stirring, the hot rousing, come from? Brenda wasn't so completely detached to believe the abduction played no part in who she was. Through several aborted attempts at therapy, she traced her ambition, her workaholic tendencies, her need for constant movement to August 2nd, 1984. She blamed it for her claustrophobia, and for her trouble maintaining close friendships and romantic relationships. She just disagreed with Emily that it was the single defining moment of their entire lives. What they went through was terrible, but everyone goes through terrible things. Three-quarters of their lives took place after the kidnapping. Its impact must have been watered down by now. Emily was successful—career, house, marriage, children. Why allow the kidnapping such a large piece of her identity?

No, Emily couldn't be serious. Unless it was ignorance talking. She must not have realized that documentaries took years to make and that they were made by *professionals*. She was an audiologist. It was arrogant to attempt making a film, let alone to think she could pull it off. Where was she going to find the time? And who was going to pay for it? A feature-length doc could run a million dollars without trying. Also—and this was by no means a minor factor—couldn't she tell that Brenda was barely hanging on? If Brenda was willing to give the short video a go, it was mostly a test for herself. She wanted to see if she could gut it out and push herself through a project that required many of the skills she needed to do her job, without the pressures of her actual job. If she could do that much, maybe her career wasn't over.

"What about the parole video?" Brenda said.

"Don't you think this is better?"

"I don't know. Maybe."

"Stop saying maybe."

"Is no better?"

Emily turned away, toward the sink. Regardless of what Brenda thought, their kidnapping wasn't just in the past, or simply a bad memory. It loomed over them to this day. The only way to dilute its power was to share the story, to spread it everywhere. She now saw the responsibility of telling their story as her fate. She also knew Brenda would tell her that fate wasn't real and laugh at her and say "trust me," her attitude so condescending, as if she knew some secret to the human condition just because she was the Catastrophe Queen and chronicling tragedies was her bread and butter.

Emily ran her hands under the water so Brenda couldn't hear her sigh. Her timing was just awful, she thought, and her style of persuasion had the grace of tripping over your own shoelaces. She knew when to back off. There would be other opportunities to talk about the documentary. She changed the subject.

"The other day a patient asked if he could film his earwax removal procedure and post it online."

"That's disgusting."

"You go into this career thinking you're going to be leading a cochlear implant team and you end up constantly telling people not to stick Q-Tips in their ear canal."

"Did you let him film it?"

"Fuck no."

That night, in the living room, they continued the drinking they'd started at dinner, their teeth stained Barolo purple, a movie on the TV that they didn't bother paying attention to. The boys were asleep, and Roger was listening to a World War II podcast and puffing on a stogie out on the back patio.

"When did he start smoking?" Brenda said.

"It's his new thing. I saw on the credit card statement how much he spends at The Cigar Lounge. I was like, 'Are you fucking insane?'" Emily took another sip and refilled her glass. "So that's what I've got going on."

Brenda took that as an opening to confess what she had going on, namely that her leave of absence from work entailed more than turning down one assignment. Some days she didn't check email or voicemail. Some days she didn't open the curtains. She streamed old sitcoms on her laptop in bed without watching them, the conversant voices murmuring beside her until the battery died. She kept waiting for someone to say something, or to check in on her, but her increasingly shrinking world went unnoticed by the few people close to her. She understood this was a consequence of the way she'd designed her life. Those who knew her were so accustomed to her traveling that they must have believed that her non-responsiveness meant she was off on another adventure. Still, it hurt to be so alone.

Whether or not this last comment was directed at Emily, she felt its sting. Perhaps she'd taken for granted just how taxing the last few months had been for Brenda since her head injury.

"Remember how overwhelmed I was after Ryder was born? I cried more than I talked," she said, offering up her own experience as proof that she could relate.

Brenda, of course, didn't remember. She tried to recall what she was doing at the time and couldn't come up with a good excuse for not knowing.

"Roger was legitimately worried about a murder-suicide. Thank God for drugs."

Brenda levered herself to her feet and found her bag. She palmed an orange plastic bottle.

"Like this?" she said, shaking it like a maraca.

"What did they give you?"

"Ativan. You?"

"Wellbutrin."

Brenda twisted off the top and tapped a couple of pills into her hand. "Want one? They work better with alcohol," she said.

Emily held her hand out, not that she wanted a pill. She just didn't want to punk out. This was another round in their forty-year contest that started with her entering the world twenty-four minutes before Brenda. Brenda had never forgiven her for getting a head start "on the outside," and went searching for accomplishments of her own. She walked and talked first and was pleased her name came first alphabetically. But Emily was first to lose a tooth. They both rode their bikes without training wheels on the same day, but argued over who kept her bike upright the longest that afternoon. Emily was first to shoplift (a cassingle of "Walk Like an Egyptian" from Sam Goody), Brenda to smoke (a Kent 100 lifted from their mom's soft pack). They got drunk for the first time on the same night, after the Fourth of July Fireman's Parade in 1988, a bottle of Boone's Farm Country Kwencher passed back and forth while they sat in the limbs of a birch tree in Abby Ballantine's backyard and fireworks lit up the sky over Village Memorial Park. Neither was sure who masturbated first, but it was Emily, at nine, who admitted to squeezing Monkey, her stuffed rhinoceros, between her thighs until her whole body started quaking, which sounded similar in result but different in method to how Brenda helped herself fall asleep. When it came to other sex acts, Brenda did everything first, proudly and with a bravado meant to conceal her nervous inexperience, except lose her virginity, which Emily did first, awkwardly and under mild coercion, with her boyfriend of six weeks, Greg Fitzgerald, in Fitzie's parents' bed—Coors Light this time, not Boone's, sloshing in her belly—in the fall of her junior year of high school.

They understood from a very early age that people viewed them in the collective and that the Mashburn Twins was a different object from the sum of Brenda and Emily Mashburn, so the point of the competitions wasn't so much about dominance but proving their independence from each other, without ever grasping that the easiest way to be seen as their own person was to stop spending all their time together.

Emily swallowed the Ativan and swirled her wine in the glass. She realized where she went wrong earlier with Brenda. She didn't need to sell her on why the documentary was a good idea. She didn't need to convince her at all.

Simply: "Together, we are safe."

It was what Brenda had said to her during the kidnapping, and what she had said to Brenda after the kidnapping. Then as now, it wasn't said to persuade or reassure the other, but as a declaration of truth, immutable, etched in stone. Brenda found the wine bottle and emptied it in her glass. Cornered, she couldn't say no. She and Emily possessed nearly boundless latitude to impose on each other. Being twins bonded them in deeper and stranger ways than regular siblings even without the shared experience of being abducted. The importance Emily heaped upon Schott's incarceration was general knowledge. Whatever she saw fit to do in the service of keeping him in prison wouldn't be too much to ask Brenda to participate in, regardless of her raggedy condition.

"I just want to punch you right in your pig face," was all Brenda said.

And it was settled.

"So, this is pre-production?" Emily asked.

"Call it what you want."

Then they dropped the subject and uncorked another bottle of wine.

By morning, they were both hungover and pretended they weren't. Brenda was writing on her laptop, trying to at least, while around her, at the breakfast table, Ryder and Sonny played "Band," the game where they pounded on their plates with utensils like drumsticks.

"Only one of you can be the drummer," Brenda said. "That's how a band works. You should stop banging until you decide who it is."

Roger joined them at the table. He took a big slurp of a moss-colored smoothie, the residue caking up in the corners of his mouth.

"Do you know why my sweet sons, who I love more than anything in the world, called me a cute little piece of shit last night?" he asked Brenda.

"Because you are."

"I hope my wife mentioned you're welcome to stay as long as you like," he said.

"Shut up, Rog," Emily said, dropping a pot of coffee down on a trivet knitted by their grandmother. She watched Brenda on her laptop, typing, deleting, typing again. "What are you working on?"

Brenda held up one finger, and reread what she'd written, mouthing the words.

She turned the screen to Emily. "What do you think?"

Were you a victim of the Brookwood Bus Kidnapping? Were you a friend, neighbor, relative, or coworker of a victim? If so, Emily Mashburn-Bauer would like to talk to you. Select participants will get the opportunity to tell their story in a major documentary project produced by award-winning broadcast journalist Brenda Mashburn. Interested individuals should send an email with their name, contact information, and a brief summary of their experience during those fateful summer days in 1984.

Emily was shaking and not because she'd guzzled thirty ounces of coffee. Her surroundings seemed to disappear, as if the room had narrowed and darkened. All she could see was the glowing paragraph on the screen.

"This is perfect," she said.

Brenda looked over her work once more and shrugged. She saved the doc and closed the laptop.

"For specific people we want to contact, I'll tailor the pitches to them, personalize them," she said.

"I want to interview Calvin and Jason Schott," Emily blurted. This was what she'd considered too dangerous to say aloud.

"That's not going to happen," Brenda said, without hesitation, scooping off the table a browning apple slice with a bite out of its corner. She dropped it on Sonny's plate.

"I want to get us all in the same room."

"We're not doing that."

"They owe us an explanation. And everyone else. Don't they?"

"It doesn't matter."

"Don't they?"

"You're not going to get out of it what you think you will."

"You don't know what I want to get out of it."

"It won't go the way you think."

"How do you know?"

"Because it's my job to know. Trust me."

And this time Emily couldn't fall back on "together, we are safe." Brenda was shutting her down.

"I want to know what the fuck they have to say for themselves now that they're not dealing with children," Emily said, her exquisite hatred of the Schott brothers ballooning in her.

"Mommy's mad," Sonny said and ran around the table and hugged his mother.

"She is. I'm going to hide from her," Brenda said, standing and tucking her laptop under her arm, starting out of the room.

Emily stayed at the table, one arm around her younger son's shoulders, her other hand tapping her thigh. She felt impatient and gloomy. Sonny dug his forehead into her ribcage. He was too young to know about the kidnapping. The boy feared raccoons and hermit crabs and garbage trucks and men with moustaches.

And yet, his brother was almost the same age Andy Kraven had been.

Interviewing the Schotts wasn't a bad idea, she thought. It was the only idea. She pictured herself and Brenda seated across from Calvin and Jason, sitting on plastic chairs that scraped a concrete prison floor. She imagined them as they'd appeared in newspaper articles after their arrest: young, sandy-haired, and big, with something soggy about them, like they had dumb wet brains leaking out of their ears.

What was the point of a documentary if it omitted a face-to-face? Emily needed to know why the Schotts took them. They said it was for money, but money wasn't reason enough. Money didn't get to the heart of their slovenly malice. There needed to be more. A genetic malformation, a disorder in the blood. There needed to be an identifiable shortcoming inborn to the Schott line. It couldn't just be greed and a lack of empathy. How could Emily protect her sons in a world where such grubby chumps could inflict untold damage and not have to explain themselves? And the Schotts had gone long enough without knowing that they were the reason Ryder and Sonny's forty-year-old mother still slept with a nightlight, and that she needed to keep the bedroom window open a little, no matter the weather, because breathing stagnant air could give her muscle tremors. It was time they learned that if her life seemed in any way normal, it came from an extreme internal demand to prove her normalcy. They didn't know that there was no higher compliment you could pay Emily than to call her boring.

There was only one way they were going to hash it out, all of it.

She lifted Sonny onto her lap, but he wiggled out of her grasp and plodded barefoot out of the room.

THURSDAY, AUGUST 2, 1984

There was no plan to meet outside the Brookwood Union-Free School District office building with the same four words on their lips, *Where are our kids?*—a request and a demand—but they drifted over there after finding Brookwood Middle closed up, doors locked, lights out, the fence to the playground chained with galvanized links, and not even peering through a window produced a janitor crooning into the handle of a string mop while wandering the dusty halls. A closed school at that hour normally meant all was well, but today it screamed negligence in the face of a crisis. An abdication of responsibility. They dispersed off school property and gathered in the parking lot outside the district office. It was a matter of style how to proceed, but the angriest set the tone, flattening the timid and taking the just polite along for the ride. They were done asking nicely, done accepting the story about Burnt Velveeta catching a flat, or overheating. Because it was just that—a story. They were willing to give the ladies in the office the benefit of the doubt that the line about a breakdown wasn't a ploy to buy time until their kids could be located, but still, they'd heard enough. They were done.

Where are our kids? they asked, roving the halls of the building, which was part of the town administration complex and which, at six on a summer evening, should have closed hours ago, their voices echoing off the floor tiles and concrete block walls painted a coffee color and hung with portraits of superintendents current and of years past. Which reminded them: Where was Superintendent Tomasetti? His portrait captured the permanent dampness of his upper lip to an uncanny degree, as though the painting were wet to the touch, along with his supercilious eyes. Was it his decision to put their kids on an ancient school bus under the supervision of a suspected creep? Was that what he considered strong policy for a well-funded public education system in a nice community?

They were met by Principal Ferguson and were taken aback by his appearance. Trevor Ferguson was dressed in the very un-principal style of a newly divorced outdoorsman, looking like he'd spent the day fishing in Stone Fort River, quenching his thirst with Miller Lite. He was sunburnt and slightly drunk, his ash-blond hair no longer captured under successive layers of aerosol spray but hanging thin and limp over his forehead, revealing his pink scalp underneath. Had they found him this way at the Fireman's Parade on the Fourth of July, they might have offered him another cold one out of their own Igloo coolers, but here in the staid district office, under the temperate gaze of three generations of superintendents, they couldn't have encountered a worse steward.

He received them with arms spread and a grimace that was supposed to pass for compassion.

"We're working on it," he said.

The vagueness, the frank cluelessness of this tipsy school administrator enraged the already angry, confounded the timid and the just polite.

Working on it? What the hell does that mean?

"We're working on it," he said again (what else could he say?), and sensing a deeper interrogation he was unprepared to address, quickly added, "We think we just got a tip that someone saw the school bus and we're doing everything in our power to get the bus back."

School bus? They glanced around at each other to make sure they'd heard him correctly.

Who gives a shit about the bus?

Where are our kids?

"I hear what you're saying," Ferguson said, nodding in his measured bureaucratic way and massaging the back of his neck with one hand. "Really, I do. I'm a parent. And like I said, we're working on it."

There was only one response they would accept, the one that reinforced the belief that the authority they had granted Ferguson and others of his ilk wasn't misplaced, the one that said, "We know where your children are. They are safe and sound and on the way here as we speak." And now that it was clear he possessed no information that might have mitigated the wholesale alarm they felt, they hammered him with other questions:

What happened?

Who did this?

Who is Pat Earl?

What are you doing to fix this? And, so help me God, don't say you're working on it.

Ferguson stood there absorbing the blows, a boxer too punchy to fight his way out of the corner. He nodded along, considering each new query, at one point rubbing his chin with index finger and thumb, saying "mm–hmm" until reprieve came in the form of recently hired Chief of Police Deke Devine, who stepped out of the men's room and joined Principal Ferguson in the hallway.

They didn't know this man well, his having come to Brookwood only three months earlier from some Midwest city, South Bend or Evansville, but he wore a uniform, a badge pinned over his heart and a gun holstered on his hip. At once, he vaulted Ferguson in the chain of command. Devine removed his hat, a red line imprinted on his forehead. He apologized for having to meet them under such tense circumstances.

"I've issued an APB. I've been in direct contact with the chiefs of police in the surrounding towns. County and state police too."

Who did this to our kids?

"We don't know that anyone did anything. Not yet," he said.

Come on, just come the fuck on, people don't just vanish without a trace.

"You're right, they don't. Which means we'll find them."

At least he was confident, unlike the principal who looked like a semi-deflated balloon next to him. They wanted to know what they should do, how they could help.

"I know this isn't what you want to hear but the best thing you can do is go home."

You're telling us to do nothing? How can we wait and do nothing?

"If you have other kids, take care of them. Make dinner. Say a prayer if you're inclined."

Devine said he hoped to have more to tell them shortly. He bid them a good evening and asked Principal Ferguson for a few minutes in private. The two men left them in the hallway, where after milling around for a moment they exited the building, back outside into the shimmering asphalt parking lot.

They climbed into their cars and began a slow canvas of town, setting aside the chief's directive without discussion. Rather than search methodically and retrace the bus's route, or start at Brookwood Middle and work in concentric circles to widen the area of exploration, or divide the town into quadrants and split up into teams, each of them felt compelled to follow paths of private importance. They drove the streets they were most acquainted with, the ones they traveled most often, checking landmarks of personal significance, the favorite restaurant, the corner playground, the bowling alley where the kids had birthday parties. They drove by their houses and houses of relatives, houses of their friends and their kids' friends. They drove through where they had built lives, powerless to imagine a world much larger than the one they had expressly created to prevent a day such as this.

Jason came to me and said, "We should start a real estate company."

"Maybe not," I said. I was too convinced of our success to give him credit for thinking it up.

"Maybe not?" he said.

"That's right."

"Maybe you were born without a penis."

"Maybe I'll beat you so bad George and Bertie will need to decide if they want to donate your organs before pulling the plug."

"No, it's not maybe. You definitely have no dick."

This was what passed for negotiations between us. Suffice it to say we were at an impasse.

Hours later: "I've been doing some strategizing, my baby brother, and I've come to the conclusion that we will make a bucket of money in real estate development."

"That sounds so familiar," Jason said.

"You said something about a real estate company. Which is kind of, I don't know, abstract. It tells me you're not a serious person. I'm talking about real estate *development*. It's more specific."

"Fine. Whatever. Let's do it."

We consummated our partnership at The Knight Spot in an orgy of ten-cent wings and mudslides, which our father found in a chunky, fly-teeming puddle in the driveway on his way to work. George stomped back in the house and woke us up where we were sprawled across the sectional couch in the family room by throwing a coiled garden hose at us, with the instruction to wash down the driveway.

But we surprised him and Bertie and, if I'm being honest, ourselves, by following through for once and incorporating Schott Enterprises Corp., a simple name that gave us the flexibility to branch out into any area of commerce we found potentially lucrative. For seed money, we drew down on our trust, our inheritance from our late Great-Uncle Fred. Fred, having no children, set us up with a sweet legacy, and insofar as we were able to think of anyone but ourselves, we wanted to do him proud. He was something of a folk hero to us. The story of how he'd survived the crash that took his legs had reached mythological proportions by the time we heard it. He died when I was twelve and had been sick for years, but I remembered him pushing himself around on his knuckles and making jokes, roaring over his onset deafness.

"Boys, what do you call a dyke dinosaur?"

We didn't even know what a dyke was.

"Lickalottapuss!"

This was the patron saint of Schott Enterprises. Why? Who knows? He wasn't even a Schott. We called him, unironically, Our Founder, and when we rented space in Fiore Plaza, a refurbished office building in town, we hung Fred's portrait in the reception area of our suite. There he was, the crafty businessman, a gimlet-eyed sentry watching over us. But like most spiritual superintendents, ours was absent when we needed him. Where was he when Lonzo Feldman Jr. paid us a visit?

We'd just hit the milestone of one month in business. We had yet to acquire a single property or parcel of land, though we'd placed bids at two foreclosure auctions where we were soundly outbid. Lonzo arrived without an appointment. He just walked in the door and gave his name to our receptionist, Erica, who we'd gone to high school with and who Jay hired because he thought his executive status would inspire her to fuck him.

Lonzo was an old guy, with oatmeal-colored hair and wide, sculpted black eyebrows. He wore dentures and dressed like George Steinbrenner, cashmere turtleneck sweater beneath a navy cashmere blazer, grey flannel pants.

We made him wait for a while to give the impression we were busy. When we came out to meet him, he said to Erica, "Do you think you would like to play road repair after work?" It seemed as if he wanted us to hear.

"What's that?" she said.

"It's a game."

"How do you play?" She was more confused than intrigued.

"You lay down and I fill your pothole."

"What the fuck, Grandpa?" I said.

Erica was already grabbing her purse from under her desk. She left and didn't even come back for her check that week.

Jay started following her, but the old man stopped him. "You don't realize it right now, but I did you gents a huge favor."

He said we needed a battle-tested receptionist, a frontline soldier who would die to protect us, not someone who would let in anyone off the street. "My girl, Denise, has a felony battery charge," he said. "She threw a process server down a flight of stairs."

He slipped into our office and waved for us to follow. "If you want to get rich, give me five minutes."

Lonzo Feldman Jr. talked for much longer than five minutes. He told us about his life. He had lived all over the world, he said, but didn't name where. He had been married four times. His first wife had nine and a half fingers, having lost two knuckles on her left index from a mishap with a watertight door on a cruise ship when she was sixteen. The injury didn't slow her down and sometimes she used to plug his butt with her nub. He told us about his family. His father was a chemist, his grandfather a glazier. His ancestors were borderline nobility prior to their expulsion from Seville during the Inquisition. The last half millennium was spent recovering all that was lost. That was his fate, he said, choking up about it. His fate was what led him to real estate. If he owned enough land in enough different places he could never again be expelled.

If my brother and I didn't contribute to the conversation it was because we had no inkling as to what he was talking about, or why he was in our office, or what he wanted from us. I was starting to think he was a crazy old man, living far longer than he ever intended to, alone and lonely and seeking human contact wherever he could find it, someone who just saw our name on the directory in the lobby and decided to say hey.

Then he produced a business card:

> Eastern Capital Development Inc.
> Lonzo Feldman Jr., President

Finally, he revealed the purpose of his visit. Three years earlier, Eastern Capital had closed on several hundred thousand acres of Hudson Valley land, zoned for mixed-use construction. The Initial Phase, whatever that was, was already complete. The Secondary Phase could not have gone better, he said. The Tertiary Phase, and again he didn't elaborate, was underway. He was now seeking investors for the Operation Phase, the production of a condominium complex the likes of which the country had never seen. Along with tasteful, modern condos—one, two, and three-bedroom models—there would be amenities that surpassed your normal luxury developments: a thirty-five-acre lake stocked with bass, a golf course that would shame the designers of Winged Foot, two Olympic-size pools, two indoor tennis courts, a multiplex movie theater, a five-star restaurant, and a supermarket. All of it one hour from Grand Central Station.

"Clean. Green. Serene," he said. "A one-of-a-kind living experience. We even have a name: Munsee Estates."

That name, Munsee. Talk about fate.

"I'd be interested in hearing your preliminary thoughts," said Lonzo Feldman Jr.

"I like what I hear," Jay said.

"Me too," I agreed, and at no point did I wonder how the president of Eastern Capital Development had found us, or why he wanted to bring us in on this massive deal.

"Who's up for a field trip?" Lonzo said.

He drove a late model Cadillac DeVille, burgundy with a white top, that inside smelled of leather polish and tea. We traveled local streets a half hour west of the office, to an area where the road bent through a copse of trees and became unpaved. We stopped just past the turnoff, a chain-link fence preventing further progress. On the other side of the fence was razed wooded land, bulldozer tracks zigzagging across dirt, and two trailers on cinderblocks.

"Isn't this part of a park?" Jason said.

"It was. We acquired it from the county. I won't tell you what we paid."

Lonzo pointed at what he said were building permits taped to the doors of the trailers.

"I want you to picture it," he said.

"Condos?" Jason said.

"No, not condos. The rarest thing in the world."

"What's that?" I said.

"A perfect happiness. That's what we're building here." He sort of traced the air with his finger, as if drawing what would one day be visible. "Initial buy-in is one million dollars," he said.

The deal he presented meshed so well with my faith in our inevitability that I was reluctant to walk away. But happiness, perfect or otherwise, wasn't part of our family's belief system, and Schott Enterprises Corp. didn't have a million dollars. Nothing close to it. We were out of our league. I said nothing because there was nothing to say.

"Have I scared the shit out of you?" Lonzo said. "Come on, gents, what did you think, you could build a utopia on the cheap?"

"What do we get for our investment?" Jason asked.

Lonzo perked right up and slapped him on the shoulder encouragingly. He said parcels would be subdivided, deeded to us. He spoke as if our partnership with him was a foregone conclusion. We would enter into a holding company.

"Eastern Capital Development will stay on to manage your property and receive a modest fee for our services."

On the ride back, he talked about lawyers. Like we had lawyers. "Have your Jews call my Jews," he said. They would send a term sheet via messenger service. Everything would be spelled out in the King's English. Then he left us on the sidewalk in front of our office.

Once free of Lonzo, Jason said we had to invest. *Had to.* I pointed out the obvious—we didn't have the money. He said that was irrelevant. Lonzo would take less than a million.

"How do you know?" I said.

"I don't know. But we'll convince him. We'll make him. We can't pass this up."

I didn't care if he got the credit this time. I wanted him to be right so badly.

"Let's see how much he'll really take," I said.

By New Year's Day, Lonzo Feldman Jr. had taken every dollar we had.

He needed a glorious night for Ultimate Hardcore Victory Wrestling.

Of course, Andy Kraven, Managing Member of Kravy Train Productions LLC, would have admitted that glory was not only an elusive bitch, but relative. For tonight, it was loosely defined as an outcome better than a total fucking fiasco. Which wasn't a given. In the run up to his first house show for the bottom-rung, semi-pro wrestling outfit he'd founded, there were times he thought a truer name for his company would have been Ultimate Career Ending Mistake. But it was his experience that dabbling in honesty might have felt virtuous in the moment, yet never settled a bar tab, let alone real debts. He'd crowed and swanked and shit-talked his way to this day. Now the day was here. Be careful what you wish for...etc.

Oh, brother, forget glory, forget fiasco, couldn't we meet in the middle, he thought. He just needed things to go moderately well. Was that too much to hope for? The fire department's sign outside the gymnasium at Our Lady of Mount Carmel High School announced a maximum capacity of three hundred. Any quasi-competent promoter could fill that space. His "intern," Boyd, was dispatched downtown, near campus, passing out flyers to the toxic fraternity set, one of the demographics Kraven was so desperate to reach. Drunken collegiate animals, along with younger teens hopped up on the promise of violence, the socially awkward but fiscally solvent, and divorced guys with weekend custody and nothing to do to entertain the kids—this was who Andy Kraven made art for.

Doors opened in fifteen and he checked in with Corine at the card table that doubled as the box office. Corine—Girlfriend? Business partner? Emotional caretaker?—a woman whose intelligence and poise were undermined by a tendency to walk face first into life, counted out the money in the cash box, seeing that there was enough to make change.

"How does it look?" he said.

Without breaking count, she nodded her head at the line forming to get in. "I need more ones and fives," she said.

He unpocketed some cash and peeled off a handful of damp bills of the lesser dominations. At thirty-seven years old, Andy Kraven considered himself neither a success nor a failure, but a survivor. In the literal and metaphorical sense. He thrived at perduring and liked to think he did so in style, with flourishes that approached originality.

He didn't have time to stand there gawking at the crowd and contemplating what they meant to his sense of self. A rented tux in the boy's locker room had his name on it. He hurried through the gym, past the ring and rows of chairs. Next to the vending machines, at a cafeteria table lined with glossy headshots, a tractor trailer of a human sat resignedly on a folding chair that strained like children's furniture under him.

Despite his gargantuan frame, there was something wasted about the man at the table, the years having punished him as brutally as he punished others. Kraven hadn't forgotten his agility and grace in the ring, a thing so incompatible with his size—to call him barrel-chested was an injustice; his thighs were barrels, his chest a refrigerator, his neck a steel-belted radial tire—that it almost required cognitive dissonance to accept his athletic prowess. Twenty years ago he was champion of the world, briefly, his fighting persona a Heel. He was never meant to hold the title for long. He won the strap just to give it back at the next pay-per-view, but did so admirably, with guts, beating the ever-living shit out of the Face for over an hour, both of them bloody and concussed, before rolling over on his back and letting himself be pinned—*letting himself*. No man walking the earth could have forced his shoulders to the mat for a count of three.

Most of the Kravy Train budget for this event was spent on getting him here. Andy knew his promotional material needed a name, a famous former wrestler to raise the profile of the entire outfit. Part of the deal was to let the champ and his weaselly representative hawk merch before and after the show, with zero percent of the proceeds funneled back to the house.

The fan in Andy didn't much care. He remembered the champ's promos from the '90s.

And I will make your women shudder and your babes cry, such is the torment I will bring to your loved ones, this Sunday, in Atlanta, where fifteen thousand screaming innocents will witness my brutality and your demise.

Talk about glorious!

Andy stepped to the table, thinking if this man had played football, he'd have a bust in Canton. Instead, he was slinging autographs in Phoenix. He must have weighed four hundred pounds. Check out the size of his noggin! Up close you could see the ruts of scar tissue across his forehead from where he bladed himself.

"How're you feeling, Champ?"

Fidgeting beside him was the aforementioned representative, a skinny, sunglassed, tracksuited interlocutor. More like a pimp, it seemed to Andy.

"Goes like this," said the greasy agent, pushing his shades onto his forehead, a thin scar segmenting his right eyebrow. "Twenty-five for a signed print, twenty for a picture with my man using my camera, ten using your camera or phone, and ten for his John Handcock," for some reason enunciating a *d* that wasn't there. He pointed to a sheet of loose leaf taped to the table, confirming the rates in blue marker. He stuck his hands in his jacket pockets and nodded so his sunglasses fell back into place.

"This is my show," Andy said. "I met you like an hour ago."

"Silly me," the manager said. "Nevertheless, why don't you grab a photo and pay the man back for all the entertainment he gave you over the years?"

"Later," Andy said, moving toward the locker room. He was glad the broken-down goliath was here, but at what cost to the morale of the organization? What message did it send to his hopeful young performers to show them that even if you were the luckiest bastard going today, who beat the odds and reached the highest highs of this dark profession, Heavyweight Champion of the World, you would wind up back in a high school gym, or VFW, or community center, your shaky signature and snarling image the only thing left of value?

The locker room was abuzz with pre-show activity: stretching, push-ups, applying makeup, arranging last-minute choreography. Most of the wrestlers were kids and Ultimate Hardcore Victory Wrestling was a thing do to right now, their long-term futures an unthinkable concept, like their own mortality. They were fans of the sport and liked being a part of it, hanging on the outskirts of the dream. A few were rough and gritty, fellow survivors like Kraven, and could maybe make a small life in the ring until it became too hard. The others were what they were—amateurs. He walked among them shaking hands, busting balls, having decided personalized attention was superior to gathering them together for a Vince Lombardian pep talk about faith and family and the Green Bay Packers, or whatever was analogous here.

As he worked the locker room, he sensed something wrong, something out of place.

"Where's Bobby? Has anyone seen Bobby?" he said in a panic.

Bobby Simmons was the one athlete in his rickety stable who had distinguished himself for his size and nimbleness, his intelligence. The boy had the unteachable quality of magnetism, the elusive "It" factor. His destiny held spandex-clad heroics, at least that was what Andy kept telling him.

Where was the star performer? He couldn't remember seeing him all day. "Where the fuck is Bobby goddamn Simmons?" he shouted.

"In here, Boss," boomed a voice from the shower room.

Bobby was pacing the tiled floor, heaving hot breath, getting himself into character, his terrifying gimmick, the Bunny Man. With pantyhose over his face, the long sheer legs sprouting from the top of his head like rabbit ears, the man was a snatcher of children, an author of nightmares, evil personified, heel of all heels. In the Bunny Man, Kraven hoped to transform trauma into cash. And, really, what was a more American way of healing than that?

He was honestly frightened to see his star in costume. "Main event. Tell me you're ready."

Bobby dropped to a folding chair and began winding a length of athletic tape around his left wrist. "What are you shouting about? You look like you might throw up. Did you eat something funny?"

"It's nerves, Bobby. Don't worry about me. Just make sure you're ready."

"No problemo." He stood and ripped a showerhead off the wall, smashed it against his forehead.

Andy jumped. "God, you're scary."

"That's the point, isn't it?" Bobby said, smiling through his pantyhose.

"Please don't break anything else. Father Garcia is going to make me pay for that."

He left the Bunny Man and donned his tuxedo, upended his flask into his mouth for a three-Mississippi count, and took a nervous piss at the urinal. From beyond the locker room walls he heard the chanting, "Start the show! Start the show!" He had another drink and another piss, a dozen or so deep, restorative breaths, and then busted out of the boy's locker room, his performers rooting him on. What he found on the other side of the door stopped him in his tracks. Every seat in the gym was filled, with more people standing behind the last rows. The chanting turned to cheers when they saw him. The show was starting!

He slid under the bottom rope into the ring. As he always did when feeling panicky, Andy relied on his ability to run his mouth, to refine whatever was unsettling him into pure trash talk. He tramped from one corner of the ring to the other, pointing and flailing about with his right arm, sweat already covering his face. Instead of welcoming the audience to the show and thanking the Arch Diocese of Phoenix, he began yelling at them, taunting them, belittling them, telling them they were too stupid and ugly to appreciate the greatness they were about to witness; and when they booed, he looked shocked, then remorseful. He turned demur and praised their intellect and great beauty, their wisdom for buying tickets and showing up tonight, the whole time yapping into his microphone. The gym was small enough that they would have heard him without the mic, but it was a prop, there to give the illusion of speaking before a sold-out crowd of fifty-six thousand at Arizona Stadium or, considering his rhythmic bark and the maniacal flash in his eyes, a crowd of hundreds of thousands in 1939 Berlin.

He stomped his foot on the mat and asked them if they were ready, and they took up their chant again to start the show. He egged them on, staring at them, uncomprehending, as if he couldn't hear them. He cupped his hand over his ear. The chanting amplified, grew louder and tribal and, finally, he said, "Alright, fine, shut up, you're wasting my precious time."

He introduced the first match. Fabulous Frankie Stylz sauntered to the ring, giving everyone ample time to drink him in, tossing his long, bleached-blond hair out of his eyes with a lurid shake of his head. The crowd identified at once that his arrogant, effeminate posturing, and the way he shooed them away with the back of his hand, was to be reviled, and they harassed him without mercy. He preened on the ring apron, and they hated him more.

Next to the ring was Sargent Psycho—J.P. behind the scenes— who bragged about having 104 confirmed kills in Iraq, a claim

Andy found prudent to neither verify nor dispute, though the fact J.P. misspelled *sergeant* in his own moniker had Andy skeptical. The Sarg sprinted to the ring, shirtless in his desert camo pants and boots, entering to music that was all crunchy guitars and heavy bass beats. He gave the impression he would need to be hit with a tranquilizer dart to rein him in after the match.

The ringsiders lost their minds when they saw him. Sargent Psycho ran around delivering windmilling high fives. He jumped into the ring and shook the ropes.

Without waiting for the bell to start the bout, Sargent Psycho dropped Fabulous Frankie with an elbow to the jaw—*Thwack!* as he hit the mat—and continued the onslaught. Boots to the chest, stomach, legs, back. He lifted his opponent to his feet by his hair and body slammed him, then lifted him again. But this time, Stylz slowed the Sarg with a knee between the legs. He now had control and pushed Sargent Psycho into a corner and, out of the ref's sight but not the audience's, gouged him in the eyes. He pummeled him with chops to the chest, the slaps echoing around the gym, and then flung him across the ring into the opposite turnbuckle.

Andy watched from the announcer's table, surprised by, and pleased with, the action. This was good entertainment, he thought, both wrestlers energetic and committed. But they were still rookies, apprentices. It was obvious in their clinches that they were whispering the next set of moves, an errant smile momentarily replacing a grimace or scowl. In those moments, there was little separating them from Andy and Kaito Watanabe and their staged brawls back in Brookwood.

Their opening act antics were brief. Sargent Psycho regained command and, gripping Stylz by the back of the neck, launched him out of the ring, onto the gym floor. He climbed to the top rope and paused, his arms outstretched, to build suspense and give Fabulous Frankie time to stand up. He was going to do a moonsault, a full backflip off the top rope, splashing Stylz in the chest. In practice, they nailed the move most of the time.

Andy clenched his tuxedo pants under the table and Sargent Psycho flung his body toward Stylz, who wobbled in a daze on his feet. He rotated in the air, his body arching, but it seemed he got stuck halfway. The gymnasium floor reached up to him. Stylz saw what was happening and rushed forward to catch him, but it was too late. The Sarg landed on the crown of his head with a nauseating thud. The chanting, heckling, screaming, cheering stopped. There was one collective groan and then silence. Andy sprinted to Sargent Psycho lying immobile on the floor. Stylz kept saying, "Talk to me, man. Talk to me. Come on, brother, squeeze my hand. Squeeze it."

Andy gave the paramedics room to work. He found the ghouls in the audience with their phones outstretched, recording. The other wrestlers had come out from the locker room and huddled together at a respectful distance. They took a knee and held hands and prayed, a gesture that looked both genuine and gratuitous, which Andy thought was fitting for a pro-wrestling event.

"Give it up for Sargent Psycho. Let him hear you," he said, and the medics wheeled the stretcher away.

The crowd delivered a somber ovation, honoring this brave, idiotic kid. And then Father Garcia took Andy aside and canceled the rest of the show.

It was inevitable that he woke to a bad morning. He opened his eyes to patent leather shoes on the pillow next to him. No sign of Corine in his sour room. He remembered arguing with Father Garcia long after the audience had filed out of the gym, saying, "Hey Padre, if you're such a man of God, why don't you stay the hell out of his way? You ever stop to think it's part of his blueprint to cripple my guy?"

The rest of the night was less precise in his memory. He tried piecing it together. He had a clear image of feasting on the teat of his flask till it was empty, and having Corine drive him to the liquor store for a refill en route to the hospital, while she kept asking him if that was really a smart thing to do. He was turned away at the emergency room under, what seemed to him now, a discriminately enforced "family only" policy. He remembered not being able to convince a nurse he was Sargent Psycho's uncle. The scene abruptly shifted in his mind to the curb by the fire lane. He was still drinking, still wearing his tux. The same nurse was threatening to call the police. Corine also insisted they go home. From there, it was bits and pieces—his head hanging out of the passenger side window because he was puking or just quaffing the night air? Had he smashed the bourbon bottle on the walkway outside his building or accidentally dropped it? Was that blood or gravy on his cummerbund?

He struggled out of bed and was on his hands and knees on the floor when he heard the apartment door open.

"What are you doing?" Corine said when she found him.

"Child's pose. Really opens up my lower back."

He decided to go back to sleep. The fallout from last night's show wasn't going anywhere and he should probably be rested when he tackled it. He put his elbows on the mattress and started dragging himself up. He stopped halfway.

"Wait, why were you out and about so early?"

"Did I leave here early, or did I not stay last night?" Corine said.

"Yes."

"Which one?"

"I'm glad we agree." He went to hug her, but she backed away.

"I'm mad at you."

"Rightfully so."

Again, she snubbed his embrace.

"Come on," he said. "You're not going to stay mad forever. At some point, you'll forgive me, so why don't we skip to that part?"

"You're such an asshole."

"I love it when we finish each other's thoughts."

"Just so you know, J.P. is going to be okay."

It wasn't what he expected her to say. He let out a long breath in relief. "Thank Christ."

"His dad says he's going to sue you, though."

She walked out of the room. The apartment door clicked shut behind her.

He lay back down and closed his eyes but couldn't sleep. He tallied the good and bad from last night to keep a loose score. J.P. not paralyzed: good. Looming lawsuit: bad. The show getting canceled before the Bunny Man could make his debut: bad, possibly very bad if Bobby Simmons lost faith in him and walked. Corine mad at him: bad also, but becoming status quo. Hangover only mild: good. The future of Kravy Train Productions and Ultimate Hardcore Victory Wrestling: TBD, but not trending in a positive direction.

More bad than good in the final count, and yet here was Andy Kraven. In bed, depleted on several fronts, but still here. Another day survived. Another day ahead of him. Living in America meant getting good at buying time between catastrophes. He eagerly wanted to know what he was capable of, what he might accomplish, without having to expend so much energy on the task of distancing himself from oncoming trouble. Who would he be if he were able to apply his creativity to something other than endurance? What could he create with a little breathing room? The unyielding hustle frustrated him, but more than anything it made him sad that there wasn't some grander function for adulthood, for life. No, the only goal was to survive it if you could, for as long as you could. He took pride in hacking it, in confounding the bandits ever nearer his door, but in considering sources of self-respect, this one was about as comforting as reheated coffee.

He yanked the pillow over his head, seeking darkness. His rancid breath made him sick, and he gave up on sleep. He found his phone charging on the night table and played around on it, scrolling mindlessly through a bunch of Facebook bullshit until—what was that in his feed? He almost missed the post, except the word Brookwood jumped out at him. Brenda and Emily? He hadn't heard their names in years. A documentary? *Interested individuals should send an email . . .* Was he interested? He thought about it. Well, was he? Fuckin' A right, he was.

He emailed at once, reintroducing himself to the twins. "As if you could ever forget your old buddy," he wrote. He sensed that this movie could be his next opportunity, though he wasn't sure in what way. He just knew he wanted to be involved, and he was a little disappointed that he hadn't thought to make a movie, but he also understood why it never occurred to him. Despite the wishes of everyone in Brookwood to get life back to normal, the truth was that those on the bus had been stained. The town had wanted nothing more than to pretend the abduction never happened, and so he and the others couldn't be embraced because they were walking, talking reminders of the one thing everybody wanted to forget. They'd ended up denying what they were going through to make life easier for everyone else, which in turn they hoped would make life easier for them too. It worked on the surface level, but they were still oddities, and they resented the subtle ways they were shown to be oddities. He and Kaito remained friends into high school, until their joint unpopularity caused them to turn away from each other and go in separate directions.

Brenda and Emily were different. They were sisters, they lived together, they looked exactly alike. They couldn't abandon each other; that would mean abandoning themselves. Probably no one was less likely to reshape their lives in the aftermath of the ordeal than the Mashburns because they couldn't look away from it. That was why they were the ones now willing to put it on film, Andy thought.

He reread the post and wondered who else would reply. Fourteen Likes, but it was early still, even in New York.

THURSDAY, AUGUST 2, 1984

Officer Al Tiles had successfully cold-turkeyed each of his vices except anger, which he often confused for his noblest virtue. Alone in his patrol car, he raged gloriously at the forced overtime he was enlisted to perform by recently hired Chief of Police Deke Devine in service of finding a school bus, along with its nineteen passengers plus driver, that somehow vanished midafternoon under bright skies. This bus situation was quite frankly as incomprehensible to Tiles as the new chief's vendetta against him. It appeared Devine had arrived via hell on a mission of tormenting him to insanity or death, whichever came first.

On his first day in charge, without trying to get to know Tiles, Devine had taken to calling him "Shingles." Tiles didn't get why, but Detective Moe Winston explained the joke to him, and he punched his locker, an outburst that only cemented his new nickname around the station.

"And let's not forget," he fumed in his patrol car and drifted southeast on Overland Avenue. "Let's not forget, it gets worse." The next part he couldn't say aloud. Devine looked the other way when the rotation schedule was posted and someone had entered the name Officer Asphalt Shingles into first shift. What kind of example of leadership did that set?

The unfairness of it all.

And now, forced overtime, on top of the nickname, when his shift ended at three and he had something going on, albeit minor, a beef short rib defrosting on the kitchen counter that would surely spoil by the time he got home.

"Whenever in the cock-shitting heck that might be," he yelled, the anger like an IV drip, sliding through his veins. He felt it cool and heavy in his stomach, a narcotic as potent as Benzedrine, with a comedown almost as sickening; and there were few things he'd loved more than crushing bennies under a paperweight and sniffing the powder. But anger came to him absent the moral failing of substance abuse, though he often suffered equally violent symptoms of shame in the throes of a hangover. Now, though, he was soaring on his high, tweaking it higher by picturing flies landing on his not inexpensive cut of meat sweating helplessly on the Tupperware cutting board his sister gave him for Christmas. "Turding out fricking purple eggs all over the beef!"

After substituting lunch with coffee, the one thing in the world he wanted more than to strangle the life out of his boss was to piss. He coasted onto Cherry Road, and into the Butler Reservoir parking lot. He skidded on his heels down the dirt path onto the hiking trail. The trees shaded the sun but did nothing for the humidity, a wet wall of air. He rested against an oak while a pungent rope of urine frothed in a puddle at his feet. The water glared silver yellow. Tiles wished he could strip out of his uniform and take a dip. He remembered floating in a tire tube in the reservoir when he was a boy. His mother called him ashore for lunch and when he climbed out, he misidentified an underwater tree root for a snake. He yelped and his father clapped him on the back of his head and said, "Keep crying like a girl and you'll grow tits." His mother, shelling a hardboiled egg, said nothing.

He thought of ditching his uniform, gun and badge and everything, and hopping in in his tighty-whities and splashing across to the other side, climbing out cleansed, a new man. There was something alluring about a fresh start, and he'd even tinkered with cleaning up his act lately. He'd kicked speed and B&B brandy and poker, his trifecta of fun, trusting that his colleagues would deem his self-improvement commendable. The only person who noticed was his sister, and she only remarked he smelled better lately. Nevertheless, in sobriety he felt like less of a dirtbag, which justified to him his impatience and quick temper with everything and everyone. It also made Devine's hatred of him so difficult to understand. The chief performed his job as an honorable man in all other areas. Why was he such a galactic prick when it came to Tiles?

He stood there in the woods with his dick in his hand, an apt metaphor for his career. He didn't know why he didn't just quit the force. An overdeveloped sense of justice or a driving need to defend the defenseless—to protect and serve, in other words—wasn't what had led him to law enforcement. He liked the power, was all. Pulling kids over for no reason if he was bored, or ticketing Puerto Ricans for open container, even if it was a Pepsi—Tiles loved that shit. But hell, if someone had graduated from Brookwood High within a couple of years in either direction of him, there was a seventy-five percent chance he'd let them off with a warning at a traffic stop, just to show he was a nice guy. That number rose to one hundred percent if they'd played football. Part of the fun of being a cop was applying the law at your discretion and knowing that you were exempt from the rules everyone else had to follow.

He understood, however, the real reason he didn't quit was that he had nothing else to do. In that case, might as well keep looking for the school bus, he thought. If nothing else, it would give him a good reason to bitch. He zipped himself back into his pants and turned to hump up the hill to his patrol car, but it was strikingly white up there and shady where he was. He decided to wait another five minutes to gather himself. He ambled along the dirt path, fists on his hips, huffing. He wiped sweat off the back of his neck. From a partially mutilated squirrel carcass wafted the sweet odor of decay, and he couldn't help but think of his beef short rib.

"Fucking Devine. Fucking overtime."

He kicked a stone and then a pinecone. He was scanning the ground for something else to kick when he saw tire tracks. The trail was for walking and the tire tracks reached the edges on either side. Thin branches had snapped from the closest trees and bark was rubbed clean off the trunks.

There was a version of what happened next that Tiles would begin to recite until it morphed into his actual recollection, in which he told people he'd been in the woods seeking the bus, that clues he ascertained in the line of his investigation led him there. In this version, he said from the moment he saw the broken branches and raw-rubbed tree trunks, he knew he was close, and his heart pumped blood so hard his saliva tasted like old pennies. In this version, he proceeded with his firearm drawn, his body crouched low to the ground. Through continued retellings of the story, he mentally eradicated the reality that when he first saw the snapped branches he laughed and thought that some jerk in Public Works was going to be in a buttload of trouble for scratching up an authorized vehicle.

Yet in both the real and embellished version of events, Officer Al Tiles followed the tire tracks. They ran to where the trail opened to a clearing. There he saw more tire tracks. And since disguising a forty-foot yellow school bus was tricky under the best of circumstances, Tiles found Burnt Velveeta, twenty yards deep in the woods, hastily obscured with bushes and saplings. It wasn't lost, it wasn't broken down, it hadn't been in an accident, it hadn't simply vanished. Someone had done this.

Here reality and overstatement merged. He unholstered his gun for the first time in his career and hid behind a wide oak. He listened for signs of human life amid the chirping of starlings in the dead air. He needed to pee again, and he realized he couldn't remember when he last felt this good sober.

There had been an afternoon that spring, when he was still using hard, that his sister asked him when he would finally quit.

"The day you find me something that feels as good as speed is the day I stop doing my thing and start doing yours," he said.

He was only being a wiseass, of course, but it occurred to him now that this excitement was what he'd been talking about. His senses felt pushed to the limits of perception, as if he could identify the individual grooves on his gun grip. He announced himself and instructed anyone around to do the same. No response. He announced himself again, this time shuffling into the open. He couldn't decide if he wanted the bus to be abandoned or not. Finding the students would make him an instant and undeniable hero. On the other hand, there was a hard boundary to the amount of courage at his disposal and he was already knocking against its upper limits.

"Last chance," he shouted.

Nearly on his hands and knees, he blitzed the bus, climbing onto the rear bumper and peering through the window. The glass was sooty with diesel exhaust that grimed the tip of his nose and right cheek, but he confirmed the bus was unoccupied. He circled Burnt Velveeta, noting the clumsy subterfuge, ferns that were uprooted whole and tossed on the roof, saplings jammed through the narrow window openings. He started to remove them but realized he needed to preserve the crime scene.

Crime scene! What else could he call his discovery?

He sprinted out of the woods for his patrol car. He no longer cared about his ruined beef short rib. He was elated, afloat. Also confused and afraid and held by a great formless sadness he wouldn't be able to put into words until much later, a dim awareness that nothing else would ever compare to this moment. He felt so many different things as he raced to his car to call in for backup, but the one feeling he couldn't locate was anger. His driving emotional companion was missing. He waited, with the lights flashing, and mourned its loss, like at the end of a relationship, and simultaneously looked forward to what was coming next.

ROBERTA

I met George Schott at my dad's Man of the Year dinner in 1952. His family operated the catering company that furnished the event. I was nineteen. George was relishing his notoriety as a war hero, having won a limp in Korea that wasn't permanent but that he exploited for attention. I guess it worked because I spent the night talking to him. I preferred his company over the granite industry people, rich but crude men, who had gathered in Albany to honor my dad with an award he had no use for from a lobbying organization he distrusted.

Garth "Skip" Clayton, president of the National Building Granite Quarries Association, honored the man of the year in his interminable speech, praise my dad never heard. He and Uncle Fred were drunkenly pitching coins into the fountain in the hotel lobby, wishing for Fred's legs to grow back. I was mortified. But the Schotts were so nice. They wrapped up my dad's uneaten meal, boxed it with his award plaque, and delivered it to him. By now, he and Fred were splashing in the fountain, retrieving their change, impatient with the slow results of their wishes.

I was surprised to receive a letter from George a week later. He said I'd made quite an impression on him. He courted me through the mail. He admitted early on that he wasn't a war hero and had never seen the Korean Peninsula. He'd been shot in his left buttock during a training drill at Fort Benning and shipped home with an honorable discharge.

George was lucky. His parents put no pressure on him to join the family business. He was the youngest of four and as long as the catering company stayed under family control, his parents were happy. I didn't understand what he meant by happy. From my parents, I understood what was meant by success, and what was required to outsmart the threats working to take it all away. I also understood bitterness and resentment.

Of which I was feeling a great deal. My dad had given up ignoring my hatred of the quarry. It was time for me to take what was mine, he said. In other words, he had a desk picked out in the Manhattan office with my name on it. But I was stubborn too, and refused. He told me this was a foolish position to take because he would win eventually. He didn't know that I had other intentions. I'd hinted in my letters to George that, if he'd have me, I'd join him upstate.

Then one day I came home and found George sitting with my parents in the dining room. Say congratulations to the newest member of the Munsee Granite family, my dad said. He'd recruited George by telling him the only way to me was through him. This was how far he'd go to tie me to the quarry. During the interview, which was supposed to be a formality, Uncle Fred asked George about his wartime experience. He still regretted not fighting in World War II and was impressed by George's service. George, not wanting to start his new life with a lie, confessed the truth of his injury, and nearly botched my dad's strategy.

In the story I heard, my dad closed his eyes and sat without speaking for almost a minute before hurling his coffee mug across his office. We've already got Legless Fred, we can't afford Assless George, he ruminated. It was one thing if George were an injured war hero, quite another if a stupid accident took him out of action. No, he said. A commie shot you in the back at the Battle of Old Baldy. That's your story. Do you understand?

George understood. If anything, he was understanding to a fault.

Right there in the house I'd grown up in, he stood from the table and proposed. My dad had tears in his eyes. George and I were married eight weeks later.

FRIDAY, APRIL 25, 2014

Brenda and Emily remembered the commercial differently. They both agreed that the ad ran on local television in the late '80s and the tagline was, "The red carpet is always rolled out for you at Tiles Jeep, Chrysler & GMC," and that Al Tiles appeared in his role of unpolished spokesman on a long red carpet that spread down the middle of the showroom. Their memory diverged at his outfit. Emily swore Tiles was dressed like a king, like Louis XIV, and Brenda was dead positive he was in a tuxedo with tails, top hat, and cane, like Fred Astaire.

In preparation for their interview with him, they were compiling and comparing their memories of the beleaguered police officer turned local celebrity, turned prominent businessman, turned beleaguered businessman. At the time he found Burnt Velveeta, Brenda and Emily were still kidnapped. They only heard about his role after the fact, but they remembered seeing him at the quarry, and at the hospital, and again at the Kids Day celebration where he was honored with the rest of them and met Vice President George Bush. For a while, they seemed to see him everywhere. Despite his ubiquity in town, Brenda and Emily realized they had never spoken to him before. They agreed this was kind of strange since they mostly remembered him talking, placing himself in the center of the conversation and holding forth. Emily's dining room table was covered with their preliminary research and notes for the documentary. They couldn't decide if they'd viewed him as a white knight when they were kids, and if they had, it was because they'd heard other people say that about him, not because they felt they owed him their lives. They had their own thoughts about how they were saved and who was responsible. Regardless, Tiles was a solid "get" for an interview, a good person to put on the record.

As for the commercial, they were both wrong. Someone had uploaded a VHS recording to YouTube, the tracking wobbly and the picture washed out, the low-budget production not aiding its attempt at posterity. The red carpet was there, and Tiles bellowed the slogan over synth-y music, snazzy with a pop groove, but he wore a ridiculously large-shouldered, double-breasted, silver silk suit, with a black shirt and paisley silk tie. With his hair gelled back and Vuarnets shielding his eyes, he looked like a wannabe drug lord from an episode of *Miami Vice*. Behind him stood the staff of his car dealership, struggling to maintain the enthusiasm required of them.

Brenda and Emily met Tiles the next day, their gear in tow. Brenda had borrowed sound and lighting equipment from techs she knew. The big misconception about her early years in journalism was that she was driven around in a news van with a whole crew, but no local TV station had the budget for that. "It's just you?" was the question she often met arriving at a location in her old Honda Civic. She wrote, shot, and edited her stories by herself. But now, despite her experience, her heart hammered with dread as Emily drove to the Jeep dealership. She was afraid of choking when the moment came, unable to perform, flop sweat drenching her underarms. She feared the interview with Tiles would confirm the end of her career, not to mention an onslaught of guilty feelings for letting her sister down. The fear had kept her awake all night while she twisted in the sheets in the guest room.

The showroom no longer displayed a red carpet. In one three-month period in 2009, during which the auto industry contracted, Tiles had lost his Chrysler and GMC franchises. His floorplan lines of credit were shut down, his inventory moved to other dealers. Five years later, he was still standing, although hobbled. If he could have found a buyer, he would have cashed out of the Jeep business in a heartbeat, but there were no takers, and it wasn't for a lack of looking.

His glass-walled office overlooked the showroom, with drawn blinds that he pulled open the minute Brenda and Emily entered the room.

"To let the light in," he said, but Emily knew he wanted his staff to see Brenda, the public person, the semi-celebrity. She wondered if he would have agreed to the interview if Brenda wasn't involved.

Tiles sat at his desk, taking a few moments to get comfortable, rearranging himself in the leather executive chair as if he had hemorrhoids.

"Thanks for meeting with us, Officer Tiles," Emily said.

"Officer? Stop right there," he said. He held up one hand. "My days of saving lives like yours are over. All that hero stuff you hear about me, that's what other people say. I'm just a regular guy."

Brenda wished he'd said that on camera. She mic'd him up quickly, before he could drop more gems, adjusted the levels on the sound recorder, and asked Emily to check that the camera lens cover was off and the memory card inserted. Brenda prepped the shot and then they started the interview.

"Mr. Tiles, please take us back to August 2nd, 1984. What stands out to you about that day?" she said.

"It was hot as shit." Tiles frowned, shook his head, and yelled, "Cut!"

"Don't say cut," Brenda said. "If you want to rephrase, just start over."

"Okay. Ask me again."

She asked him to recall the day of the abduction.

"I wasn't even supposed to be on duty. My shift was over. But the second I heard about the missing bus and you kids, I told Chief Devine I didn't care about the schedule, I didn't care about overtime. I just had to help. I love Brookwood. I would do anything for this town."

Emily watched the picture in the monitor and listened to Brenda and Tiles talking. He was a jerk, but Brenda showed patience with him, coaxing out answers about the kidnapping when he just wanted to talk about himself. It was exhilarating to be a part of the process, Emily thought, exhilarating to be doing something for the first time, when there was something at stake. She also felt somewhat jealous of her sister in a way she couldn't remember ever feeling at any time since they were adults. She'd always thought that for all their twinness, Brenda proved her individuality with her job. Chasing around the country in pursuit of danger and calling it journalism, when it was plainly reckless, was anathema to everything Emily valued. What she saw now, however, was the attraction of inquiry, of being there first and finding out, of placing yourself as a conduit through which information flowed. She understood how this could be addictive, and that Brenda's renowned bravery might have been but a side effect of obsession.

Tiles then said something that caught her attention and brought her back to the moment.

"My only regret is that I didn't find the bus when you guys were still on it. If only I'd gotten there sooner."

"What would you have done?" Emily said unexpectedly. They had agreed Brenda would conduct the interviews, but she couldn't help herself.

"What's that, sweetheart?" Tiles said. His face looked playful in the monitor.

"If you were at the reservoir before they moved us, what would you have done?"

"Isn't that obvious?"

"I guess not. I guess that's why I'm asking."

"Emily, I got this," Brenda said.

"I would have brought them to justice," Tiles said, a clearly rehearsed line.

"There were two of them. They had guns."

"So did I."

"Don't you think that might have made things worse? It might have turned into a standoff. They might have started killing us."

Tiles leaned back in his chair and crossed his arms over his chest. A vein protruding on his high forehead pulsed vehemently.

"Those two dumb shits? I sincerely doubt it. But, since we're speaking as old friends..." He uncrossed his arms and leaned forward with his elbows on his desk, tapping his fingertips together in a triangle. "Let me tell you this. If Calvin and Jason Schott had done anything to hurt you while I was around, right now we would be damn close to celebrating another anniversary of their deaths." He grinned, tremendously pleased with himself.

"You're saying you would have killed them?"

"Emily," Brenda said, and told her with her eyes to back off. She returned to Tiles. "I want to jump ahead to the granite quarry, Mr. Tiles, if that's alright with you."

"It's your show," he said.

Afterward, when they were in the car heading home, Emily massaged the steering wheel as she drove.

"How did you think it went? I think it went really well," she said, mentally reliving the moment sher pressed Tiles. She couldn't wait to get home to watch the footage.

Brenda came away from the interview feeling good, not so much having assessed meaning in the work (come on, she once interviewed Ban Ki-moon), but she perceived herself reset to an earlier time when she was a functioning journalist. She'd been going through the motions with Tiles and yet, while the camera was on, she'd focused on the task at hand. She could view that only in terms of success. She cupped the bottle of Ativan from her purse and dry swallowed a pill before realizing she hadn't needed or even wanted it. The important takeaway from the interview, she thought, was that what she feared hadn't come true. If she could get in the habit of reminding herself of this fact, if she could manage it on a regular basis, perhaps she could get back to real work.

"One thing, though," she said. "I'm not sure arguing with the police officer who worked the kidnapping is helpful."

Emily made the turn onto Underhill Terrace. "He was talking so much shit."

"So?"

"And you..."

"Me?"

"Didn't push back."

"That's his truth."

Emily stopped behind a silver SUV at a red light. She faced Brenda.

"His truth?" she said.

"How he sees things."

"It doesn't bother you how arrogant he is, acting like he was our savior when we know he wasn't?"

"People can only tell their version of things."

The light turned green, the SUV drove off, but Emily's car didn't move.

"He didn't mention Pat Earl or Martin, what they did. You were in the other van. You didn't see Lindsey. We thought she was dead. Martin took care of her."

The car behind them honked its horn and Emily took her foot off the brake.

"It's like the commercial. You remembered Louis XIV. I remembered Fred Astaire," Brenda said. "Al Tiles remembers himself a hero." Then she said something else that finished the debate because it upended Emily and left her speechless. "Our kidnapping was the best thing that ever happened to him."

It was so plainly true. How couldn't Emily have seen it? The worst thing that ever happened to her was the best thing that ever happened to Al Tiles. A low poisonous fog settled in her chest. She turned up the radio and didn't talk for the rest of the ride.

THURSDAY, AUGUST 2, 1984

They bought the vans at a New Jersey auto auction for two hundred bucks a piece. Jason was convinced they overpaid. The grey van's engine knocked so loudly it sounded as if a piston would break free and rip through the hood. It almost stalled at a red light on Jackson Avenue. He shifted into neutral and kept his foot lightly on the gas to hold the idle. When the light changed, he dropped it into drive and the van bucked forward through the intersection. There was no air conditioner. The vent blew a steady hot current at his face and body, and the fan made one of the belts squeal.

Of the many ways he could get caught, the van dying was high on the list. He imagined a good Samaritan or a cop pulling over to lend a hand while he was disabled on the shoulder and hearing the kids screaming for help, pounding the walls. The surge of adrenaline that propelled him onto the school bus had ebbed. Sweat rolled down his ribcage and he shivered. His mouth was dry and the only thing to quench his thirst was a warm two-liter bottle of Pepsi on the passenger seat next to his pantyhose. The thought of drinking it made him want to vomit.

The dashboard clock read 3:52. Jason focused on the orange clock hands, reminding himself that by this time Saturday, the plan would be completed, the kids home safe, and he and Calvin on the way to New Orleans. He softly incanted the word "Saturday," a now magic word whose significance calmed him.

From the reservoir to the meeting place was 10.3 miles, but it was too early to reconvene. The plan necessitated that he and Calvin hunker down separately until the time was right to transfer the kids and the driver to the final stop. He drove the rest of the way to Pheasant Hill Park. Due to a stalled revitalization project, the dredging of eighty county lakes and ponds that made the entire park smell like decomposing fish shit, hardly anyone came here, which was why they decided it was a safe place to wait. There was something dreamlike about pulling off the busy street and entering the semi-abandoned park. Jason took comfort in the scenes of neglect, grass overgrown and sunburnt brown, trash barrels brimming with trash, a twin mattress stained the color of iced tea leaning crumpled against a bench. He parked in the rest area. The engine shuddered to a stop. He heard birds nearby and street sounds in the distance, but nothing else. He turned on the radio—static through the speakers—and turned it off.

He wondered how Cal was doing. Had he made it to his waiting place, Lewis Brook Nature Preserve, a twenty-acre patch of mixed hardwood owned by the county land trust? Or had he been caught? If so, how much longer until Jason and the primergrey van were found?

He got out to stretch his legs. The stench from the dredging was putrid. The men's room was locked, so he peed behind the building and wandered back around to the front. Inside a glass cabinet covered with marker graffiti, the park map was tacked up, the red circle and You Are Here below it. It read as reassuring, a statement of being. *That's you, Jason, you are real*, the red circle a radius of his existence.

The water fountain worked and he took a long drink and cupped his hands under the stream and poured it over his head and the back of his neck. Then he just stood there, as a swarm of midges found him, listening unhappily to the quiet. He had a sudden and lurid image of finding ten dead children in the back of the van, their brains boiled in their own fluids, and he ran to get his pantyhose mask and the Pepsi bottle, pouring out the soda and refilling it at the water fountain.

He yanked open the cargo doors, daylight exploding the darkness inside, and the children recoiled, squeezing away from the doors. They looked awful—red-faced, sweaty, weak—but alive. They reminded Jason of the time he found a nest of baby raccoons under the front porch of his house. He rolled the Pepsi bottle of water into the van. The children retreated as if he'd tossed in a live grenade.

"Drink up," he said, and slammed the doors shut. He sat on the bumper, holding his head, breathing through the wet mask, listening for voices, or for the van creaking on its springs, but still nothing. He opened the doors again. The soda bottle was lying where it had rolled to, and the children remained pinned in one corner.

"It's not poison," he said. Like the baby raccoons, they squirmed away from him, hiding behind each other, defenseless. It seemed that no matter how they responded, they upset him. They kept responding the wrong way. When he wanted to scare them, they looked confused and slightly entertained, and now, when he wanted to reassure them with a small gesture of comfort, they were terrified of him. Why the misunderstanding, he wondered, when everything about this situation was clear cut?

"Who needs the bathroom?" he said. It was important that they appreciated when he was being generous. The odor wafting out of the van alerted him to the fact that it was already too late for some of them, but he repeated his offer. "Who needs to go?"

They looked at each other, sensing a trap but unsure how to act, and stayed quiet.

"Now or never," Jason said.

A girl, the one he called a bitch earlier, whose name he didn't know was Lindsey Robinson, raised her hand.

"Come on," he said. "Let's move."

She crawled forward on her hands and knees, her cheeks flushed red as blown glass, her hair matted with sweat, the neck of her T-shirt stretched and wrinkled. She gulped the fishy, hot air, desperate for it. Jason pointed to the back of the rest area building and she walked in the path of his finger, occasionally glancing over her shoulder at him. Once she realized there were no facilities behind the building, she stared at him, and he stared back.

      TIME WILL BREAK THE WORLD

"Here?" she said.

"The bathroom's locked. You're going to have to pop a squat."

Shards of glass glittered between clumps of crabgrass at their feet. Lindsey was almost crying.

"Please, don't," she said.

"Christ, I'm not going to rape you," he said, breaking a cardinal rule of the plan. Keep the threat of violence in the front of everyone's minds. Then the students would behave. They would obey. Jason had just given away his leverage. He wished he were holding his shotgun.

She didn't seem to believe him. She was still almost crying.

"Do you have to go, or not?" he said.

She shook her head no and Jason said, "Waste of time," and started back for the van. Lindsey ran in the other direction. Jason was half-around the building when he saw that he was alone.

"Goddamn idiot," he said to himself, and started running.

He checked in and around the dumpster, but she wasn't there. A paved path led downhill through a stand of sycamore trees to the ball fields. Jason heard the echo of footsteps. He got her back in his sight, but the girl was quicker than he expected; although if he'd thought about it, he would have understood that running for your life gave you an extra kick. But he wasn't thinking that. He was thinking he had to catch her. Catch her right now. He couldn't expect the park to be entirely empty. A DPW employee, a dogwalker, a vagrant, lovers, anyone, it didn't matter who, anyone could wander by and blow a hole through his and Calvin's plan.

At the bottom of the hill, she hugged the tree line rather than bursting out into the ball fields where the afternoon light bathed the turf in an unsettling diaphanous glow. Jason made the turn in time to see her right arm windmilling over her head, but didn't see the rock. It struck him on his forehead, above his left eye. A drop of blood squeezed through the mesh of the pantyhose. He swayed but kept moving forward. Lindsey, who had stopped to watch her handiwork, looked surprised that she hit her target and that it hadn't been enough to bring him down. She ran, but Jason closed in on her and without thinking about anything besides getting her to the van before anyone saw them, punched her in the back of her head, near the base of her skull, propelling her face-first into the low, crooked branch of a crabapple tree.

He was queasy with remorse and his head stung. Her snoring was how he knew he hadn't killed her. He lifted her under her arms and got her over his shoulder, like a sack of potatoes, and labored up the paved path. His legs quaked under him and he felt a tightness in his chest. If he had a heart attack right then he hoped he died. Behind the rest area building, he propped her against the wall and she slid to the ground. He staggered off and threw up, forgetting to remove his mask, the pantyhose like a cheesecloth separating the undigested food from the liquid of his stomach. He yanked the mask off, bits of the food getting clumped in his hair, and wiped his mouth with his hand. He shook out the pantyhose and put it back over his face and carried Lindsey to the van.

The kids thought she was dead. He shoved her in torso first but couldn't manage to get her all the way inside.

"Grab her arms and pull," he said. "Right fucking now."

One of the older boys came forward. He put two fingers on her neck to find a pulse and whispered, "Alive."

"Good job, Trapper John. Just pull her."

The boy heaved backward until she slid into the van.

Jason closed the doors and weaved to the fountain and splashed his face and rinsed out his mouth. The swarm of midges found him again. He swatted at them thoughtlessly and climbed back in the van, where he sat, for how long he couldn't remember, testing the soreness of his forehead with his fingers. After a while, he looked at the dashboard clock.

"Saturday," he mouthed. "Saturday, Saturday, Saturday." But this time his incantation failed him. He was trapped in the present.

Neptune Diner was Bertie's favorite restaurant. She considered it a bulwark against the trendy, upscale eateries cropping up on Milford Avenue and Brookwood Boulevard—sushi, tapas, farm-to-table, artisanal everything. The new restaurants brought snobs and yuppies and their obnoxious progeny to the area, she complained, making the town so crowded you couldn't breathe; but her main grievance was that things looked and felt different, unrecognizable to her. The diner, with its chrome and glass façade and neon trident over the entrance, signified permanence in a shifting world. And she loved their eggs.

She and Jason and Angie took a booth close to the restrooms in case she needed to make a pit stop. She commanded Jason to sit on her side but carped that he was taking up too much space. And when he slid to the edge of the banquette and the vinyl groaned, she accused him of farting.

"It's moments like these I'm going to miss when you're gone," he said.

"I'm not going anywhere," she said, lifting her reading glasses from their chain around her neck and studying the laminated menu, though her order was the same each week.

When their meals arrived, Bertie's world was once again contained and orderly. She told Jason to get on over to the other side of the table and sit with his lady. She offered Angie a bite of her fruit salad. She was in such a good mood that when Jason cut her off after one Bloody Mary, she didn't carry on about it.

Angie squeezed Jason's thigh under the table. She looked forward to a time in the not distant future when a weekly meal with Bertie was the only time investment they would have to make. She and Jason would live together, in her condo, or perhaps a house of their own. Sometimes on the weekend, for the hell of it, they visited open houses for properties they could never afford. Angie put her last name as Schott on the sign-in sheet, and they toured the home as a married couple.

Bertie was wiping her plate with a piece of toast. "I hate to say it, but the best eggs I ever had were your grandmother's," she said. "George's mom, not mine."

Jason knew the story, Angie too. Bertie disclosed it on most trips to the diner. Each new retelling was almost identical to the previous ones, and yet she treated the memory like a sudden and unexpected recollection.

"That woman got the freshest eggs. They were bought directly from a farm. She used to fry them in creamery butter *and* bacon fat. That was the trick, I think. A sprinkle of salt and pepper. A hunk of peasant bread. It was heavenly."

While Bertie was lost in her reminiscence, Angie checked her phone for something fun or interesting for her and Jason to do later. She scrolled Facebook and noticed her cousin Lisa had tagged her in a post. Lisa commented: *ur boyfriends gonna be a moviestar lol!!!!!*

She read the post, a casting call. Someone was making a documentary about the Brookwood Bus Kidnapping.

"But these eggs are terrific too," Bertie continued, and Angie attempted to get Jason's attention without interrupting the story.

Jason was listening to his mom as though her report about his grandmother's eggs unlocked a compelling piece of family lore and wasn't just a groove in her mental record the needle periodically got stuck on. Angie saw him nodding along, asking questions, a good son. Why would someone want to make a movie about him and Calvin? It seemed impolite to pry into their lives. What was the point of dredging up ancient history?

Bertie finally wrapped up the story in the usual fashion, by pointing out that Jason's grandmother also made the worst meatloaf she ever tasted, swearing, honest to God, that it contained mule. She wiped her lips with the paper napkin and tossed it on the plate. She wiggled her way out of the booth and shuffled off to the ladies' room.

Angie held up her phone. "Is this bad?"

Jason squinted at the screen, but his face gave away nothing. He smoothed his eyebrows with the condensation of his water glass and waved to get the attention of the waiter, signing an invisible check in the air.

"Is it?" she said.

"How could it possibly be good?"

"For Calvin? Or you too?"

"There is no difference between me and Cal when it comes to this."

Because Angie was in love with one brother, and the other brother was in prison, she tended to blame Calvin for the bus kidnapping and disregard Jason's role in the crime. He seemed incapable of menace, or lawlessness. She couldn't locate in his soft, middle-aged face a corrupt moral center. She had observed him working in other people's yards, his proud toil and the gentle way he had with their plants, and wondered: How could this man have hurt children? She wasn't in denial—not quite, Jason wouldn't allow it—but she was convinced that whoever he'd been at twenty-three was alien to who he was now.

"Do you know these women?" she said.

"Yes," he said.

The Mashburn twins—Jason knew them. It was he who yanked them apart and forced them into separate vans, kept them locked away from each other for hours and made them think they might never be reunited, for no reason other than he'd felt they were challenging him. The motive for the abduction was money, always money, but if Jason wanted to really make plain why he and Cal did it, it was because they were the kind of men who could feel confronted by two scared-to-death ten-year-old girls.

"What are we going to do about it?" she said.

"How the fuck should I know?" Jason said too loud and at an

inopportune time. The waiter dropped the check right as he hit the plosive *f* and there was Bertie, just steps from the table.

She eased herself back into the booth. "Something the matter?" she said.

Jason ignored her. He counted out enough cash for the tip and placed it under the ketchup bottle. It seemed counting dollar bills was the one thing within his control. He hadn't meant to yell. Angie's question just made him feel helpless. What were they going to do about it? What kind of question was that? He asked Angie to help Bertie to the car, overcome by a desire to be left alone, to not have to face this, whatever this was, to pawn it off onto someone else and make it their problem. It was a childish wish, he knew, and an impossible one too. Like it or not, he was going to have to deal with Brenda and Emily Mashburn.

He took the check to the register and helped himself to a toothpick and a handful of mints. The cashier laid his change on the counter. He waited an extra moment, gazing at the autographed headshots of famous diner patrons on the wall behind the register—Sade Baderinwa, Dee Snider, James Gandolfini, Joan Rivers—before scooping up his change and heading out to the car.

THURSDAY, AUGUST 2, 1984

They showed up at Butler Reservoir with flashlights and camping lanterns and walking sticks, thermoses of coffee and canteens of water. Cherry Road was closed to cars, so they walked the rest of the way, working through a scrum of reporters lingering at the outskirts of the taped-off area, then past emergency vehicles from local, county, and state agencies—police, fire, EMT. Officers from the K9 unit disgorged a team of German shepherds from a dark van. The people arriving were there to help. In whatever capacity they could. Members of the Brookwood police broke them into groups, handed out maps, and assigned a "map holder." Chief Devine and Sergeant Adamski from New York State Police Troop K took turns explaining that the searchers should move slowly through the area at the same pace, trying to keep no more than an arm's length apart. "Be mindful of trees, rocks, roots, hills, and animals," Adamski said. "Regard anything suspicious as such and tag it with bright-colored tape. Officers are handing that out now. Do not touch anything that could even remotely be evidence," Devine said. "Stay focused, mentally prepared, at all times," added Adamski. A helicopter passed overhead and Adamski repeated the last part to make sure they heard him, "At all times." "Thank you for your assistance," Devine said, and set the ground searchers loose.

"We agreed I was taking the point," he said to Adamski, once the groups dispersed.

"How do you figure?"

Devine's case was compelling. Burnt Velveeta was property of the Brookwood Union-Free School District and Pat Earl was a district employee and the students were Brookwood residents and a Brookwood police officer had found the bus in the town of Brookwood.

"The reservoir is state land," Adamski said.

Then two agents from the FBI field office arrived and rendered the conversation moot.

Liz and Phil Mashburn followed their group into the woods. Liz didn't wish harm on anyone, and of course it went without saying that she hoped for the very best possible outcome. But if two people, and only two, were returned home alive, it had to be Brenda and Emily. Maybe later she would feel selfish and ashamed to think this way, but right then she didn't care. She would rather cope with survivor's guilt than arrange two funerals. She assumed every other parent creeping through the woods felt the same way, whether or not they admitted it.

Their group's map holder brought them to a stop on the hiking trail. He spoke to them around a penlight in his mouth, the thin beam dancing with his words.

"The bus was found sort of over there," he said, motioning to an unseen spot behind him and to his right. "We should probably head that way."

They followed with neither enthusiasm nor complaint. Phil took Liz's hand and they moved off the trail, through some plants he hoped weren't poison ivy. Around them, the other searchers speculated.

The bus driver did it. Who else? You didn't need to be Columbo to figure it out.

What Pat Earl had done with the children was less clear, but the portrait of him that emerged as the search party fanned out into the woods, cutting a wide berth around the yellow police tape cordoning off the bus, was one of a disgruntled creep with poor hygiene and dark, though unsubstantiated, rumors swirling around him like litter in the wind. All of a sudden, many of them recalled how their kids criticized him, how, according to the younger ones, he urinated on the bus seats before they got on in the morning, and how, according to the teens, Burnt Velveeta was his girlfriend and he made love to the tailpipe. They'd ignored their children's gossip because those were the same stories they themselves told about him, or whoever their school bus driver was when they were growing up. Now they regretted not listening, not taking their children seriously. Even if the stories weren't true, the kids had sensed something not right, something off about the man. It *was* obvious. And by obvious, they meant Pat Earl was dangerous.

Liz and Phil slowed their pace and the search party drifted ahead of them. She stopped walking altogether and he kept going a few more yards before he turned and looked back. She was firing up a Kent 100.

"This is so stupid," she said. "You really think someone's going to look under a shrub and the girls will jump out?"

"We have to look."

"This can't be happening."

Phil took a few steps toward his wife.

"Where are they?" she said.

"I don't know."

"Where are my girls?"

He started to say he didn't know but stopped himself.

Liz looked up and Phil thought it was to keep tears from falling down her cheeks, but she just exhaled a large plume of smoke. She smoked and he watched her smoke. What did it even mean that their daughters were missing? Missing—it felt like the wrong word. Brenda and Emily and a bunch of other kids weren't missing. They were somewhere. They were hidden. Someone or something was hiding them. Like a goddamn prank. The real question, Phil knew, wasn't "where are they?" but "are they alive?" But that was too close to "are they dead?"—the flip side to the same coin—which was why nobody asked it. "Are they alive/dead?" was a bad question anyway. Once asked, it begged an answer. And what if the answer was the impossible one, the world-shattering one? So, "where are they?" was safer. It was what they said aloud while they thought of the unspeakable question. They thought of the unspeakable question while they made up stories about the bus driver. It was easier that way. But who knew? Phil thought. Maybe Pat Earl was the guy they were looking for, maybe Pat had answers to all the questions.

"Want to pray?" he said, the suggestion unexpectedly coming to him.

"Why start now?" Liz said.

"I saw other parents doing it. It might help."

"To who? To what?"

He was looking at his feet. "I don't know, God?"

"God?" Liz said. "Get real."

In the parking lot, Chief Devine and Sergeant Adamski briefed the FBI agents, whose names were Griffin and Dunbar. They shared a passenger list from the bus:

Robert Avery—9	Brenda Mashburn—10
Christopher Armbrust—11	Emily Mashburn—10
Jennifer Bartoli—8	Martin Mendoza—13
Thomas Burke—11	Sean Price—10 (Absent)
Brian Davidson—10	Lindsey Robinson—12
Gregory DeVito—9	Sarah Ramsarup—9
Patrick Earl—59 (Driver)	Jennifer Strauss—9
Nelson Garcia—10	Heather Sussman—12
James Harris—8 (Absent)	(Absent)
Jodie Hoffman—12	Jennifer Taylor—11 (Absent)
Andrew Kraven—7	Lance Viscuso—13
Jonathan Medina—7	Kaito Watanabe—8
	Paul Zamfino—10

Agent Dunbar ran his index finger down the list and said, "Twenty. That's confirmed?"

Devine said it was, unfortunately. Twenty people, Jesus Christ. He felt dwarfed by the magnitude of the situation. He couldn't tell you why Adamski, Griffin, or Dunbar had become cops, but he knew that at this point in his career he was an administrator, a bureaucrat, not a crime fighter.

Al Tiles sidled up to them and stood there with his arms crossed.

"Need something?" Devine said.

"Good evening. Officer Alphonse Tiles," Tiles said, holding out his hand to the agents. "I found the bus."

"Does he know anything we should know?" Agent Griffin said.

"No," Devine said.

"Chief, how can you say that? I found the bus."

"I know you did, Al."

"I think I could shed a little light," Tiles said.

"Take a breather, Shingles," Devine said.

"That's not fair, Chief. That's really not fair," Tiles said, and skulked away.

The agents wanted to see the bus. Devine and Adamski led them into the woods.

Agent Griffin asked what the local cops knew about Pat Earl.

"I haven't been here long, but I was told we sent a car to his house a couple of years ago," Devine said.

"Domestic situation?"

"Yes and no. Seems like he woke up from a nap disoriented, started shouting, and punched his hand through a window. His wife made the call."

"Was he brought in?"

"There was no need. He was calm by the time they got there. Said he had a bad dream. Refused medical attention for his hand."

"What do you think about him?" Griffin said.

Devine didn't know what to think. He knew of abductions that ended in grisly discoveries days or weeks later, or that were never cracked, forever mysteries that haunted everyone involved, but he had never worked that kind of case. His experience was limited to fathers unhappy with their custody agreement taking their son or daughter on unauthorized weekends, or a child temporarily separated from his mother in a department store.

"I think it's Earl," said Sergeant Adamski. "Think about it. He's been driving that ratty bus his whole life, eating kids' shit every day, it's about two hundred degrees out, and he finally snaps."

"No, that's not it. This was premeditated. This is a hostage situation. There will be a ransom demand," Dunbar said.

Ten days before the 1968 games, Mexican soldiers gunned down hundreds of student protesters in the Plaza of Three Cultures in Tlatelolco. "We don't want Olympics, we want revolution!" the students chanted while tanks surrounded them. On October 16th, after Tommie Smith broke the world record in the 200-meter dash, and his teammate John Carlos finished third, they stood on the winners' podium and raised their gloved fists in the Black Power salute as the national anthem played, a political statement that got them kicked off the team, barred from the Olympic village, and caused their relatives back home to receive death threats. These were events I didn't know about when I was eight and watched George Foreman win the gold medal. Nor did I know, four years later, in Munich, that on September 5th, in the hour before dawn, eight Palestinians climbed the fence of the Olympic village, took eleven Israeli athletes hostage, and then murdered them. It was months after the 1976 games that it came to light that the politically peaceful sports spectacle almost bankrupted the city of Montreal. I didn't know that East German trainers gave steroids to fourteen-year-old female swimmers. I didn't know what blood doping was. I didn't know about the rank hypocrisies and moral failings of the International Olympic Committee and its chairman Avery Brundage, who after World War II allowed known Nazis and Italian Fascists to remain on the committee. This was the same governing body that expelled Ernest Lee Jahncke for suggesting a boycott of the 1936 Berlin games. I didn't even know that the concept of amateurism was created to prohibit the working class from the pastimes of the leisure class.

This is the problem with fandom of any kind—if there are people involved, the human tendency toward corruption will follow, and you must find a way to reconcile your pure love with disappointment. You must compartmentalize the parts that give you joy from the parts that make you cringe. In other words, the adult in you needs to look the other way so that the child in you may rejoice.

That I would see Lonzo Feldman Jr. again, in Auburn Correctional Facility, where he landed after his arrest and conviction and the media dubbed him the Godfather of Land Fraud, in no way made me feel better about being swindled. Eastern Capital Development was one fragment in a mosaic of companies he used to sell land he either didn't own or misrepresented as having livable accoutrements—little things like water and electric—or that he did own but that he sold to multiple parties, forging titles as needed.

The Munsee Estates scam was pure fiction. The site he drove us to in his Cadillac turned out to be part of an ongoing project to dredge eighty lakes and ponds in the county. *Due diligence* weren't words in Jay's and my vocabulary. Maybe it's true that Lonzo only fast-tracked the inevitable, that we were born to lose, but if we'd failed on our own we wouldn't have had the excuse of victimhood that supercharged our self-pity. We believed we were honorable businessmen defrauded by the scum of the living earth. Under fairer circumstances, we would have succeeded. Rationalization at this level requires but the smallest of delusions.

Because we couldn't tell George and Bertie the truth, we had to let them believe we'd given up on our business, meaning they thought worse of us than usual. Because we couldn't tell them the truth, we had no choice when George put us to work at the quarry. We were groundsmen. Ten-hour shifts removing mud and muck from stones with a steam hose, and chipping irregularities

　　　　TIME WILL BREAK THE WORLD

off slabs with a pick. We loaded broken rocks into boxes with a stone fork or with our hands. After a month, we were assigned to start the day by filling the water tank truck, although we weren't allowed to drive it.

It didn't have to be a terrible job. Or it wouldn't have been a terrible job if it were just some company we worked for. Busting rocks wasn't a profession either of us would have pursued on our own, but once there, we fell into the routine of the day. We got along with the other groundsmen, many of them Salvadorans or Guatemalans, and we drank cans of beer with them at lunch, huddled around an open cooler and leaning against a tailgate, not following along with their conversations. But then, when we got paid, we had to see our father's signature stamped onto our checks. It was a biweekly reminder that we weren't in control of our lives and that these migrant men, our coworkers, had accomplished more than us because their daddies didn't give them their jobs. After our first payday, Bertie started charging us rent to live in their house. She was making a point about us pitching in, contributing to the family, and not leaching off it. When I mentioned that I didn't remember seeing her hammering slabs of granite, she told me the quarry had taken more from her than I would ever understand. She said I should shut my goddamn mouth about it and be grateful for what she and my dad had given me and Jay, which was, in a word, everything.

Even our advancement within the company was engineered from above. George promoted us against the recommendation of the site manager. We saw a quarter-per-hour bump in pay and could drive the water tank truck. We took turns driving, the other riding shotgun, and got to see the whole sprawl of Munsee Granite, the farthest reaches of land surveyed by geologists and deemed profitable 150 years earlier and purchased by the oldest Reilly generations. We hauled four thousand gallons of water, spraying for dust control. Creeping along the roads leading from the pit to the processing plant, we passed the stockpiles, the weigh stations, the sharp downhill turn (now secured with a guardrail) where, once long ago, Great-Uncle Fred drunkenly took a dump truck over the edge. Some mornings I looked at the guardrail and thought about testing it.

I wouldn't go as far as to compare our predicament with the tragedy of the '72 games in Munich. No, I wouldn't compare us to slaughtered Israelis, but I would say that what we were dealing with was similar to the fate of Jim Thorpe. King Gustav of Sweden called him the greatest athlete in the world. In Stockholm, in 1912, Thorpe won gold medals in the pentathlon and decathlon on the same day, wearing mismatched shoes. He returned home in triumph, until his former college coach let slip to a reporter that Thorpe played a couple of seasons of semiprofessional baseball in the Eastern Carolina Association, and was paid two dollars per game. After the story was printed in the *Worcester Telegram*, the New England Association of the Amateur Athletic Union retroactively contested his amateur status, though the deadline to challenge the games' results had ended. Long story short, the IOC stripped him of his medals.

I was at the wheel when I told Jay my theory.

"Wasn't he an Indian?" he said.

"Sauk and Fox."

"Didn't he play football?"

"Hall of Fame running back. Also played baseball for the Cincinnati Reds."

"How are we supposed to be like him?"

"The man was robbed of victories by forces beyond his control."

"Lonzo wasn't beyond our control. It was my fault."

Jay took responsibility for our fleecing, his logic being cause and effect: if he hadn't proposed the real estate company, we wouldn't have lost our inheritance. He never brought up that I claimed credit for starting the business. It was his fault, all of it, he said. I knew it wasn't true, and his accountability depressed me.

　　　　　　　　　　

I was fixated on our lost money. If we could get it back, we could have a successful second act like Jim Thorpe and wind up in our own hall of fame. The heater cranked on full blast, the windows fogged with condensation, a thermos of lukewarm coffee rolling back and forth on the dashboard.

"Let's rob a bank," I said.

"Why not?" Jason said, his voice distant, uninterested.

I sketched out a loose plan. I wasn't serious, but we had time to kill. We'd strike on the fifteenth or thirtieth of the month, payday in other words, when a bank would be ready to cash checks. Get there the moment the guard unlocked the door at the start of business. Crack him in the head. Grab the branch manager. Gun to his temple. Take the cash in the drawers. Disappear like phantoms.

"Sure," he said. He rolled down the window, poured out his stale coffee, and let his hand surf on the air.

"You're letting the heat out, dickwad," I said.

"It's stuffy. Pull over."

He started opening the door before I could come to a stop.

"Pick me up when you're done."

I finished the loop and got him. He hadn't moved an inch from where I'd left him.

He climbed in, heavy in the passenger seat, and slammed the door. "It won't work," he said. "Bank robbery."

"I was just bullshitting."

"It's not enough money," he said.

"Alright, let's rob a bunch of banks." I parked the truck in the equipment depot. We got out slowly, reluctant to start shoveling rocks.

"Do you know how many banks we would need to rob to get our money back?" he said.

"Do you?"

"Too many."

That night, at home, Bertie stopped us at the front door. She was wearing slacks and a blouse, like she was expecting company, a Solo cup of white wine with lipstick smears on the rim in one hand.

"From now on, you get undressed in the garage before you come in," she said.

"Mom, we're tired," I said.

"You've been tracking shit into the house for weeks."

We smelled food cooking and knew it was warm inside. We wanted showers and beers and to be left alone.

"Get out of the way, Mom," Jason said.

"When I was a little girl, I used to make your grandfather wash up before he came in and he was the president of the god-damn company. You two grunts can strip in the garage or live in the backyard. I don't really care."

It was around that time the idea occurred to us that kidnapping a rich or important person and holding him for ransom was a better way to get our money back than robbing numerous banks. The right victim could make us financially whole.

"We're not going to risk our lives for chump change," Jason said.

We joked about it constantly. Whenever work got us down or Bertie and George were riding us, we would say, "All our problems would be solved." We didn't have to say the word kidnapping. We knew what we meant. We fantasized about our post-ransom life—Mexican beaches via New Orleans, a road trip for the ages.

The alternator on the water tank truck quit one morning. The headlights began dimming and the front spray bar stopped working and the power light on the CB radio flickered and went out. Then the engine died. We jumped ship and started walking. On foot, you got a good look at how bleak and deserted parts of the quarry were, the old backfilled pits, abandoned trailers and outhouses. We hoofed it to the equipment depot and brainstormed potential targets. I thought we were finding a dark-funny way of surviving the morning. I realize now that we

　　　　　　　　　　　　　　Time Will Break the World

were letting the idea take hold. The longer we joked, the less it sounded like a joke. We were talking ourselves into it.

New York Yankees right fielder Dave Winfield. "Nope, he would kick both our asses," I said.

Mayor Ed Koch. "Too much security," Jay said.

Lee Iacocca. "Is Detroit a big city? How would we find him?"

Lonzo Feldman Jr. "Now we're talking."

But we quickly dismissed Lonzo. Honestly, I feared seeing him again. If we kidnapped him, I worried he'd turn the tables on us, hold us for ransom, take more from us than he already had.

"How about George Schott?" Jason said.

We debated this one for a while. Our dad could afford a ransom and deserved a little torment in his placid life. He was also tough enough to handle a hostage scenario. But we backed off. He would know it was us. He might not press charges, but he would fire us.

Jay had drifted behind me. The morning was overcast but smelled sweetly of spring. He had stopped walking and seemed rooted to the spot. I doubled back to him.

"This would be a good place to hold someone," he said.

"Where?" I looked around. There was nothing but flat land in each direction.

"Here," he said, pointing down.

Liz Mashburn (68) sits next to her husband Phil (69) on their tan Bridgewater sofa, beneath a framed watercolor landscape Liz bought at an estate sale. Their daughters, Brenda and Emily (both 40), face them on two chairs they carried over from the dining room, the camera on a tripod between them.

It is a warm, luminous afternoon and, after the interview, the Mashburn family has reservations for a late lunch.

Emily Mashburn-Bauer (EMB): Can you and Dad sit closer together? I need to fit you in the shot.

Liz Mashburn (LM): This is so exciting. This is fun.

Phil Mashburn (PM): I love seeing my girls work together.

Brenda Mashburn (BM): I'm glad everyone's enjoying themselves.

PM: Why wouldn't I be? I'm being interviewed by the famous Brenda Mashburn. Just like Qaddafi and Paul McCartney.

BM: I never interviewed Qaddafi. Are you nuts? And it was Paul McCartney's daughter.

PM: Is she in a band?

BM: She was raising money after a tsunami in Indonesia.

LM: Sometimes I think about it, you know?

BM: The tsunami?

LM: No, the bus. It's not often, and I don't try to think about it. It just comes to me. Usually something will remind me. Like that song.

BM: What song?

LM: Phil?

PM: Yes, honey.

LM: What song am I thinking of?

PM: You want me to guess?

LM: What, guess? You know.

PM: I do?

LM: You know what I'm talking about... the one about magic, just a little magic. The guy sings *Oh, oh*, a lot. Don't you all look at me like that. You're pretending you don't know the song to make fun of me.

PM: "Magic"? The Cars song? That reminds you of our daughters being abducted?

LM: It was a very popular song that summer.

BM: I think we should get started.

PM: I'm at your disposal.

BM: Dad, how did you first learn that we were missing?

PM: Easy. Your mom called me at work. Next question.

BM: What about you, Mom? How did you hear?

LM: I was home from work when I got the call. From the phone tree... Just like we did on snow days... It went alphabetically. But I already knew there was a problem before I got the call.

BM: How did you know?

LM: Because I'd just called Mary Galvano at Save Mart and asked her if she could light a fire under your skinny butts and send you home ASAP.

EMB: Why did you think we were at Save Mart?

LM: You volunteered me to make cookies for a party on the last day of summer school and didn't tell me until that morning.

EMB: We did?

LM: I used to think you did things like that on purpose to stress me out. You were so bad. I gave you money and said that if you wanted me to bake, you'd better run and see Mary when you got off the bus and pick up supplies.

BM to EMB: Do you remember this?

EMB shakes her head no at **BM**.

LM: I'd send you there all the time for groceries or a carton of cigarettes, which Mary knew was okay to sell to you because she and I went to high school together. Anyway, Mary said you hadn't been to the store.

BM: Did that worry you?

LM: Not really.

BM: Shouldn't it have?

LM: Don't second-guess me, Brenda.

BM: It's a significant point. We were supposed to be at one place, and we weren't. I'm asking you why you weren't concerned.

LM: As long as you were home by dinner, there was nothing to worry about.

PM: Kids had more freedom back then.

BM to EMB: (Inaudible)

EMB to BM: (Inaudible)

BM: Fine. Back to the phone tree. What was the message?

LM: The bus ran out of gas. That was what they told everyone.

BM: When did you find out that wasn't true?

LM: I started getting calls from other parents, not on the phone tree. And then we went down to the main office to find out what was going on.

EMB: Were you still at work, Dad?

PM: I met your mom there. There were two cop cars in front of the building. That's when I knew something big was happening.

EMB to BM: (inaudible) this part. We (inaudible) the same (inaudible) Al Tiles.

BM to EMB: (inaudible) *my* job, okay?

LM: It's rude to whisper.

BM: Looking at things now, we know that Emily and I survived and our family has done its best to put the incident behind us. But I'd really like to drill down into what you were feeling at the school district office and later that night, when everything was still unknown.

LM: You can imagine how worried we were.

BM: Explain it to me.

PM: A parent's worst nightmare.

BM: Specifically, though, put me in your head once you knew that your daughters were kidnapped.

LM: I felt the way any parent would.

EMB: How would any parent feel?

LM: You have children, Emily. You know what it's like.

BM: What about you, Dad? What did you feel?

PM: What your mom just said.

BM: Would you like to add your own comment?

PM: I wouldn't want to go through that again.

BM: That's it?

PM: Uh-huh.

BM to EMB: (Inaudible).

PM: More whispering.

LM: Rude.

EMB to BM: (inaudible) Push (inaudible) won't, I will.

BM to EMB: Be my guest.

EMB: Did you look for us?

PM: We went to the candlelight vigil at the reservoir.

EMB: What vigil? I've never heard of it.

PM: The whole town was there.

LM: Phil, honey, it was a search party.

PM: It was both.

LM: It was just a search party. There were helicopters.

PM: You don't remember the—what do you call it?—prayer circle?

LM: Oh, yes, okay, that's right. There was a prayer circle and some singing, I think.

PM: We said some prayers and shed some tears. It was cathartic.

EMB: You prayed?

PM: Does that surprise you?

LM: Your father and I are spiritual people.

BM: No, you're not.

PM: There's a lot you don't know about us.

LM: The main thing is we never gave up hope that you'd be brought home. And we were right.

PM: Well said. You guys ready to eat?

EMB: Not yet.

LM: All I had today was an apple and a piece of toast.

BM: Did you think we were hurt? Let me say that differently. When you had no clue where we were, did you think someone was hurting us?

LM: You try not to think about it.

EMB: Did you think we were being raped?

PM: Jesus, Emily!

EMB: Tortured? Murdered?

PM: That's very dark.

EMB: We were hostages, Dad! Of course it's dark!

LM: You can't give in to negative thoughts.

EMB: So, you had negative thoughts? That's what we're asking.

LM: Of course.

EMB: What were they?

LM: Who can remember? It was so long ago.

EMB: Seriously?

PM: Stop interrogating your mom.

EMB: You can jump in anytime you want. What negative thoughts did you have?

PM: The same as your mom.

EMB: You're allowed to talk for yourself.

PM: I know I am.

EMB: So, do it.

PM: I thought you were dead.

EMB and BM look at each other, about to say something, but neither does.

EMB: (Quietly) You thought we were dead?

PM: Just you.

BM: Just her? Why just her? Why was I still alive?

PM: I didn't say you were alive. I didn't know what you were.

BM: You weren't even thinking about me?

PM: I didn't say that. I just thought she was dead. I can't tell you why. That's just what I thought.

LM: I made a bargain with myself that I didn't care if everyone else on that bus died except for you two. If I had the power to bring that about, if it meant saving you, I would have done it.

PM: There. We answered. Are we good?

LM: I hope you never feel that helpless.

BM: Do you mind if we take five? I have to change the battery on the recorder.

PM: We don't need a break. We're done.

EMB: We're not done.

PM: Okay, then I'm done.

EMB: The interview isn't over.

PM: Interesting theory. Now watch this.

Phil stands, unclips the microphone from his shirt collar, drops it with the battery pack on the couch, and walks away. Liz follows.

*

The footage was hard to look at. It was late and they were in the living room. While Emily watched, Brenda cleaned receipts and gum wrappers out of her purse. She found three tubes of ChapStick. She didn't want to deal with the interview, not right then, but decided it was best that Emily wasn't alone. She popped an Ativan for the hell of it. She needed a good night's sleep.

Emily rewatched the moment their father walked out of the room. "I was counting on them."

Brenda didn't say it, but this was the reason you didn't go into an interview with expectations. She didn't say that you had to uncover the story that was there, not the story you wanted to be there. She didn't say far better journalists than her had ruined their reputations by shoehorning their desired outcome into a story where it didn't belong. Everyone was biased, but the trick was not to be so desperate about proving your point of view.

"It was pretty funny when Mom was talking about sending us out for cigarettes," she said, trying to lighten the mood.

"Totally normal parenting. Jesus." Emily restarted the video from the beginning and paused it on a shot of their mother's face, frozen at half-blink, like she was sneezing, their father looking passive and tired beside her. "These aren't the same people we grew up with."

Brenda glanced up from her purse. She was going to say that maybe Emily should wait a few days and approach the interview with fresh eyes. Let her get a little distance and she might have a different opinion about the work. She might end up being less critical of their parents. Instead, what she said was, "Can you give me a ride to the train station tomorrow?"

Emily shut the laptop and drummed her fingers on it, a bitter little laugh escaping her mouth. "You're going home?" she said.

"I have to water my plants."

"You have plants?"

"If I did, they would need watering."

Emily slipped her computer into its case. "I guess I'll do the Andy Kraven interview by myself."

"Don't do that," Brenda said. She wished she hadn't said anything.

"Don't do what? You're the one quitting."

"When did I say that?"

Brenda had decided to go home because she was thinking of ending her leave of absence.

She planned on easing back in, until she was sure she could handle a full workload. It would take a while. Until then she would have time to work on the documentary. She told Emily this.

"I'm glad you're feeling better. I was worried about you," Emily said, and stood up.

"How about before I go, let's drive around and get footage down at the reservoir."

"I'm pretty busy. Maybe call a taxi," she said, and went to bed.

I'd been with three other men before my husband, but none was as large in the pants. Let it be known: George Calvin Schott had a humongous member. The first time we slept together, I prayed for it to end because of the pain. I clawed his shoulders in self-defense, not passion. He mistook my whimpering for pleasure. I sat gingerly on the toilet the whole next day.

George adjusted to his job at Munsee Granite in no time. He loved it. I'd predicted my dad would put a pickaxe in his hand, but George started in administration, destined for management and executive status in the midtown office. He got the career that was meant for me. We bought a three-bedroom split-level near my parents', probably a bit too near, but I made the most of my new freedom. I took up smoking. I loved cigarettes, the heat, the taste, the lightheadedness of the first long drag, the tingling in my fingertips. George bought me a carved ivory cigarette holder that I never used because I even enjoyed picking tiny bits of tobacco off my tongue and lips.

But strain worked its way into our relationship. I got pregnant not long after our wedding and miscarried in the second month. George didn't want to know anything about it, the messy human aspects. He just wanted to start a family. It was a yes or no proposition for him. Pregnant or not pregnant. Not pregnant ruled the day. Two more miscarriages over the next year and a half. Then I stopped getting pregnant. My mom thought it was God's revenge for the way I destroyed her body. During the worst of my infertility, I agreed with her.

And then: Calvin Daniel Schott, born December 8th, 1959. He was six pounds, two ounces. I don't remember much about the delivery once the scopolamine kicked in and the doctors went to work on Cal with the forceps. Poor boy's head got mushed into the shape of an overripe avocado. Twenty months later, we welcomed Jason George Schott to the family. This boy was a galoot, nine pounds, nine ounces, a head of hair like an alpaca. I really could have used drugs this go-round but refused, and by the time I asked it was too late. Who knew Jason would be so damn big?

That summer I assembled both sides of the family for a week on Cape Cod. I rented a house in Wellfleet that looked right out of the Kennedy Compound. It was no easy trick for the Schotts to walk away from catering gigs in the height of July, but they came—parents, siblings, nieces, and nephews.

For three days, George was the happiest I'd ever seen him. He was a husband and a father, with a career far afield of anything his own father understood. I realized he was proud of himself. At night we stood on the deck beneath a sky baring layer upon layer of stars. Out past where we drank and smoked and played cards, the tide in the bay rolled silently in.

In the mornings, we moved from the house to the beach to wash away our hangovers in the salty current, or to sweat them out under the sun. Uncle Fred had rigged up a wheelchair with skis and my mom pushed him around in the sand. Well into one afternoon, I realized Calvin was missing. I looked to where the children played and couldn't see my son. I shielded my brow with my hand, looking for Calvin among the tan and wet legs.

George, I said, and the quiver in my voice got him to his feet. We fanned out over the beach. There were no lifeguards, and I couldn't bring myself to look at the water. Panic welled up inside me. We trampled sandcastles and interrupted volleyball games, disrupted other families' picnics, screaming Calvin! I began crying.

Then we heard the shouts. We got him! Over here! Uncle Fred

waved from his chair, my mom behind it. Calvin was sitting on a blue blanket with another couple.

I hugged my son until he squealed. The woman on the blanket said Calvin had just wandered over a few minutes earlier. Her husband told us his name and stuck out his hand.

Looks like you got yourself a real sneaky one, he said.

George punched him in the nose.

Way to go, Assless George, Fred said. My mom said Shhh! and slapped him on the shoulder.

Nothing was the same after that. We did our best to enjoy the rest of the vacation. But something had changed and didn't unchange when the week was over. I couldn't help but think that my family had finally put its mark on my husband, or worse, the quarry had contaminated him. My childhood suspicions about the granite pit flooded back to me.

George never spoke about what he had done. I never brought it up. All I can say is that if he was eager to show off what kind of man he had become, he got what he wanted.

Jon Stern greeted them in jeans and a faded Dartmouth T-shirt.

"Ever the professional, I see," Bertie said.

"I wish I could roll out of bed looking like a million bucks like you, Mrs. Schott. But, alas," he said, and winked at her.

"That's pretty good," she said, and winked back

He shook Jason's hand. "How are you?"

"Sorry about my mom," Jason said.

Jason had reached out to Stern about Brenda and Emily Mashburn's documentary, not knowing where else to turn. Bertie, upon hearing about the casting call from Angie, gloated that she was, as usual, right. "What did I say? What did I say from the start? Cal is never getting out." She reveled in her bitter victory just long enough to spark her sense of persecution. Galvanized by the latest Carlo Rossi vintage, her voice unsteady, she complained about this latest intrusion into their lives until she was shouting at Jason, "Haven't we paid enough? We lost everything. What more do these sluts want from us?"

Jason had said he would call their lawyer.

"You do that," she said.

Stern sat at his desk. He pulled up the Facebook post about the documentary on his computer. He made slight wincing faces while reading it.

"What can we do to stop them?" Jason said.

"Our options are limited, unfortunately," Stern said.

"Would a better lawyer have more options?" Bertie said.

"Maybe a lawyer who practiced in a world with different laws."

"Don't we have a right to privacy?" Jason said.

Stern made a vague hocus-pocus motion with his hands, as if

seeking to pull an acceptable answer out of thin air. He understood where they were coming from. The problem, he explained, was that a right to privacy didn't extend to people involved in a matter of public interest, which the Brookwood Bus Kidnapping was.

"Incredible. Just incredible what this country's turned into," Bertie said.

"So, there's nothing we can do?" Jason said.

"Waste of time," Bertie said. "Let's go home."

Jason put a hand on her shoulder.

"Jon, there's got to be something. Please."

Stern stood up, not to signal the end of the meeting but because he communicated better on his feet. He leaned one buttock on the edge of his desk to seem casual, like a friend giving advice, instead of what he was, a man paid to represent their interests. "Here's what I can do. I will send the filmmakers a cease and desist letter. I'll make it threatening. I'll use words like unauthorized and defamatory and egregious and bad faith."

"And that will make them stop?" Jason said.

"The letter will have no legal effect, but it might scare them."

"And if it doesn't? What then? Nothing?"

"I understand where you're coming from. The timing is unfortunate, but I would caution against drawing more attention to this. I don't see how they can finish making a movie before Calvin's parole hearing."

Jason didn't know how to tell Stern that Cal's parole was only one issue at stake. This documentary was going to ruin his life. It would put him out of business and put Bertie in the ground. Already he'd noticed a change in Angie, a protective distancing. She hadn't answered his texts in two days, and perhaps she was using this time to reappraise their relationship.

"What about one of those things… an injunction?" Jason said.

"Let's start with the letter and see how it goes," Stern said, and now he was standing because the meeting was over.

Bertie muttered something else about a waste of time and

Jason couldn't stand to hear her thin, nasty whisper, even though he was having trouble disagreeing with her.

What good was a cease and desist letter if it didn't stop the Mashburns? If the law wasn't on his side, what was he supposed to do?

# CALVIN

Jason was munching a wet tuna sandwich in the passenger seat of my Cutlass and I didn't kick him out. What more proof could anyone need that I was a good brother? We had stopped having lunch with the other groundsmen, isolating ourselves not only from them but everyone. We arranged our comings and goings at home to limit interaction with George and Bertie. We were waiting. For what, it was hard to say. A chance, I guess.

We were pulling away from each other as well. We read the paper while we ate to avoid talking, the low buzz of WNEW ("Where Rock Lives!") trickling out of the speakers. Our conversations of late were inadequate and left us wanting. It seemed that when we did talk, we talked about the kidnapping but could never find its center of gravity. So much of it was focused on the aftermath, on smoky, brassy New Orleans nights, and the coral reefs and mangroves of Costa Maya, on women and food and our sloppy luxury. Kidnapping simply became another word for better days ahead. It almost felt outside of our immediate control. The way I saw it, an opportunity would present itself and we would take it. We just had to wait. We waited for the right moment. We waited. But we were bad at waiting. It agitated us.

I fell into my comfortable distraction of the Olympics. I was reading about this sixteen-year-old gymnast from Fairmont, West Virginia, who had been training in Houston for the last year and a half—Mary Lou Retton. I'd had my eye on her for a while. She was the best vaulter in the world. She possessed the rare combination of power and finesse, and she'd come out of nowhere last year winning the all-around competition at the McDonald's American Cup at Madison Square Garden as a substitute. That one put her on the map. Then she dominated the Chunichi Cup, in Japan, with another all-around win.

I rolled down the window for a breeze to carry away Jay's fishy sandwich odor. A runnel of mayo flowed from his fingers down his wrist. He had his face buried in the newspaper, oblivious. I went back to my own reading.

The article said that Mary Lou had a very real chance of being the first American woman to win an Olympic medal in gymnastics. Her coach, the Romanian Béla Károlyi, said she was unbeatable. Don Peters, coach of the American women's team, said, "Watching her perform is like seeing O. J. Simpson run. Everybody else seems to be standing still."

I was in the middle of reading about how Retton's compact, muscular build—which was uncommon for gymnasts, who are traditionally long and elegant—could alter the entire approach to the sport. Then Jay said the sentence that changed everything.

"Did you know the state just passed a $35.6 billion dollar budget?"

Of course, right then the significance of what he said escaped me.

"What's your point, Dick Cheese?"

The fact was I didn't get it. Schotts weren't civic-minded people. Jay had never even voted. Why did he suddenly care? What was his hobby really about? He said it wasn't a hobby. He said we knew jackshit about the way the world worked. It was shameful. None of the information was kept secret from us; we were just too lazy to look. That was why Lonzo took us without a fight.

"Do you have any concept of how much money thirty-five billion dollars is? You really don't care?" he said.

"In ten minutes we'll be breathing dust for the rest of the day. So, no, I don't care."

"That's where our money's going to come from, Richard Cheddar."

That shut me up. I laid the paper on my lap. I realized I was looking at the kidnapping the wrong way. I thought our participation would be as passive as finding a dollar bill on the sidewalk. But Jason, he wasn't waiting. He had stopped dreaming of tequila and carnitas. He was laying the foundation and spoiling to get to work. Instead of seizing a rich person for ransom, he said we could take just about anybody and make the state pay. He decided five million dollars was the magic number. The budget was seven thousand times more. We were asking for chump change in comparison. The catch, as he saw it, was that the state wouldn't lay out seven figures for just one person. We needed to kidnap multiple people to get multiple millions.

And then he said it: "Kids."

Children were precious. New York would pay vast sums for children.

"We get some kids. Hide them. State pays the ransom. We let them go."

"Then what?" I said.

"We're happy forever."

"You really think we can do this?" I said. If he said we could, I would believe him.

Jay smiled like he felt a little bad for me and folded up the rest of his sandwich in the wax paper. He got out of the car and went to clock back in. I pretended what he'd said hadn't made much of an impact on me and I returned to my article. The Olympic trials were in June, and Mary Lou was unfazed by the pressure.

"It doesn't bother me," she said.

I reread the sentence several times, hoping it would rub off on me and make me unbothered too, or at least distract me from what I was really thinking about, which was that it didn't matter if we believed we could go through with the kidnapping because I knew, in a spine-deep way, that my brother's words had just bound us to it.

THURSDAY, AUGUST 2, 1984

Lindsey Robinson wasn't dead. Martin Mendoza kept checking her pulse anyway. The steady throb in her soft, wet neck that had relieved him when he first felt it, now startled him. He thought about what the sensation really was: blood. Blood swelling through the arteries in her neck. An echo of her heart contracting a moment earlier. Her head was in his lap and her hair unspooled over his thighs. It was, obviously, the closest he had ever been to a girl, but his erection predated their touching. His was a terror boner, straining at his tighty-whities for hours, not your standard-issue horndog hard-on. For the first time since they were crammed into the grey van, he was thankful for the darkness. He was positive everyone was staring at them. He didn't like being looked at, even in the complete dark, and he wanted Lindsey to wake up so she could move off him. He considered shaking her shoulders a little bit, gently, to rouse her, not rude like when his mom tossed a glass of water in his face that morning, but chose to leave her alone. He had this cool thought that when she finally opened her eyes and heard about how he'd helped her, they could be friends. He would have a partner for the rest of the ordeal. If they lived, they would have their own inside jokes, like Scott and Brian at Camp Wanaksink. They would have stories nobody could top.

The van was moving again. It went fast, then slow, then stopped. Then fast for a while. It made turns. It slowed and stopped. The motion felt endless, as if the driver were trying and failing to find his way out of a labyrinth. Martin heard coughing and gagging. Someone was barfing. Car sickness, he thought. He leaned away from the sound and sensed others doing the same, no one wanting to get hit with the splash back.

The barfer, Emily Mashburn, wasn't car sick. She just didn't believe Lindsey was alive and the thought of being locked up with a corpse turned her stomach. She saw the way the man in the pantyhose mask dumped the girl's body in the back of the van, like a duffel bag of dirty clothes. That wasn't a sleeping girl. Why would a girl be napping in the first place? She was dead. How didn't the others notice it? Emily pictured a green sick-making vapor rising off the dead body that she was breathing in. It coated her mouth and throat, filled her nostrils and lungs, spun her dizzy. She retched to get it out. Peanut butter and jelly sandwich and Oreos and orange juice. She was on her hands and knees, her head hanging between her shoulders. She missed her sister. If Brenda were there, she would have rubbed Emily's back. But no one was rubbing her back. She hoped that if a dead girl in Brenda's van made her sick, someone would rub her back.

They turned yet again, and she lost her balance. Her hand slapped into the warm puddle. She scooted back to her spot against the wall, holding her slimy hand away from her body. She put her head on her knees and cried.

Lindsey heard Emily crying. No one knew that she had regained consciousness while she was still outside. She remembered hitting the kidnapper with a rock and turning to run. There was a gap in her memory and the next time she opened her eyes she was being carried. Once she realized whose sweaty shoulder she was riding, she chewed the inside of her mouth until she tasted blood, so deep was her disappointment. She'd closed her eyes and pretended to sleep. But now the spell was broken. She couldn't playact any longer. She rolled off Martin's lap, which was, she hated to admit, a surprisingly nice place to rest, and propped herself up on one elbow.

Martin said, "Hey, welcome back."

"This totally sucks," she tried to say, but her voice came out a croak. Her throat was dry and sore, the back of her head ached, and her face, on the left side, where it struck the tree, felt weird, larger, her skin hot and sensitive.

"Want some water?"

She took the Pepsi bottle of water and drank some and then crawled up beside Emily.

"Here, drink this," she said.

Emily raised her head off her knees, sniffling up snot. She could barely make out Lindsey's shape but recognized that the girl talking to her wasn't dead.

The warm water retained the faintest flavor of cola. She drank a little more and spat a mouthful into her barfy hand and wiped it on the sole of her Keds. She stuck her hand in her pocket. "Thank you," she said softly.

The van wobbled on, and the children resettled into their quiet torpor. Several had urinated in their shorts. The stress put Robert Avery and Paul Zamfino to sleep. Others fixated on the heat, hunger pangs, headaches, muscle cramps, urgent, yet unmeetable physical needs, to distract from murkier fears. They turned again, this time onto a dirt road or a street in really bad shape, Martin thought. They hit a pothole or divot and he banged his head against the wall and his jaw snapped shut, his teeth clacking together. When they stopped next, the driver shut the van off, the engine ticking as it cooled. Lindsey worried he was coming back for her.

But he didn't come back for her because he was waiting for the van the color of pistachio ice cream. The dashboard clock told him he was ten minutes late, but he'd arrived first. He rubbed his face with both palms and looked down the road.

A waxing crescent moon was perched above the trees when the green van turned the corner, two dim headlight beams flickering before it.

"Took you long enough," Jason said when Calvin joined him.

"Just don't, okay."

"Did something happen?"

"Let's just get to work."

They threw open the doors to the green van. The smell wafting out made them turn their heads.

"Driver, out," Jason said, his hand over his mouth and nose.

They walked Pat Earl behind a sagging plywood fence stenciled with words he couldn't make out, but that read MUNSEE GRANITE CO. One of the men lit a propane camping lantern. Once Pat's eyes adjusted, he saw within the short circle of lamplight that he was standing on hard, broken ground. He thought they were at a construction site. The two men were taller and bigger than him, especially the one with the shotgun. Pat saw no way of overpowering them and getting away.

The one with the black pantyhose mask sat backward on a folding chair, holding his pistol on Pat.

"What's your name?"

Pat told him and the other man wrote it on a sheet of paper on a clipboard.

"Take your pants off."

"What for?" Pat said, but he untied his boots, freed his feet of them, and let his pants slide to his ankles. "Those kids are sick. They need fresh air. They're dying for water."

"You didn't give them water?" Jason said to Calvin.

"Why, so they could piss all over the floor?"

"I got bad news for you," Pat said.

"Shut up and put your boots back on," Calvin said.

"You really didn't give them anything to drink?" Jason said.

"Maybe I should have taken them to Village Memorial Park Pool and let them swim a few laps to cool off."

"They need water. We discussed it."

"A few more minutes and they won't need anything."

Jason lifted the pants by the belt loops. They were wet and smelled like mildew and ass. He pinched the wallet from the back pocket and thumbed through its contents. He lifted the driver's license and read Pat's address aloud.

"The slums of Brookwood," he said, and handed the license to Calvin, who pocketed it. "Come on," he said to Pat.

They came to a backhoe with dried mud splattered on the

tires and cab windows. Two shovels and pickaxes leaned against the loader bucket. The one with the shotgun pushed Pat toward a hole in the ground, its symmetry and evenness he immediately took for a grave.

"I'm telling you, fellas, there's no need for this."

"Duly noted." He jabbed Pat in the spine with the shotgun barrel.

Pat shuffled to the edge of the crater and saw a metal ladder protruding. It wasn't a grave, but he didn't know what it was.

"How dumb are you? Get in the hole," Jason said.

Pat threw one leg over the top of the ladder, then the other. The hole was narrower than a grave, and he brushed his shoulders against the sides. He counted the rungs as he descended. The hole opened up into—what? A cavern or a room of some sort? He reached the bottom and said, "What is going on?"

"There's a lantern next to you. Check out your digs."

Pat swept the light over the area and still couldn't figure out what he was standing in. It was a rectangular box, possibly a shipping container or the inside of a moving truck. But why was it buried like an underground bomb shelter? He saw ventilation pipes with slow-turning fans in the ceiling. There were eight mattresses on the floor, three buckets with plastic toilet seats affixed to the tops, four five-gallon water coolers, and, on a folding table along one wall, food. Pat inspected the goods: Wonder Bread, Oscar Mayer bologna, mayonnaise, Mr. T breakfast cereal, powdered milk, Ritz crackers, peanut butter, jelly, and cans of Juicy Juice with triangular holes punctured in the tops. There was another lantern, a box of candles, a book of matches, and a disposable lighter.

He slumped onto the bottom rung of the ladder, trying to piece it together. The gunmen intended to keep them down here. Past that, he was stumped. Pat Earl was a man who took things at face value and his lack of introspection, a quality that hadn't necessarily hurt him over the years, left him unable to process

     TIME WILL BREAK THE WORLD

what was going on, beyond a lifetime of experience that taught him good and bad were doled out lopsidedly.

Vibrations on the ladder made him stand up. Down came Doodoo Viscuso.

"Those dick weeds stole one of my sneakers. My sister is going to kill me," he said, before noticing that the bus driver was in his boxer shorts. "Damn, they got your pants, Mr. Pat?"

Pat Earl nodded.

"Smells like my basement down here," Doodoo said. He spied the water coolers and placed his mouth right under one of the taps. "I was thirstier than a mummy."

More kids climbed down the ladder. Jodie Hoffman. Andy Kraven. Jonathan Medina. Jennifer Strauss. Brenda Mashburn. Each child was missing one article of clothing or a personal item like house keys or a watch or, in the case of Kaito Watanabe, eyeglasses. Emily entered without her plastic hair clips, her braid unraveling. She ran to Brenda and they hugged, a violent embrace that put them off balance, and they staggered into one of the walls.

"Together, we are safe," Brenda said.

Pat inspected each student in the lantern light and then sent them for water. Besides Lindsey Robinson, who had a swollen cheek she refused to talk about, they seemed mostly fine, really better than fine considering what they had been through. Which was of little relief to him. He never should have tried to help the stalled van. He never should have, he never should have—the words repeating in his head. He should have continued his route and watched Eddie's baseball game. Had he done so, had he done his job and nothing more, they would be home now. He would be in his chair, in front of the TV, and the worst thing he'd have to worry about was a campaign commercial that annoyed him.

"Can we make you a sandwich, Mr. Pat?" Brenda asked, arm in arm with her twin. Their simple courtesy, when it was obvious he deserved none, shamed him.

"No, thank you," he said. "I'm not very hungry."

"I'm starving," Emily said.

They moved on to the food table where Martin hovered beside Lindsey. She spread mayonnaise on bread with a plastic knife. Someone had lit a few candles, the glow warm and gold over her hands. He wanted to talk to her. To make friends with her. But he didn't know what to say.

"Would you rather be buried alive or drowned?" he said.

"I don't know," she said.

"Drowned or blown away with a shotgun?"

"Those are all terrible." She pressed two circles of bologna onto the white bread. She handed the sandwich to Sarah Ramsarup and faced Martin.

"Can I ask you something?"

"Sure."

"You have to promise to tell the truth. Can you do that? Earth to Marty. Do you copy?"

No one called him Marty, not even his friends. He kind of liked it.

"Copy," he said.

"Does my face look A. bad, B. really bad, or C. totally wrecked?"

He studied her swollen cheek. "You look fine," he said.

"Okay, sure. Thanks for nothing."

"Can I ask you something?" he said. "What happened when you got out of the van? Did he...?"

"I hit him with a rock and ran away."

"You're lying. Right?"

"Why do you draw whales?"

"I like whales."

"I like elephants. But I suck at drawing." She turned back to the table. "I guess I'll eat cereal," she said.

Martin opened a sleeve of Ritz. He wanted to tell her that drawing was pretty easy once you got the hang of it. He could show her some tricks he'd learned. If she wanted. Instead, he stuffed his mouth with crackers and stood there chewing.

They might not have noticed when the ladder was pulled up if they didn't hear the voice of one of the men shouting down at them, "Citius, Altius, Fortius." The hole was covered by something that scraped the earth as it was put in place. The students started yelling to be let out. Machinery sounds came from outside. There was a metallic scratching noise above them, and Martin heard the roof of the container creak and thought he saw it sag under the weight.

"I think the roof is going to cave in," he said, in the same matter-of-fact way he explained that killer whales weren't fish.

In the last month, Martin Mendoza had begun waking at 4:00 a.m. because he'd read a blog that said four o'clock was when CEOs and billionaires and other iconoclasts started their day. What they did once awake depended on the person. Some meditated, some exercised, some journaled, some communed with a spiritual higher power, and some wasted not a minute before getting down to business, using the extra hours to gain an edge while their competition slept. Martin was looking for any edge he could get his hands on. And by edge, he didn't mean an advantage but an actual place of purchase, something he could cleave himself to, to prevent himself from falling.

He stood dazed and blinking in the kitchen while the Keurig fired up. Upstairs, Alexandra was on her side of their bed, and the kids were in their rooms, and he knew the one thing he shouldn't do with this time was ruminate. He'd be better served by accomplishing a task with definite results, for example, working on his petition to get his name on the ballot for the Glenville Village Council. Getting on the ballot was his main electoral obstacle since there were three council members retiring and the council wasn't a hotly contested position. It was his neighbor Jerry Woods who suggested that he enter local politics. Martin's successful crusades to have the tree with Dutch elm disease on Lindell Drive removed and a stop sign installed at the corner of Bird Street and Rose Lane hadn't gone unnoticed.

"It would be a good thing to have a guy like you with his eye on the neighborhood," Jerry had said.

Martin, at forty-three, wasn't completely sold on what kind of a guy he was, but he appreciated being thought of as the right kind of guy.

He carried his mug to the breakfast table and sat down

facing the window looking out on his slim side yard. He could put together a list of prominent residents he might appeal to for endorsements—that was something he could do while his little world slumbered around him. And yet, despite his best effort to busy himself, his only thought now was how it had been inevitable that the instant he showed the slightest interest in advancing himself in a public way, he would reencounter and be confronted by "That Thing." The timing was almost perfect. He announced on his Facebook page his candidacy for village council and that night, the same goddamn night, as he was tallying Likes and comments of encouragement, enjoying the quick but fleeting dopamine hit of social media engagement, he discovered the post about a Brookwood Bus Kidnapping documentary in the works. Discovered wasn't even the right word. He hadn't gone looking for it. The post just appeared on his timeline, conjured by dark magic, it seemed, right there below another of his mom's constant reposts, this one a heartbreaking plea from an animal rescue group to save a hard luck canine from imminent euthanasia.

Were you a victim of the Brookwood Bus Kidnapping?

Define *victim*, he thought. Better yet, define *were*. Define *Brookwood*. It all seemed so far away. Another boy's life. Which was precisely the way he'd engineered it.

He kept reading.

...friend, neighbor, relative...survivor... Select participants... award-winning... Interested individuals...

He knew what each word meant in isolation, but this particular arrangement baffled him. And then, the kicker:

... a brief summary of their experience during those fateful summer days in 1984.

The producers were two women he knew a long time ago, when they weren't yet women. They, too, *were victims*. That they were making a movie about "That Thing" was almost funny, were it not an active threat to the life Martin had built.

It was after the kids were in bed when Alexandra stumbled

upon the post and asked him about it. They were alone in the kitchen. He was leaning against the counter, sipping a bottle of beer, relaxing to the sloshing rhythm of the dishwasher.

"There was some kind of mass abduction in your hometown?" she said, half statement, half question. "In the eighties, I guess?"

"I guess," he said.

Sip. Another sip. An ersatz inspection of the dishwasher's progress, running his finger over the blue cycle light.

"How come you never said anything about it?" she said.

"I must have," he said, shrugging.

"Did you see someone is making a movie about it?"

"I don't know." More shrugging, sipping, the sudden recollection of a cast iron pan in urgent need of seasoning.

Not even Alexandra knew what he experienced the summer he was thirteen. It wasn't part of a grand design to keep it from her. By the time they met in their twenties, he'd been omitting this detail from his biography since decamping to Ohio for college. It had been easy to withhold that in August of 1984 he had been infamously abducted, mostly because it was what he wanted to be true. He told the story of his life as he wished it had happened, as it very well could have happened, if only things had turned out a little differently: he spent the summer before ninth grade at Camp Wanaksink with his best friends Brian and Scott, feeling up girls and winning Color War, forming some of the best memories of his childhood. It didn't feel like a lie; it felt like a vital correction. He found that once he excised the kidnapping from his past, he was free of its hold over him.

Martin peeked up from the cast iron pan and saw Alexandra reading something on her phone. He knew it would be a fruitful search engine experience—the Wikipedia page, the *Daily Times* digital archives, the *A.P.* photograph of him that night at the quarry and again when he met George Bush at the Kids Day celebration. He waited, rather than confess. Then she was horrified by his casual ability to create such a lacuna in his personal history. It was a betrayal on par with having a hidden second family, she told him.

The kitchen lights had never seemed brighter. It felt like he was arguing in an operating room.

"It's nothing like a second family," he said.

"I feel like a fucking idiot," she yelled.

Yelling—he couldn't handle it, ever. He would shut down during his parents' fights before they split, literally turn away from the sound and freeze, unable to escape. Something about the violence of loud noises immobilized him.

"You shouldn't," he said, focusing on the mouth of the beer bottle.

"Shouldn't what?"

"You know, feel like an idiot," he said, almost too softly to be heard, as if trying to average out the volume in the room.

"Wouldn't you feel stupid if you married a psychopath?"

"That's a bit overboard. I think so, at least."

"At your dad's funeral, the priest kept talking about what your family went through, some hardship. I had no clue what he was talking about. People kept coming up to me saying you were a hero," she said. "I was like, 'Martin, a hero? What?'"

"It's just something I don't like talking about. It's not a big deal."

"You were kidnapped! That's a huge fucking deal. And I don't know anything about it."

Alexandra looked like a natural disaster, a hurricane or flash flood, nature unleashing itself and bearing down on him. He stared at his feet and that did no good; the bright lights reflected off the kitchen tiles. When he looked up again, she was gone.

The next day his mom texted. Alexandra had sent a lengthy email accusing her of abetting her son's duplicity. *Secrets don't stay secret. Busted!* her text read.

That was how Martin felt—busted. Not as in caught, but as in broken or dented. The façade he'd constructed was crumbling.

There was also the matter of his marriage, which felt busted also. More like ruptured, a fissure rent between them. Martin was on one side, Alexandra and the kids on the other (though she was merciful in not telling them), and he was looking at them and then at the wide crack separating them, and he could just wonder how they were ever going to be reunited.

His coffee had gone cold, the milk an oily sheen on its surface. He made a mental list of people to contact for his campaign— Joe Lockhart, Eileen McElhenny, Margaret Josephson, Ted... something. He thought he should write the names down to have proof of his progress. He jotted them on the back of an AEG bill envelope. The list was real and gave Martin that edge to hold on to while his relationship with his family hung in uncertainty.

Although, that wasn't true, and he knew it. There was no uncertainty. It wasn't as if Alexandra didn't tell him what she wanted from him. After two days of radio silence, during which time he truly worried she might be retaining the services of a divorce lawyer, she softened. She hugged him and told him how sad she felt for him, how she had read up on the kidnapping and it made her cry whenever she thought of what it must have been like for him. She loved him and it broke her heart that he carried around this terrible thing all by himself. Martin thought their fight was over, but Alexandra wasn't done. He was leaving to take the kids to school when she staged her request so there was no time to debate. She was very composed. The kids were in the car waiting. First, she said, he needed to tell her everything about the bus hijacking, everything he remembered. There would be questions and he would need to answer them thoughtfully, patiently. This conversation—though to Martin it sounded like an interrogation—would go on for as long as it needed to go on. It would be over when it was over. She hoped he saw the conversation as a cleansing. It would bring them closer together if she shared in his history. Second, he had to participate in the documentary. In whatever way he could be of use to the production, he needed to assist the Mashburns.

"All I want from you is honesty," Alexandra had said and let him leave.

Oh, is that all? he thought, and walked to the driveway. He hadn't lied when he said he didn't like talking about the kidnapping, but the truth was, after so many years, he wasn't sure he could talk about it. How could he explain to her satisfaction that the man she'd married and was raising a family with, wasn't, in a very real sense, a passenger on Burnt Velveeta? He didn't know who that kid grew up to be. That kid was obsessed with orcas, a bully's easy target, and wanted nothing but to be simply accepted by his classmates. When suddenly he was praised after all he did to dig everyone out, his newfound popularity made him feel more uncomfortable. And guilty. Having gotten what he wanted, he was still unhappy.

Martin had locked that boy away inside himself and let him wither with neglect.

He heard Alexandra on the stairs. The other problem was that he wasn't convinced she was entitled to know about the kidnapping. She owned exclusive rights to his present, which extended into the future in perpetuity, but was the past hers as well? How could she claim authorization to his life before she knew him?

Martin crumpled his list. He'd squandered his extra time. It seemed unlikely this was how Richard Branson spent his early hours.

"Morning," Alexandra said.

"Can I get you some coffee?"

"I'm going to make tea. How was CEO Time?"

He didn't answer. He heard stomping from upstairs. The kids were awake. He wanted to clarify one aspect of her request before they came down.

"Why do you want me in the documentary? If I tell you every-thing, isn't that enough? Isn't that enough punishment?"

"It's not a punishment. It's an honest accounting."

"An audit."

"Being in the movie means you're not keeping a secret anymore," she said. "You'll be free."

And with that last part, it occurred to Martin that Alexandra fundamentally misunderstood the concept of freedom. He had rearranged reality to grant himself a clear path away from his past. What was freer than that? Yes, they would have the conversation she desired, taking place more or less how she wanted it, but only because the pain of losing his family outweighed his unwillingness to let that other thirteen-year-old Martin Mendoza, the one who begged his mom to keep him off the school bus, speak again. The movie, however, didn't matter to him. It was none of his business.

"We'll talk tonight," he said.

"Yeah?"

"Of course."

Outside was full daylight. The kids were on their way downstairs, the house again noisy, full of life. Alive.

"Do you have time to make me a tea?" he said, yawning. He thought if he could get through the conversation, finally putting "That Thing" behind him forever, he would sleep in tomorrow.

"Of course," Alexandra said.

FRIDAY, AUGUST 3, 1984

Pat Earl woke to a rat chewing a smudge of peanut butter off his lower lip. The pinch and sting brought him around. He dabbed at his face and his hand met fur, warmth, the twitch of muscle, and sharp, bony feet. He recoiled from where he was passed out, sitting with his back against the wall of the buried box, his uniform shirt a balled-up pillow.

He tried to complain. A phlegmy yelp caught in his throat.

He stood up and another rat slid off his lap, tumbling down his bare legs. He kicked at what he couldn't see, missed, and heard scurrying, the sound on the metal floor like someone had scattered a handful of uncooked rice. He licked the wound reflexively and, realizing what he had done, spat, and wiped his mouth on his undershirt. He pictured rodent germs sliding into his bloodstream to contaminate him with the plague or some other disease that caused the death of his living tissue, starting with his face but moving swiftly down his neck and fanning out across his chest, prune-colored, crusty lesions that seeped when he moved.

He found a Bic in the pocket of his uniform shirt and flicked it open, running the flame low to the floor. The rats had disappeared. He inspected the food table. The kids had left an incredible mess and if the rats were hiding among the trash there was no way of knowing. His lip was a dull ache and he thought that was better than losing feeling and going numb. Feeling beat no feeling. It meant his flesh was still alive.

It seemed ass-backwards to take solace in pain. The notion of feeling beating no feeling was an exception to a personal maxim dating back forty years to the Battle of Monte Cassino. After the abbey was bombed out, SPC Pat Earl, part of the 34th Infantry Division, was dispatched to secure what was left of the 1400-year-old monastery. What he found there was among the worst he saw in the war. The abbey wasn't a German artillery position, as military intelligence believed, and the dead inside, numbering in the hundreds, were shelter-seeking civilians. Among the survivors was a paralyzed young woman, barely more than a girl. She was blanketed in rats. She couldn't move to save herself. They took her earlobes and fingertips, the meaty part of her nose. Bites and scratches covered her face and throat. Pat had blocked out much of his time in Europe, but that image stuck. He dragged the woman out from under the rodents and prayed her condition kept her from feeling, that if she could close her eyes it would be as if the rats weren't there. No feeling beat feeling.

He groped his way to a water cooler and cupped his hand under the spout. The water was hot, with a thin plastic flavor. The kids had claimed the mattresses, spacing them out where they could, or laying them end to end, side by side. He hoped they were resting but assumed some were sleepless despite their exhaustion. Earlier, right after he'd turned out the lantern, before he'd drifted off, Jodie Hoffman started singing. In the suffocating darkness, out came this voice, plain and clear, singing a song he didn't recognize. He knew it was Jodie, she was always singing on the bus, and he never knew any of her songs. Tonight, unlike on the bus, no one asked her to stop, then begged her, and finally yelled at her to shut up, that she wasn't Madonna. Not even Doodoo threatened to stick something in her mouth if she didn't close it.

Pat didn't have the ear to tell if she had a nice voice, she probably didn't, but her singing was a comfort.

All he heard now were the fans rattling in the vent and the box creaking. He sat with his shoulders slumped, head hanging, the heels of his hands pressing into his eyes, a burst of color behind his lids. Red, purple, yellow, white. He always thought this was the last thing you saw as you died, a final explosion of color before the lights went out for good.

THURSDAY, MAY 1, 2014

From: Dr. Lindsey <lindsey@lindseyrobinsonphd.com>
Sent: Thursday, May 1, 2014 1:55 AM
To: Emily Mashburn-Bauer <emb412@gmail.com>
Subject: Documentary

Emily and Brenda,

How great to hear from you! I think of you and the others often. We're a fucked bunch. It makes me happy to know that you are both well. I wanted to reply sooner but I needed to sit with the information and breath into the emotions it brought up. I immediately commended you on naming your pain and your approach to dragging it into the light, but I wondered if I could be one of the "interested individuals" that you seek. I was in the nasty quandary of wanting to help but not knowing the right way. I decided that if I could be useful to your documentary project it might be through describing my experiences in the aftermath of those "fateful summer days."

It's not a metaphor and far from exaggeration to say that part of us died in that hole. Whoever crawled out was not the same person who climbed in. It was like one of those makeover shows, but in reverse and with our souls. For me, my childhood ended down there. I came out knowing that everything I believed real was in fact fraudulent.

As a teen, I struggled with insomnia, depression, eating disorders, and unhealthy relationships. Maybe you can relate. I was seventeen when Geoff Miller broke my heart (we weren't even dating, but I thought I loved him) and I tried suicide by eating an entire package of Benadryl. I took the time to pop each tablet out of the foil before washing them down with a warm can of orange Slice. I can still remember vomiting up the sticky soda and how it felt on my tongue mixed with the half-digested pills.

But I was high functioning. I got good grades. I was popular. I was the starting goalie on the lacrosse team (Go Indians!). I presented myself as happy and lived in terror of being found out. I was at Skidmore when my mask started slipping. I lasted three semesters, then dropped out to marry a man whom I met on campus. My marriage was shorter than my first stint in college, but my son Ezekiel was the bright spot of that brief union. Zeke and his partner just had their first child. I'm a grandma (What?!?!).

That early period of being a single mom ranks among my most shameful days. I lost track of how many times I pawned and bought back our little thirteen-inch TV with a VCR built in so I could buy a pint of vodka or six pack of beer. I can't remember how many times we ate cereal with powdered milk, the same meal I ate with you in the hole, because I couldn't afford real food. I couldn't tell my parents what was really going on. I was still trying to fool people into thinking I was capable.

Have you ever felt like you don't belong or that if people knew the real you they could never love you?

If you had told me then that I wouldn't rise higher than working at an upstate Kmart, not only would I have agreed with you but secretly I would have believed I didn't deserve that much. I was blessed to cross paths with someone who saw my inherent worth. She showed me that I was enough for the world, that I deserved love just by being me. This woman owned a ramshackle Victorian in town that she had inherited from her aunt. She let me and Zeke stay in one of the bedrooms. We were her tenants, but she soon became our family. She introduced me to the practices of meditation and yoga, and encouraged me to reenroll in classes, this time at community college.

My twin interests (no pun intended) in mindfulness and neuroscience drove my academic studies, my search for answers. By merging Eastern and Western traditions I've attempted to activate the awakened mind. Incidentally, *The Awakened Mind* is

   TIME WILL BREAK THE WORLD

the name of my podcast. Please pound the subscribe button to my YouTube channel at the same name.

My journey has taken me from being buried in a rock quarry to building a house atop the Blue Ridge Mountains, from pawning TVs to earning a PhD, from an unhappy marriage with a closed-off man to a loving relationship with a woman. That is why when I tell people in my practice that their lives can be different, it is because I speak from experience.

I would be humbled to be a small part of the story you are telling.

Respectfully,
Dr. Lindsey Robinson, PhD

We almost lost Uncle Fred in the winter of '66. His trademark smoker's cough, the sound of crumpling newspaper that erupted during fits of laughter, turned wet, aquatic, as if his lungs were a swampy habitat. On Christmas Day, a frightening coughing spell, where his face turned red as the cranberry sauce, sent him reaching for his handkerchief. We saw pink blood smears on white linen.

Jesus, just kill me already, he wheezed.

He spent New Year's Day at New York Presbyterian. Soaked in cold sweat, his fever spiked at 103 degrees, he packed a suitcase and called a car. Pneumonia, Dr. Gelman said on the phone to my dad. More worrisome from the doctor's point of view was that when Fred was admitted, nurses had to cut off the socks he wore over his stumps. They were crusted to his skin with dried pus and fluid. His body was a carnival of infection.

My mom visited him the next day. She reported back that it was best to start making arrangements for the wake.

His doctor said that? I asked on the phone.

She said you didn't need a medical degree to know when a man is dying, and in an uncommon break in her steely façade, began crying softly, so softly it took me a minute to realize what I was hearing.

What does Dad say? I said.

He can't believe UCLA won the Rose Bowl.

The first day back to work after the holidays, George came home with a promotion. He was distressed about it. Calvin's G.I.

Joe motorcycle was in the front hallway and George kicked it into the wall, telling Cal the next time he left it lying around it was going in the trash.

My dad gave George Fred's job. He was being made managing partner. The lawyers were drawing up the paperwork.

My dad can't do that, I said. He and Fred are equals. It doesn't work that way.

George suggested I shouldn't tell him how things worked at the office.

Fred was in the hospital for five weeks. He dropped twenty pounds and aged twenty years. His unwillingness to die, but inability to get well, irritated everyone.

Shit or get off the pot, read the card my dad sent with flowers and a box of Peruvian cigars that was confiscated by hospital staff. It was a sentiment shared by my mom who, having consigned Fred to the grave, also grew tired of his lingering, his reluctance to prove her right. George, meanwhile, chafed at wearing another man's suit. Fred's limbo existence hung over his coronation and left him worrying about cheating a man out of his life's work when he was too weak to defend himself.

My uncle lived, however, and we denied ever speaking of his death. Of course Fred Reilly would pull through; he'd been in tougher jams than this—that was our line. Still, the illness had done irreparable damage. We lied when we said he just needed a little time and fresh air for a full recovery. As if to prove our lie, George's ascendance was made permanent. Fred put in the briefest appearance at his own retirement party, my mom taking him home after just one boilermaker and a slice of cake.

What followed was an uneasy partnership between my husband and my dad, one that I feared would endure for decades. I was wrong about that too. Less than five years later, the company was George's.

Brenda was just in from a run on the first spring day worthy of the name gorgeous. Sweaty and exhilarated, she bore the pleasant burn in her lungs, her Achilles tender. Vigorous exercise was still a restricted activity in her recovery, if she remembered correctly. Or perhaps it was at her discretion, that sounded right, depending on how she felt. And right now, she felt startlingly euphoric, the best she'd felt in months, which put her in a grateful kind of mood, and she meant to thank Emily for pushing her to work on the documentary. The time she spent at her sister's house helped her no longer see a stranger when she looked at herself.

She faced the open living room window, the warm, sweet breeze cooling her damp torso. She wrestled off her sports bra, flashing 84th Street from the sixth floor. Her phone rang. It wasn't the call she was expecting. She was awaiting reinstatement from her leave of absence, but Gennifer Mullen, a senior producer, was hoping for a little clarity regarding a cease and desist letter the legal department received from Calvin Schott's lawyer. That was how she phrased it, "a little clarity."

"I'm emailing you the letter now," she said. "I'll stay on the line while you read it."

Little in the letter was unclear, but it was the first Brenda was seeing it. She hadn't received a copy in the mail and doubted Emily had and didn't mention it. She placed her foot on the windowsill and stretched her hamstring.

In terms of C&Ds, this one had a theatrical energy to it.

"'You, therefore, proceed to disregard this letter's demands at your peril,'" Brenda read aloud.

"That's pretty good," Gennifer said.

If they weren't cowed immediately it was because they had both received this type of letter before, and Jon Stern, no disrespect to whoever he was, didn't even have an office in Manhattan.

"I'm helping my sister with a project of hers," was all Brenda thought to say. She turned away from the window and sat on the vintage pouf, the cracks in the leather mirroring the ones now surfacing on her good mood.

"She's a filmmaker?"

"Emily is an audiologist."

"I don't follow," Gennifer said.

Annoyed that she might have to explain the whole story, Brenda stood and paced. "I don't think I ever told you what happened to us when we were kids."

"I Googled Calvin Schott. I had no idea," Gennifer said. "Just remarkable how you came through it. Humans are so resilient."

Brenda relaxed a little. Platitudes meant Gennifer didn't want to dig too deep.

"I'm sorry you got dragged into this. I don't know why the letter was sent to you."

"The Schotts are probably trying to get you fired."

"That's silly. No real lawyer would think that."

There was silence on the other end. For a moment Brenda thought the call dropped.

"What does your contract say about freelancing?" Gennifer said.

"Excuse me?"

"I'm asking because I don't have a copy of your contract in front of me."

"This isn't a commercial project," Brenda said.

"And you're on medical leave?"

Brenda crossed her arm over her chest, unready to hold up her end of the conversation with her tits out. She looked around for something to cover herself with and settled on the alpaca blanket on her love seat.

"My sister is making a video for her victim impact statement to the parole board. I'm helping her," she said.

"Brenda, it's okay. I'm just showing you why their lawyer sent the letter to Legal. To stir the shit. Listen, I love the concept. I should have just come out and said it."

"That would have been nice," Brenda said, but... the concept of what? Now she was asking for a little clarity.

"A news doc about the crime. A first-person experience with historical background, in the lead up to the parole hearing," Gennifer said. "You should have brought this to me. We know this C&D is a non-starter. What do you think?"

Brenda hesitated. What *did* she think? She thought she would wait a day or two and politely decline. What Gennifer was putting forward wasn't an offer, but an expectation. And Brenda, regardless of how she was feeling moments earlier, was still not completely healed. Anxiety slipped right through the cracks in her good mood and took up shop in her chest, a tightness in her sternum. She tipped her head back and exhaled to the ceiling.

"I think I need to discuss it with Emily. I'm just lending her a hand."

"That's fair," Gennifer said, sounding as if Brenda was being totally unfair.

After a shower and a clean outfit and a trip to Shake Shack on Columbus for a root beer float, Brenda began putting together a pitch, an anti-pitch really, to convince Gennifer of why it might not be wise to come on board and produce the documentary. She composed her thoughts, considered the best way to proceed— and came up empty. Maybe she was looking at the situation the wrong way. The Catastrophe Queen had long contended that a good story was usually someone's tragedy. The kidnapping certainly qualified. It took her a minute to realize she believed some professional assistance might not be a bad idea. What had bothered her all along about Emily's vision for the documentary was its hobbyist enthusiasm. She looked down on it because it was amateur shit. She took a table on the sidewalk patio, gazing at the Museum of Natural History across the street, trying to carve out distance between herself and what she was really making. If she didn't take it so personally, she was finally able to see the concept of investigating the Brookwood Bus Kidnapping in a fresher, compelling light.

It might work, she thought. She just needed to decide if it was worth it.

need to talk re: doc she texted to Emily while walking home.

That evening, on the phone, Brenda said, "I want you to know I owe you so much for helping me. I'm really feeling better and it's because of you."

Unaware this was preamble, Emily thought she'd been right and Brenda was quitting on her. She looked helplessly at the boys eating dinner at the counter bar.

Brenda segued and told her about Gennifer. Made it sound like it was a done deal. Wasn't that incredible?

"That's... not what I expected. That's, I don't know," Emily said.

"Big is what it is."

"Yeah, big."

It was definitely big. Big news. But Emily couldn't help but wonder where this keenness was when they started. She'd hoped Brenda would hook them up with pros and instead her sister had shown up with borrowed equipment and a slack-ass attitude that couldn't hide the fact she was only there as a favor. What had changed? Did it really matter?

"How will it work?" Emily asked. She felt like she should have a million questions, but this was the best she could come up with.

"We'll show Gen what we've got so far. She'll have notes, etc."

"Notes? Sounds intimidating."

"How so?"

How wasn't it intimidating? She would have felt more comfortable exposing her C-section scar than showing her interview footage.

Sonny knocked over his cup of milk, a frothy white waterfall over the side of the counter.

"Shit, I got a mess here I got to take care of," Emily said.

"I'll let you go. I hate your pig face."

"I hate yours more."

"This is going to be amazing. You have no idea."

Emily agreed. She had no idea. She really didn't.

FRIDAY, AUGUST 3, 1984

Andy Kraven had a mondo poop ready for launch but so far no one had pooped in the buckets and he couldn't be first. He stood by the food table. One of the older girls handed him a Styrofoam bowl of Mr. T cereal, which was an exact rip-off of Cap'n Crunch, it was so obvious. He pitied the fool who didn't know that.

He held the bowl, not eating because the mondo poop needed no additional help. If he could have gone to the buckets when everyone was sleeping, that would have been a real slick move. Too bad he'd been asleep too. He had to admit that pooping in a bucket sounded kind of cool. Kind of like an outhouse, which he wanted to build in his backyard but his mom and dad wouldn't let him. When he reminded them that he peed on a tree that time they went hiking, or that he peed in the Long Island Sound when they went to the beach, they told him that was different. An outhouse was different. They said it was against the law to put one in your backyard. They said that about a lot of his ideas, that they were against the law. He couldn't tell if they were lying to him.

It was just too risky to hop up on one of the buckets with so many kids around. He needed someone to go first, then he could go. Unless whoever went first was made fun of, then he'd hold it. Problem was it hurt to hold it and the more he held it the harder it was to keep farts from coming out. The best thing would be if one of the older kids went first. Or Mr. Pat. Mr. Pat looked like he always had to poop. That was why he was mad every day, Andy thought, and laughed to himself. A man who was mad every day because he always had to poop was absolutely hilarious. If someone made a movie about that, he would see it a hundred times.

Kaito walked up with his hand over his head. Andy high-fived him. "How's it going, Switchblade?" he said.

"Does my breath smell?" Kaito said, and blew in Andy's face.

"Gross. What about me?" And Andy blew in Kaito's face.

"Very gross."

"Do you have any gum?"

Kaito shrugged.

"Me neither," said Andy. "Want my cereal?"

"Ok."

Andy gave him the bowl. He drank all the milk first, then picked out each soggy piece with his fingers and ate them one by one.

"Do you always eat like that?" Andy said.

"No." Kaito kept eating until the bowl was empty. "Do you think we're going home today?"

"Mr. Pat said the Bunny Man isn't playing a game."

"I hope I'm not in trouble," Kaito said. He looked around for a garbage can and then let the empty cereal bowl fall to the floor. "Want to wrestle?"

"Not now."

Kaito deepened his little voice, made it menacing, or what passed for menacing to a seven-year-old. "Scared, Stingray? Weak?"

"I can't right now." He had a sharp pain in his stomach.

"Come on. All those mattresses. We could do a battle royale."

The mattresses were tempting. Andy had noticed them when they came down into the hole. If not for Mr. Mondo in his butt... It wasn't fair. He was trying to make the best of it. That was his father's advice for when things didn't go his way, but his dad never told him how to make the best of it, which explained why he wasn't good at it.

He had an idea, though.

What if he could get the Blade to use the bucket first?

"Do you have to go to the bathroom?" he said.

"Gross," Kaito said. "Don't be weird."

"Don't call me weird. I'm your gang leader."

"Then don't be weird."

Andy saw the twin girls walk beside each other to the buckets. Well, hold the phone. This could be it. They were only going into fifth grade. If they got away with pooping then the coast was clear. He didn't want to be weird, like Kaito said, so he looked away, but his eyes wandered back. He saw one of the girls disappear behind a beach towel held up by the other girl. He couldn't believe it.

"No fair," he whined.

Where did they get a towel? The Bunny Man took his book bag when he came out of the van. Andy kept two dollars in his right sneaker that the Bunny Man didn't find. He thought he could use it as a bribe later if it came to that. He didn't know the word *bribe*, so he thought of it as a trade: I give you two bucks, you let me go home. He wondered if there was another towel around or if he could borrow the one the girls were using. Who would hold it for him, though?

"Come on, let's rumble," Kaito said, raising his hands up, fingers open, an invitation to play Mercy.

"I can't now."

"What's your problem?"

His stomach was really beginning to hurt. He started pacing. The worst thing in the world would be to have an accident. Then he had another idea. He could drag one of the buckets into a dark corner, away from the lanterns and the candles, where no one could see him. He was waiting for the girls to finish up so he could make his move. The one behind the towel reappeared. She traded places with her sister.

"Hurry up," Andy said.

The pain was getting so bad he couldn't wait any longer and he walked closer to the buckets, ready to grab one and move it somewhere private. He was bouncing on the balls of his feet, his butt clenched so tight the little muscles shook.

Then Kaito's voice was in his ear, "No more hiding, Stingray. Let's brawl."

Kaito grabbed him around the waist, spun him, lifted him, dumped him on the nearest mattress, and belly flopped on top of him. And all of Andy's efforts to this point proved useless. The worst thing that could happen to him did.

How many people did it take to tell one story?

This was what Emily thought watching the crew set up in her home for the shoot. The changes to the production were obvious and impressive. There was now a sound tech whose name Emily had been told but didn't catch. She didn't know the gaffer's name either, but she knew he was called the gaffer and she was pretty sure he handled the lighting. There were a lot more lights now. And cables. And the cases the lights and cables came in. And metal stands and wooden crates and sandbags. There was a camera operator who had his own set of cases. He acted like an old war buddy of Brenda's, which Emily guessed he was. There was a director too. Her name was Tamara. Andy Kraven was talking to her.

Andy had brought with him a woman who he introduced as his partner. Emily couldn't decide if he meant business or romantic or both. The third person in their group was the largest human being Emily had ever seen up close. When she asked what he had to do with the interview, Andy said, "This man is integral, I'm sure you'll agree."

The enormous man was sitting on her couch solving one of Ryder's puzzles. He looked like a bouncer, or Andy's bodyguard. Is that what made him integral? At least he kept himself out of the way, which was more than Emily could say for Andy's partner, who had been standing near her for ten minutes, giving off an attention-craving vibe while staring at the ends of her hair and humming-whispering something (song lyrics?) under her breath.

Emily could have avoided the woman's murky neediness if she had a job to do, a task active to the proceedings, but her title now was "producer," meaning she stood around while everyone else worked. No one even asked if she minded the way they messed with her house. The crew's cold professionalism rankled her. They treated her home as if it were just another location. For weeks after today, she would discover gaffer's tape stuck to her walls, long after she'd thought she'd found the last piece.

If there was an upside to the larger production, it was that it helped Emily understand that the cease and desist letter was toothless. How could she fear Schott's lawyer with so much activity going on? And that led to her newest question of how many people were required to tell this one story. And what would stop them from twisting its meaning away from her, making it unrecognizable? Or strip-mining it for a garish reality show? The project still belonged to her and Brenda, but not exclusively. They had control, up to a point. Emily didn't understand all the details. She left it to Brenda.

The woman next to her was squeezing the last life out of a tube of hand lotion. She rubbed it in and brutally cracked her lubricated knuckles.

"I'm Corine," she said finally. "You have a lovely home."

She looked younger than Emily. Much younger. There was something juvenile about her. It was the way she dressed, Emily thought, like she was still in college, unless that was just the style in New Mexico or Arizona or wherever she lived. Could it be possible she was in her twenties?

"This is my first trip to New York," Corine said.

"We told Andy we would Skype-interview him."

"He has his own plans."

"That sounds ominous."

"I just mean he wanted to visit his mom and show me around."

"Who's the big guy?"

"That's Bobby. I want to say he works for us, but I'm not sure he's ever been paid."

Andy was talking to Tamara, gesturing with his hands and pointing repeatedly to the door to the backyard. He wasn't what Emily had expected. He looked like someone who would find a wallet and not return it to its owner. She tried picturing him as he'd looked when they were kids, mentally photoshopping away the years until his face was a version more compatible with her memory of him.

"Were you guys friends in school?" Corine said.

"My sister and I are a few years older than Andy, but we got along."

"Do you mind me asking what he was like back then? I can't picture it."

I can't either, thought Emily, still struggling to see the boy's face in the man who kept talking and talking to the director. He wouldn't stop talking, fidgeting, and pushing up his sleeves.

"What do you mean?"

"I thought he was joking about being kidnapped," Corine said.

"Is that something he would joke about?"

Corine blew out a puff of air, her wide eyes showing the whites. "He once told me that on a class trip to the zoo an elephant gored him with its tusk. It's clearly an appendix scar on his stomach but he won't admit it. He also likes to say he got a varsity letter for lovemaking."

"Are you asking me if our high school had a lovemaking team?"

"I'm asking if he was always this weird."

"I don't know. Probably."

Tamara and Brenda walked up to them. Tamara said that Andy requested permission from the lady of the manor—those were his words—to shoot his interview on the back patio.

"Is that a problem?" Emily said.

"You tell us," Brenda said. "You're the lady of the manor."

Emily didn't have a problem with it. The crew did though. They had to reset everything outside. Tamara gave them the go-ahead and the gaffer bitched about it, but then scrambled to get to work. Corine walked off and sat with Bobby on the couch.

"How do I look? Like shit? I'm exhausted," Brenda said.

Brenda looked the opposite of exhausted. Focused, engaged.

Alive. Emily couldn't remember when she'd last seen her sister so animated.

"Promise me, you won't let them turn it into a freak show." Emily said.

"Who's them?"

Emily gestured around at the strangers in her house.

"You're the reason they're here."

"They're here because of you."

"You're the reason I'm here. If P then Q."

"Just promise me."

When the scene was set, Tamara found them. They were ready to go.

Andy was already seated on the patio and Brenda took her seat near him. Emily watched the ease with which she conversed with him. She could talk to anyone. It was a skill she'd always had. She and Andy laughed at something she said.

Tamara told everyone to get ready. Then she said action.

Brenda asked Andy to introduce himself, and he jumped up as if she'd thrown a bowl of soup in his lap. He pointed at the camera over her shoulder.

"Kravy Train Productions is proud to present, a collaboration with—"

"Stop, Andy, Jesus, what collaboration? Don't say collaboration," Tamara said, and cut the take. "Also, maybe stop all the yelling."

"I bring energy to my promos. You should know that about me."

"We love the energy," Brenda said. "We love your passion. But we're just getting started. This is just a conversation between you and me. Forget everything else. Just you and me."

They continued in a normal tone after that. Andy was a willing and, Emily had to admit, funny interviewee. More likable than Al Tiles and more forthcoming than her parents. He had a solid grasp of the child he was before the kidnapping.

"ADHD, no doubt about it. But back in the eighties, I was just a pain in the ass. I feel bad for my parents."

He corroborated details about August 2nd. He and Brenda had been in the green van with Pat Earl. Their driver hadn't assaulted anyone, unlike the driver of Emily's van who beat Lindsey Robinson unconscious. Like Brenda and Emily, Andy never knew if his driver was Jason or Calvin Schott. Also like them, he spent the rest of his time in Brookwood feeling like an outsider.

"I probably would have moved away no matter what, but the way everyone treated us sealed the deal."

"How else do you think the kidnapping changed you?" Brenda said.

"Would I have turned out the same if I skipped summer school that day? I can't say. I was seven. Maybe something else would have come along and made me who I am. But I will say this. I am haunted to this day by the Bunny Man."

"The Bunny Man?"

"That's what I called them. The pantyhose on their heads. I thought the legs hanging down looked like rabbit ears."

"Holy shit," Corine said, and covered her mouth.

"What do you mean he haunts you? Like in dreams?" Brenda said.

"Real life," Andy said. He sighted the camera and talked directly to it. "The Bunny Man is actively terrorizing me."

Brenda paused. She was thrown. She looked to Emily to get her read on what Andy had said. What was he talking about? Before she had the chance to ask him what he meant, Bobby tore into the backyard, ripping the screen door off its hinges, a pair of sheer pantyhose yanked down over his face. He was panting and snarling, as if sleepless pursuit of Andy for days had brought them face-to-face, and he pulled up short to appreciate the moment before his kill. Brenda jumped out of her chair and the sound guy dropped a boom mic and backed away. Andy stayed where he was, startled but not surprised.

"There he is," he said, a man resigned to his fate. "That's him!"

The Bunny Man grabbed him around the neck and lifted him over his head. Andy's legs kicked and twitched. He tried clawing the Bunny Man's face, who turned and drove Andy onto his back on the lawn. He began crawling away, only to be hoisted up by his belt. The Bunny Man spun him around and the belt broke free of the loops in his pants, centripetal force sending him flying. Earlier, Andy had told Bobby to keep going until the director called cut, but Tamara seemed to be coaching the camera operator into position, moving her index finger in a circle, instructing him to keep shooting.

Emily watched this giant lunatic stomp back onto the patio for the screen door. Integral, sure, she thought. He beat Andy with the aluminum door frame, and she realized that perhaps her fear had been placed on the wrong party. It wasn't Brenda's coworkers degrading the documentary, but one of the other survivors. She couldn't sit there waiting for Tamara or Brenda to stop these assholes, so she threw herself between the Bunny Man and Andy. Bobby immediately backed away, tugging the pantyhose off.

"Sorry, ma'am, sorry. Was that no good?" he said.

Andy staggered up, cradling his ribs with his arm. "That is what I'm talking about!" He searched around for the camera.

"Next month, Friday the 13th, at VFW Post 549, Tucson, Arizona, Kravy Train Productions brings you Ultimate Hardcore Victory Wrestling, The Brawl for It All. Tickets are still available. Doors open at six thirty. All ages show, folks, so bring the whole family."

He dropped to one knee on the grass. "I thought you were going to kill me."

"Sorry, Boss," Bobby said.

"Hey, Brenda, you think I can get a copy of that to throw up on the old social media?" he said.

"You're a crazy person," Emily said.

"Apologies for the screen door. That's my bad."

     TIME WILL BREAK THE WORLD

Corine ran up to them. "You guys were so, so good," she said. She helped Andy to his feet. "How are you feeling?"

"Like I'll be pissing blood. Let's celebrate."

He put himself next to one of the water coolers, as if it were another child, so he wouldn't look so alone. He was really starting to worry that he was going to be in trouble when he got home. Kaito knew that trouble was different for him than it was for his classmates. That time he was at Stingray's house, they stole a can of diet soda from the fridge and took it outside. Stingray shook it up and called it a hand grenade and threw it down on the driveway to watch it explode all over his mom's car. She came running outside and instantly Stingray was Andy again—Andrew Kenneth, she called him. Mrs. Kraven yelled, right there in the driveway where anyone could hear, that Andy could forget about playing with his toys or watching *Dukes of Hazzard* anytime soon, and that he better apologize to his friend for misbehaving.

Kaito's mom never yelled. And she didn't take away his toys because when he was in trouble, he knew they were off-limits without being told. He wouldn't further disappoint her and have her exclude him from the family. This was what she said would happen. If he were disobedient, or didn't keep his room tidy, or was disrespectful to his teachers at school, in short, if he did anything that would make people think less of his family, he would cease to be a part of it. That time he missed the school bus—Stingray told him that the buses ran on a schedule and the next one was ten minutes away—Kaito's mom wouldn't unlock the front door to let him in. He had to wait outside, quietly of course, not pounding the door or ringing the bell incessantly. When she finally brought him in, she sat him down with a snack and explained the mistake he'd made. She then left him with a pencil and paper and had him write a letter to his ojiisan, asking to be reinstated. Kaito had never met his grandfather, so writing him for permission to stay in the family seemed like appealing to God. Or at least Santa Claus.

"Move, ass wipe," said the big sweaty boy, shoving him out of the way. Kaito watched him guzzle from the cooler, bending down and clamping his lips around the spigot and slurping the water. The boy stood up and asked what he was looking at. Kaito smiled and walked away to one of the mattresses. He sat down by himself. It was too dark to see where Andy had gone after he slammed him, but he was probably in one of the corners. The Stinger was mad at him. He'd told Kaito to leave him alone so that was what he was doing. He'd been less scared when he was with his friend, and now he didn't have anyone else to hang out with. He leaned back and lay down. The mattress smelled like old fish. His clothes must have smelled like that also. It was his responsibility to keep his clothes clean. But what was he supposed to do? He was trapped in a cave or whatever the word was for where they were.

When the Watanabes first moved to Brookwood, his parents taught him that in this country he needed to be careful of adults who steal children and hurt them. They modeled for him how to stay alert while walking down the sidewalk, and they tested him by pretending to be strangers who volunteered to give him rides in their car, or money or food. They taught him to say "no, thank you" to any offer made by someone he didn't know, unless that person was the police. People in uniforms could generally be trusted. Mr. Pat, for example, wasn't a policeman but he wore a uniform and Kaito trusted him. He wondered if Mr. Pat could talk to his mom and tell her none of this was his fault.

What could he have done to stop it? He was just sitting on the bus. The man had a shotgun. It was like a scene from a movie he wasn't allowed to watch but that Andy told him was on TV if he stayed up late enough. Since he didn't have an excuse he believed his parents might find acceptable, he decided to get a jump on his letter to his grandfather.

He found the sisters on a nearby mattress and said, "Excuse me," but his voice was too soft and one of the girls told him to speak up. He tried again. They gave him a sheet of construction paper and a marker that smelled like cherries. They told him if he lost the marker he would have to buy them a new one. He thanked them and retreated to the wall of the container, away from the others, and squatted down to write.

Dear Ojiisan, he began. The dirt on the floor interfered with his penmanship. He lifted the page and brushed the floor with his hand. In past letters, he'd asked for forgiveness, swore to improve, never blaming others for what he was responsible for. This situation felt different. He changed his mind. He turned the paper over and started again.

To Stingray (Andy),
I am sorry I hurt you. You are a good gang leader. You are my friend. One day we can play again.
From,
Switchblade (Kaito)

He recapped the marker and folded the note in half, making sure the edges were even. He searched out the darkest corner and that was where Andy was, with his face to the metal wall. Kaito didn't say anything. He tapped Andy on the shoulder and waited for him to turn around to hand him the note. The big sweaty boy then interrupted them, wanting to know what they were doing back there—kissing?

First pitch of the A's game was 7:05 in Cleveland, making it after one in the morning in Amsterdam. By the time Sean Doolittle closed out the ninth to give Oakland a 6-2 win, it was 4:15. Kaito sat mutely on his black leather sofa, one of the only objects in his Jordaan neighborhood apartment, with his MacBook Pro open on his lap. If he were aware of the time, he didn't seem bothered by the lateness of the hour. Neither did he seem happy that his five-hundred-dollar wager on the A's had won. His fandom to the Athletics held no contemporary significance for him. They were his team because he'd started rooting for them when the Bash Brothers led them to a World Series victory twenty-five years earlier, and because he'd had cousins living in the Bay Area.

He clicked on the browser tab open to hockey. He'd been riding the Rangers throughout the playoffs. The score remained unchanged from the last time he checked. New York took game one, blowing out the Canadiens. This news also failed to stir him.

What roused him was a coolness on his neck, and he closed the window behind him. He was vaguely cognizant of a craving that was either hunger or horniness. His appetite for food and sex was practically mechanical, like the beeping of a smoke detector needing its battery replaced. Without checking, he knew there was no food in the kitchen. It was too late to order anything. It was also too late to call Jort. Jort probably wouldn't come over. At any time. Not again. He didn't care that his name was an American portmanteau for an unfashionable article of clothing, and he was tired of Kaito laughing at him about it. Besides, he never liked this apartment, hated it, in fact, the bare walls, the lack of furniture, the windows uncovered of blinds or curtains.

"My aesthetic is spartan," Kaito had said.

"You live like a serial killer," Jort replied.

How was one supposed to respond to that? Kaito had laughed, of course, and tried coaxing his friend into the shower, but Jort was serious. That was two weeks ago. They had been incommunicado since.

It didn't occur to Kaito to sleep. Or to try to. He opened another browser tab to an online poker room, low stakes, thinking he could stay busy with \$1/\$2 blinds until the sun rose and he could go out for breakfast. He would nap for an hour or two before tipoff for the NBA playoffs. If it was possible for him to have a desired outcome, he was looking to make up for the losses he took in the previous round. He'd really thought the Nets would hold their own against the Heat. He was down, he wasn't sure how much. Safe to say in the ballpark of ten grand. Not that it mattered with the kind of money he was making.

Hey, Jort, would a serial killer work in the bond market for one of the largest banks in Europe and Asia? Don't answer that.

He played a few hands of Hold 'Em, his mind half on the card game and half on... nothing, everything, something else. He stayed in when he should have folded because he was impatient for the next hand to be dealt and didn't have the energy to sit in on more than one game at a time. When his phone vibrated beside him, he felt something uncharacteristically approaching hope, a prickling on his skin like a nearby phantom.

Jort!

It was Akira. His younger, much younger, brother had just graduated from Michigan, spending the summer in Futako-Tamagawa at their parents' house. It was noon, Akira's time, but it was well-known that Kaito never slept.

Was Kaito coming in August? Akira was asking for their mom. Would he be there for Obon? He could stay for the month.

A month!?!?! lol Kaito texted back.

Come! We'll get fucked up you can pick up the tab I'm broke.

Get used to poverty with a degree in environmental science. He couldn't think of anything cleverer. A soft buzzing sound filled the room, like his neighbor turned on a blender, but Kaito realized that that was impossible at this hour. His phone vibrated again.

Akira said their mother had heard there was going to be a movie about the day Kaito disappeared. The day Kaito disappeared—this was what the Watanabe family called the bus hijacking.

His phone seemed incredibly heavy in his hand.

His parents never fully acknowledged the scale of the abduction. They refused to include the other kids. It wasn't as though they didn't know better. But their version of events completed the larger story they told of those first years in America. It was a story of dislocation, confusion, and homesickness. It was a story of anxiety. The kidnapping became the emblem of this story, the vessel into which the Watanabes could pour every aspect of their immigration experience, including their money, since their financial wellbeing in Brookwood—the inground pool and Mercedes sedan—didn't otherwise jibe with the obstacles they faced. They were convinced it was his father's position with Mitsui Fudosan that made Kaito a target. It was only several years ago, long after they had moved back to Japan, that he tried to disabuse them of this misunderstanding. He hadn't been targeted. He was just on the bus that day. And there was no way, absolutely none, zero, that either of the Schott brothers had ever heard of the company that employed his father. His father told him simply that he was wrong, and his mother changed the subject, asking when he was going to get married.

He started texting Akira back to tell him he couldn't take that much time off work, but then put his phone down. This wasn't a pressing issue. He had pocket queens that demanded his attention. He knew some of the others were telling their stories for the documentary. It made sense to think that their stories would be as personal and therefore erroneous as his parents'. For years after, Andy would tell people Kaito was kidnapped because he was descended from a notorious ronin, and their abductors were settling a centuries-old grudge. Sometimes he went along with it, adding little flourishes to improve the tale, but what was his real story? What did he think of it? He never personalized it, never made it about him. Whenever he thought or spoke about it, he used the first-person plural. *We were taken off the bus and put in vans. We climbed down a ladder into a hole. We slept on old mattresses. We.* It was strange to admit, but his inclusion had felt like an achievement, as if he had won something when the Schotts took the new, foreign kid in school along with everyone else. It made him feel like one of the gang.

Another queen and two nines on the flop. Full house. He really needed to focus on this hand.

Once we settled on taking a group of kids, the school bus scenario just presented itself. Where else could you find a couple dozen children in the same place with nowhere to escape?

At every step of the way, as the plan moved from daydream to possibility to likelihood to certainty, we could have backed off. I held two opposing thoughts in my head at the same time: there had to be a better way out of our troubles; this was the only way out. In my mind, I tracked these two thoughts that never intersected. If Jason had doubts, or thought of changing his mind, I didn't want to know. I never asked him. When we began plotting in earnest, our brotherhood and, more crucial, our friendship, didn't know how to accommodate obvious shifts in our attitudes. Everything about us was becoming unpliable, and we took it out on each other.

Example: The pyramidic display of plastic eggs rose up over the shelves of deodorant and skin lotion at Ballard's Pharmacy.

Give your legs a refreshing massage—L'eggs.

I grabbed two packages of the pantyhose and tossed them to Jay.

"You're buying them," I said.

"Fuck you, I'm tired of paying for everything."

"You're such a little Jew. I'll give you the money. We just both shouldn't go to the counter. In case Ballard remembers seeing us."

"I honestly don't know why we're even buying them. Mom's got a bunch at home."

"You're a disgusting human being."

"What?"

"Did I just hear you say you want to wear our mother's underwear on your head?"

"I never said that."

"They touched Mom's pussy."

"Don't say 'Mom's pussy.' That's sick."

"What you said is sick."

"I didn't say anything. You did."

"You said, and I quote."

"Don't."

"'Hey, know what we—'"

"Fucking don't," Jason said.

"'Should do? For fun?'"

"Don't say it, jerkoff."

"'Let's rub our faces on Mom's pussy!'"

I headbutted him over the bridge of his nose.

He tackled me into the pyramid of plastic eggs, a wild thrashing on the pharmacy floor.

Ballard ejected us. Outside we sat on the curb.

"I'm sorry," I said, and spat blood on the street. "I shouldn't have called you a disgusting human being. My mistake was calling you human. You're an animal."

"You want me to beat you into a coma," he said, massaging a sore shoulder.

"There should be an island for animals like you. For sex perverts, such as yourself. Not as a punishment, but so you can be with your own kind. Wouldn't you like that, Jay? An island where you won't have to live in shame?"

"One more word and I'm going to cave your fucking face in." He kicked me in the spine and walked away.

We were turning cold and hard by necessity, but it was easier for me. Jason needed to put aside who he was to do the crime. For him, this scheme was always one of desperation. For me, it was different. I didn't need enticing to become my worst. What I needed was a place to put my anger. Blaming others for my problems felt good. Taking out my trouble on the world felt good. I was releasing a small, but permanent, part of myself that no longer needed to be hidden. Life was easier when I didn't think about those around me.

In other words, we both did the kidnapping. My brother never liked it. I did.

Andy Kraven didn't have to be an expert in body language to know Corine was mad at him. It was becoming a distraction when she reacted this way to everything he did. What little he'd accomplished in his life was a result of his capers. At a certain point, taking exception to his style of work was just a bad synergy between them.

She moped in the backseat of the rental, next to Bobby, from where she periodically lodged complaints.

"You said they knew. You said you cleared it with them," she said.

"Slipped my mind," he mumbled.

"What was that?"

"I said it slipped my mind."

"I feel so stupid. I'm out there congratulating you and Emily was ready to call the police."

"It's fine," Andy said, meaning it was fine that she felt stupid. He felt stupid all the time.

"You know they're never giving you that tape," she said.

"I don't know about that." He peeked in the rearview mirror. She was looking out the window. "Brenda didn't seem to have a problem. As a matter of fact, Tamara said she loved it. Once I promised to replace the screen door, Emily was cool too."

"She was definitely *not* cool."

"I don't even know why I should replace it."

"Because you broke it."

"She has insurance. You think that production isn't covered?"

"I really can't with you right now."

"Bobby agrees with me, don't you, big guy?"

"He's asleep."

Andy checked in the rearview again. He figured Bobby was

faking it, like he used to pretend to sleep when his parents fought.

"By the way, it's totally sick that you named his character after the guys who took you," Corine said.

At his mom's house, she left them in the car and sequestered herself in the guest bedroom.

Andy trailed her at a safe distance, leaving Bobby to decompress in the backseat. On the table by the front door where Jean kept her keys and dropped the mail, he saw the framed needlepoint reading "Easy Does It." He wondered if there was an AA gift shop where you could buy this shit, an online store to help fund the free coffee. The house he lived in on August 2nd, 1984, was no longer the house his mother owned. His parents divorced when he was in seventh grade. Craig Kraven moved to Philadelphia for work, but Jean stayed with Andy in Brookwood. It turned out the motivating factor for owning the needlepoint was also the catalyst behind his parents' split.

By the end of the eighties, Jean's alcoholism had become too much for Andy's dad, and when a job opportunity came his way, he took it. Jean later made the breakthrough in recovery that her son's abduction loomed largely in the story of her drinking. She had other triggers, of course, but the strain of Andy being taken from her was the event that pushed her fully into addiction. And wasn't that just a delightful fucking anecdote, Andy thought, waiting for Bobby to join him inside. As if his own scars weren't enough to bear. His mom's drinking and parents' divorce weren't his fault, obviously, he was just a kid—this was what everyone reassured him. Of course, to believe that he would have had to deny cause and effect. Maybe anything could have given Jean the excuse she needed to slug vodka until she was snoring fitfully on the couch while he scribbled math homework at the coffee table, but it was the kidnapping that did the trick.

She was in the backyard, starting her vegetable garden, her legs folded under her, her wide-brimmed hat shadowing her face. Her arms were lightly muscled, golden, freckled from wrist to shoulder.

"How did it go?" she said, not looking up. "Feels good to talk about it, doesn't it?"

"I feel ten pounds lighter and five years younger."

"You don't have to be defensive with me."

"Expecting a bumper crop?"

Jean straightened, sitting back on her heels. "I know exactly what I'm eating. What do you eat?"

"The flesh of infidels," he said.

"We're all out. Want a sandwich instead?"

"Sure."

She'd been sober so long Andy had stopped worrying about seeing her in a condition less than totally clear, and no longer lugged around that apprehensive twinge he'd get in his gut when he would come in the house not knowing what he would find. Sometimes, though, when he was at a bar or restaurant or party, he would catch the scent of vodka in his nose and remember what it felt like living with her, the nights he made himself dinner and hoped he had clean clothes for the morning.

"Where's your entourage?" she said.

"Scattered."

"Is Corine your girlfriend?"

"She checks a number of boxes at the moment."

He slumped down the doorframe and sat on the stoop, trying to find a position easy on his ribs.

"Did you get hurt?" Jean said. She unfolded herself in several rusty jack-knifing maneuvers to get to her feet. She removed her work gloves and came nearer.

"I think your emotional pain is manifesting itself as physical," she said.

"Bobby choke-slammed me. What I have is most definitely physical pain."

"Why would he do that?"

"I told him to."

"You were seven when you left that morning. My college

friends came back from Vietnam less devastated."

"About that sandwich," he said.

"If it had happened now, I would send you to therapy. But back then, conventional wisdom said to put it behind us. It was just what we did."

"You did your best," he said, which was true, but stopped himself from finishing his thought, which was, "unfortunately for me, your best was piss poor."

"What about now? It's never too late."

"For what?"

"To talk to someone."

"I think there would be unintended consequences."

"What do you mean?" Jean said, now squatting in front of him, her elbows resting on her thighs.

"Most days I feel like a Jenga puzzle halfway through a game. One bad move won't topple me, but I'm at the point where a little strategy is required to keep me standing."

"Jesus Christ."

"We should have stuck with talking sandwiches."

"Do you still like turkey and Swiss?"

"My favorite."

"Is Corine hungry?"

"You'd have to ask her. You know what? I'm going out for a while. I'll get something to eat there."

"Where?"

"Wherever."

Pat Earl woke this time to yelling. The sound couldn't echo. Beyond the box holding them was tons of earth to muffle the ringing outburst of Doodoo Viscuso.

"Shit stain," Lance chanted. He needled the air with his forefinger at someone or something in the dark. *"Shit! Stain!"*

Pat asked himself if he was awake or dreaming. His answer disappointed him.

"What's this about?" he said, creakily getting to his feet. His rat-bit lip still stung.

"Shut up, Lance," said a girl. Pat couldn't see who.

"Little man plopped in his pants, Mr. Pat." Doodoo forced a hideous laugh.

Pat came closer and became an unwilling participant in the scene. Andy Kraven had his back to the dark corner of the box. He tried in gulp-breaths to tell his side of the story, to set the record straight.

"I sat in something. That's all. It's so dirty down here. I just sat in dirt."

"That Chinese kid karated this dude onto a mattress so hard he crapped. I can't believe it."

"Shut the hell up, Lance," the girl said.

"That's not true. That's not true," Andy said.

"Shit stain!"

"Guys, it's just dirt."

Doodoo got louder by galling degrees and Pat cleared his throat and pondered something to do besides what he wanted, which was—he wasn't proud of it—to smack Lance in the mouth. How easy it would be to split his lip. How good it would feel. If there were ever a time for Martin Mendoza to take vengeance on this punk, it was now. From the look of things, Martin was, per usual, nowhere. "That's enough," the bus driver said. His head hurt from thirst. "I'm serious."

"I'm serious too, Mr. Pat. You didn't see it. This kid—"

Doodoo was shoved in the chest by the girl who had told him to shut up, who turned out to be Jodie Hoffman. As he fell, he became entangled with the Mashburn twins busily drawing in the dirt on the floor, his body corkscrewing for what couldn't have been more than a second, and he landed with a sound like someone kicking a rotten jack-o'-lantern. The flow of laughter reversed course, swam upstream to Doodoo.

The laughter subsided and Pat said, "Alright, someone help him up." He was satisfied with the outcome and sensed a return to the quieter equilibrium of their captivity.

There were no takers. Doodoo had gone too far tormenting Andy, when the truth was the hierarchy had been leveled once they went subterranean. Everyone was equal in the box.

"Lance, quit playing around," Pat said. He helped him up.

In the lantern light, it was obvious Lance wasn't playing. His right shoulder wasn't where it should have been, and his arm on that side looked several inches longer than on the left. Something was separated or dislocated. When Pat touched him, the boy went down again in agony. Pat left him there and hopped over a mattress to the metal plate in the ceiling covering the hole they had climbed through. He yelled up at it that there was an injury, someone was hurt, hurt bad. Could anyone hear him? He ran to a ventilation fan and tried his luck there, hoping his voice traveled up through the pipe and to their abductors.

He checked the time. He thought his watch was broken. How was it possible they had been entombed less than a day? It felt eternal. And Pat was old. Time didn't represent the same thing to him as it did to the children. A day out of sixty years didn't have the heft of a day out of ten or twelve. Hours were weighted differently, heavier for the kids because they owned fewer. All other things being the same, time will break the world, but its elasticity meant the damage would be less for Pat. It might have been true they were going to die in this hole, but he'd already had his one chance in his one body, so that much of what he would call his life was burning the inertia of the past. These kids, on the other hand, couldn't accept the end of a life they never had. That they didn't know what they were going to miss was in no way a blessing. It was larceny.

They had to escape.

The actual mechanics of the date were to not call it a date. It was nothing fancy anyway, just dinner at Brookwood Bar & Grille. Jason didn't thank Angie for accepting his invitation. Doing so would have put a spotlight on the un-date, anti-date, though he felt true warmth that she had come out with him after the distancing, which he couldn't call subtle, that she had placed between them once she learned about the Mashburns' documentary from her cousin. He suspected this same cousin counseled her privately about their relationship, but he couldn't tell if her appearance at dinner complied with or disregarded the advice.

The hostess showed them to their table, Angie ahead of Jason, her hair lifting at the top of each step she took. They sat and she told him a story about the other day when, on her way to meet her cousin Lisa (Ha! He knew it!) for a drink after work, she watched an old man park his car and not feed the meter on purpose. He hung around on the sidewalk ("Right there on Milford.") for parking enforcement and spoke up only after the officer placed the ticket under his windshield wiper. He didn't do the expected thing, which was to ask her to rescind the summons, but instead chatted her up about her job, if she enjoyed it, if she had other dreams, if she had a family, if they were in good health. He buttonholed her for a good five minutes.

"Isn't that incredibly sad? He must be so lonely," Angie said.

Jason approximated all the gestures of listening with attention, the perfectly timed nods, the frowns of comprehension, even as he searched the middle distance behind her for the server. Mostly he thought, God bless Jon Stern. If anything was responsible for defrosting Angie it was the cease and desist letter. The letter eased her concern about the documentary, vis-à-vis their future, but the aggressive legalese also reassured her that Jason and, to a lesser extent, Calvin were also injured parties. The force with which their lawyer demanded capitulation was written proof that her boyfriend, the man she loved, wasn't an unrepentant criminal, as she'd begun to fear he was.

Hence, two starters (fried calamari and French onion soup). Jason wanted to believe that Stern's magic with the Mashburns was but a precursor to his getting Cal paroled. And after that, he thought, looking at the woman in question, he and Angie could move in together, and Calvin and Bertie could get reacquainted, mother and son, companions, roommates—however they wished to categorize their relationship. It was remarkable the future he sketched out in the brief interval between courses, while they awaited their second drinks and entrées. Stern had cautioned that his letter was unenforceable, but the last time Jason checked the Facebook post, the casting call was removed. Brenda and Emily Mashburn had surrendered. Even Bertie announced her reluctant approval. "About time he did something right," she said of their lawyer.

Dinner hit all the markers of a successful date (but he was careful not to call it that): a comfortable meal, a few drinks, the anticipation of sluggish, full-bellied sex back at Angie's within the hour. The server went to run his debit card, and Angie slipped out of the booth to the restroom. Jason was calculating a tip when she returned.

"There are three of them, at the bar," she said. She measured her words, as though it took great courage to speak them. "I passed them on my way to the ladies'."

"Who's at the bar?" He didn't understand what she was talking about but could tell she was upset.

She blotted tears with the side of her index finger.

A wooden column hampered Jason's line of sight. He dodged a busboy to get a clear view. One of the sisters, the one from TV if he had to guess, held a glass of red wine; the car dealer was drinking white. There was a third guy with them, with his back to Jason.

Angie looked on, half-hidden by the wooden column. Jason asked what precisely she had seen.

It wasn't what she saw, but what she heard.

"They were talking about the movie," she said.

"What about it?"

"You said it was over. Your lawyer's letter?"

"It's supposed to be," he said, and sidestepped a man carrying two pints of beer to his buddy at a bar table. He knew it was bad judgment to approach a woman he'd kidnapped, the ex-cop and local hero (if he heard that one more time in his life he would jump out a window), and whoever the guy was with them.

But it was already too late and he was at their side, a late-comer to the party. He didn't know what to say. Could they have a calm chat? Was that possible?

It was the unknown third party with Brenda and Al Tiles who spoke first.

"Now we've got ourselves a real reunion. Pull up a seat, Mr. Bunny Man," he said, without conviction, gazing into his glass of brown liquor.

It was the weird little boy from the bus, the one unafraid of Jason, his Adam's apple dancing in his throat as he drained his glass down to the ice.

"Please leave us alone," Brenda said. She was composed and polite, just like when she'd asked Jason not to be separated from her sister on the bus. The car dealing ex-cop appeared checked out, recessed into himself, a smudgy old man rendered unchar-acteristically mute.

"My lawyer sent you a letter. I know you got it. You need to stop the movie."

"What movie?" Andy Kraven said, playing dumb.

"Just stop, okay?" Jason said, a request, not a command, but he knew they had no intention of stopping just because he asked them to. It wasn't spite, or payback, for the way he hadn't considered their feelings on the school bus. It didn't rise to the level of spite. His feelings were beside the point. The sisters were simply doing what they wanted, and what he wanted didn't matter. He didn't matter.

He walked out of the bar and past Angie, past his leftovers boxed on the table, through the dining room, pausing at the hostess stand for a toothpick and matchbook, and out to the street where clouds bunched together to conceal the evening sky.

Now our little family was well off. I was the wife of an executive. It was my job to demonstrate the importance of his work with material goods. That suited George. Like most Americans, he reduced self-worth to affluence and made them interchangeable. Calvin and Jason were spoiled because of it. I admit it was my fault. I never felt bad giving them what they wanted. We bought a new house, and I filled their parts of it with toys, bicycles, BB guns, roller skates, a trampoline in the backyard. I bought them clothes they didn't need. I fed them. Boy, did I feed them. Ham and eggs. Toast with butter and honey. Grilled cheese and potatoes. Hamburgers. Fried chicken. Tuna casserole. We went through three gallons of whole milk a week. Our grocery bill looked like we were providing for the Brookwood Fire Department.

My sons grew bigger, ravenous. Their heads! Their feet! They had so many teeth! They required biweekly haircuts. They were uncoordinated growing into themselves. I don't remember them having friends besides each other. When I set them loose, they tormented the neighborhood children and weren't invited into their homes. At school they linked up at recess and hunted the weaker ones. Maybe it was the only way they knew how to show affection. They were no better with me. Calvin wasn't yet nine the time I found my Bulova stashed in a shoebox in his closet. I spanked them often with a leather strop. Even this they turned into a game, the lashings converted into points, a scoring system in which I could never figure out who was the winner, me or them.

It's possible that if Calvin had been a different kind of boy, quieter or kinder or just not so blunt, Jason would have followed suit. The thing was, Jay soon pushed the envelope further than Cal, as if he had learned all he could from his brother and needed to strike out on his own.

One Sunday my parents and uncle visited for lunch. They arrived straight from mass and Fred was complaining from the moment I heard the car door open. Calvin and Jason were hungry and had been whining at me nonstop to feed them, but I could see that everyone needed a few minutes to decompress.

Fred said the body of Christ was gummed up under his bridge and he begged for a drink. He was losing his hearing and spoke in a near shout. He left his wheelchair in the foyer and dragged himself over the wall-to-wall carpeting in the living room to the bar cart, where George was setting up a round. Fred took his glass to the couch and hoisted himself onto a cushion. He summoned the boys around him, bellowing Jalvin! Cason! Where are you?

My sons hovered over their great-uncle. He was always a mesmerizing sight.

Those aren't our names, Cal said.

Fred said the boys looked like sports fans, so he posed a question: Why are there no midgets in the NFL?

Jason said that it was because they were too small and would get hurt by the big guys.

No, dummies, screamed Fred, the grass tickles their balls! And he burst out laughing.

Meanwhile, I finished cooking. I hefted the Pyrex dish from the oven, the cheese browned and bubbling, steam rising off the dish. I laid the lasagna on a trivet on the dining room table and hurried to the kitchen for the salad. The aroma must have attracted the boys. They were kneeling on their chairs, leering at the meal.

I told them don't even think about it.

Jason pled his case to his father. George wisely answered that he should do whatever his mother said.

But I'm starving, Jason said, and here he paused, just for a moment, then smirked, and plunged his hand to the wrist in the still boiling lasagna. He yanked up a fistful of cheese, sauce, ground beef, ribbons of noodles. After the fact, we saw he bore second-degree burns on his hand. The skin blistered like tiny water balloons, then dried up and peeled, and he had to wear an ointment-filled glove to prevent infection. The pain must have been excruciating. Even Cal couldn't believe what he'd done and jumped off his chair to stand with the rest of us. But Jason didn't say a word. With his smirk perfected on his face, he stared at his hand as tears dripped from his eyes. He lowered his mouth and ate, lasagna and tears, out of the palm of his hand.

Emily was too upset by the broken screen door to appreciate how captivating the interview was. Brenda couldn't make her see that they were finally getting somewhere. Beneath Andy's shtick laid real pathos. Not all trauma is processed the same way. "Depression is violence," Brenda said. But Emily kept saying that what took place at her house was a joke.

"A fucking mockery," she said. And the worst part was that it was Brenda selling them out. Brenda was selling herself out. For what?

"Look, I'm sorry about your door but you know what, who fucking cares?" Brenda said, and took a cab to the train station, even though her train wasn't for an hour. She stopped across the street at Brookwood Bar & Grille. Halfway through her first glass of wine, she remembered she hadn't eaten anything but a cranberry muffin in the morning. She ordered artichoke dip and another glass of wine, fiddled around on her phone, not paying attention as the bar area filled up with the happy hour crowd.

The bartender served the dip and warned her that the dish was burning hot. She touched it to see just how hot. A man took the seat next to her and placed his order.

"I'd like to sample this fine establishment's worst bourbon. Double, rocks," he said. He reached out and helped himself to one of the crusty pieces of bread that came with the artichoke dip. "Don't mind if I do."

Brenda followed the thief's hand up his arm to his face—Andy Kraven.

"I was about to stab you with the serving knife," she said.

"I've never been stabbed. I guess I wouldn't mind if it were you who put the blade to me."

"That's oddly sweet."

He asked about Emily. Was she pissed off about the screen door?

"What do you think?" Brenda said.

"I was just trying to put on a good show. I take things too far." He buried his drink, as though it were a penance, and waved the empty glass at the bartender for a refill.

Brenda picked at the appetizer, thinking of conversation topics. Small talk constrained her. Everything else she thought to say to him, though, was about the only other thing they had in common. She didn't have the energy to go down that road.

"I got served here when I was fifteen," Andy said, studying the dark wood bar. "Remember Kaito? Freshman year his mom had a kid, and one night we were babysitting. I took his brother in here with me and said he was my son."

"You pretended a Japanese baby was your son?"

"I told the bartender, 'This little one's been keeping me up for days and my wife wants a divorce and I just need a drink.'"

"What did you order?"

"A gin rickey."

Brenda's train was just then squealing into the station across the street, but she stayed at the bar, where the dim lights and glowing TVs mounted in the corners, the susurration of voices and the warmth of pinot noir, comforted her.

"Kaito was on the bus," she said, in something of a murmur, to herself.

"Sure was."

"Whatever happened to him?"

Andy shook his head, unsure. "He's probably not getting choke-slammed for a living. He never reached out about the movie?"

"Did I just hear someone say something about a future Oscar winner?"

Al Tiles swooped into the narrow space between their knees, almost spectrally, a phantom with a golf tan and an aura of spicy cologne. He'd wrapped a paper napkin, damp with condensation, around his glass of white wine.

"All I want to know is when's the premiere? I got to pick out my red carpet outfit," he said. He fidgeted with a button on his shirt. "Do I know you?" he said to Andy.

"We're acquainted."

"No shit?"

"He was on the bus," Brenda said, and ordered another glass of red.

"Which one were you?" Tiles said to Kraven.

"Which one was I?"

"I'm asking your name, Stretch."

Andy bantered with Tiles. Brenda listened and sipped her wine. It never dawned on Tiles that Andy was mocking him. He kept his bullshit going and grinned at Brenda the whole time. He was being an asshole, but since he knew he was an asshole, and she knew he knew he was an asshole, somehow that absolved him.

He asked Tiles for a good deal on an El Camino.

"I'm a Jeep dealer, I told you that," Tiles insisted.

"I'm looking for something with a six-disc CD changer. I should tell you up front that I've never trusted power windows."

Peripherally, Brenda noticed a large man standing in front of them. She thought he was squeezing in to get a drink. The change in Tiles's face, however, to a look of scrotum-tightening concern, was what made her pay attention to who it was. She didn't place him right away. He looked familiar, but this was her hometown. Everyone looked familiar, everyone an older, meltier version of someone she'd grown up with. Then it hit her, and she was promptly clammy. Her throat tightened and the edges of her vision narrowed.

Andy was the only one holding it together enough to simulate ease.

"How's it hanging, Bunny Man?" he said, or something to that effect.

Jason Schott was middle-aged, chunk-bellied, thinly hirsute, gray stubble around his mouth, tired in all the places middle-aged men were tired. Brenda grasped that he posed limited danger in the crowded neighborhood bar. They weren't on a remote road like last time. And she wasn't a child anymore. She reminded herself she'd faced serious threats to her safety her entire adult life, sought them out in the name of journalism, or maybe just to prove she could. What she was unable to account for was the boldness of his showing up at happy hour. Why was he there?

"We would like you to leave us alone," she said, speaking for the group, strength in numbers.

Schott said something about the documentary, the cease and desist letter, expressing his displeasure not quite calmly, but like a parent arguing with his spouse in earshot of their child, not wanting the kid to overhear.

"Just do what the letter says," he said, and stalked off through the crowd, the negative space where he'd stood the only evidence of his being there.

Brenda took her purse from the hook under the bar, and rooted around in it for her Ativan. She remembered she no longer carried the pills, not even for an emergency like this, not even as a talisman, a security blanket. She'd thought she didn't need them anymore. Down went the remainder of her wine, the only medicine on hand, a drop spilling out of the corner of her mouth and sliding down her jaw.

"About that release I signed, I'm sure it's not too late to back out, right?" Tiles said.

Brenda wiped her chin.

"Just so there are no hard feelings, put those drinks on my tab," Tiles said, peeling off cash from a wad in his pocket, stacking the bills on the bar. "We're all good?"

"Thanks, Sal. You're a peach," Andy said.

"It's Al, but okay, nice seeing you guys. I've got to hit the road."

And he left.

"What a dildo," Andy said, gazing wistfully at the liquor in his glass.

Brenda examined and reexamined the previous two minutes, putting them to memory, but they wouldn't stay fixed. She couldn't correctly order the few things Schott had said. While he was with them, the moment seemed crisp with definition. But now that he was gone, the details, she couldn't swear to them. Her mind was protecting itself by making Jason Schott's reappearance into a psychic maze. This was why it was so important to record interviews, for everyone's sake—video and audio, to verify what really went down. She imagined watching the scene as an impartial third party. Would she have known that what she was seeing was a threat? Did it look dangerous?

"What was that? What the fuck was that?" she said.

Andy repositioned himself on his stool, aiming for a posture that didn't hurt his ribs. "We're having a fucked-up day, that's what."

"But that was him? You said Bunny Man."

"Are you okay, dude?"

She wasn't. She asked the bartender for water.

"It's funny, I woke up feeling great," Andy said. "I don't know what your spiritual leanings are, but I think we might be cursed. All of us on the bus."

"Do you think about it a lot?"

"That I'm cursed? It's a plausible explanation for my life."

"No, the bus. Do you think about it?"

"Not really."

"I don't either. Emily lives with it every day."

"I'm going to have another drink. Want one?"

"I have to go," Brenda said.

"Back to the city?"

"I need to see Emily. I need a cab."

"Let me give you a ride."

Though neither said anything, they hesitated on the sidewalk,

　　　　TIME WILL BREAK THE WORLD

surveying left and right for Schott, expecting him to be leaning against a parking meter, swinging a length of chain. Brenda hoped the fresh air would clear her head but instead she felt lost in the openness. She put her arm around Andy to convince herself that she wasn't alone.

"Easy, I think I cracked a rib," he said.

She held on and they walked a few steps and then Andy abruptly turned and kissed her, catching her off guard, and she went along with it, kissing him back, pressed against someone else's car, before pushing him away, the palm of her hand gently on his chest. He mumbled an apology and they made it to his car, a mid-size sedan from an airport rental counter. He fumbled with the key fob to unlock the doors and then just stood by the open driver's side.

"You know what, I probably shouldn't be driving. My mom would kill me if I caught a DUI in town."

"Want to split a cab?" Brenda said.

Andy looked up at the sky and took a deep breath. "It's shaping up to be a nice night. I think I'll walk," he said.

They said goodbye and Brenda watched him walk right back into the bar.

FRIDAY, AUGUST 3, 1984

The groundsmen were morose and subdued. They huddled in their shy conglomeration. Most had kids. What if theirs had been taken? Even the childless grasped the severity of the day. They waved Jason and Calvin over to join them in pre-shift prayer. One of the groundsmen, a pious man off-duty, spoke to God in Spanish while the rest of them lowered their heads.

"Amen," Calvin said. "I hope they find the scumbags who did this and string them up by the nuts."

This was a big hit with the laborers, vengeance a topic that bridged cultural and economic divides.

Jason and Calvin took the water truck out to spray down the dirt roads. They were on no sleep. How could they sleep? Still, Calvin, behind the wheel, was acting as if it were just a regular Friday.

"The women's individual all-around is tonight," he said. "I can't wait. Mary Lou Retton has a very good chance to medal."

Was he really talking about the Olympics?

"Listen to me, Cal," Jason said.

He worried that his bother wasn't acting nonchalant, that Calvin had somehow compartmentalized or disassociated from the fact that the kidnapping was frontpage news in not only the *Daily Times*, the local rag, but that it captured the imagination of the headline scribes at the *New York Post* and *New York Daily News*, who wrote, respectively, "AFTER-SCHOOL DREADFUL: Students and driver missing, feared kidnapped," and "TRAGICAL MYSTERY TOUR: School bus disappears in broad daylight." The story appeared below the fold in the *New York* goddamn *Times*. Even Scott Shannon, host of Z-100's *Z-Morning Zoo*, dropped his zany persona to offer solemn words of support to the town of Brookwood.

Jason gulped coffee from the thermos and scalded his mouth.

"We took silver in the men's individual all-around in gymnastics last night. Peter Vidmar came in second for us. Not bad," Calvin continued.

"The FBI is looking for us."

"The FBI is not looking for us. They're looking for the kidnappers."

"That's us!"

"Fucking Japanese."

"What are you talking about?"

"Japan got the gold. The women are tonight. I am *not* missing the women."

"I know you're stupid but are you also insane?"

"Do you know how many individual medals American women have ever won in gymnastics? The answer is zero."

"Let's get back to work," Jason said.

"Mary Lou Retton has a very real chance to change that. That's not just me talking. Everyone says so."

How did Calvin not understand that things were worse today than they were yesterday? Their situation would continue worsening until they collected the ransom, released the hostages, and were gone from Brookwood forever. Did Cal fail to comprehend what it meant that every agency of law enforcement was using the full power of their authority to hunt them? Here he was, bumping along in the truck, still talking about the Olympics.

"Gymnastics starts around eight. We'll have this wrapped up by then, you think?" he said.

Wrapped up? Like with a neat little bow? Jason closed his eyes. There was no reaching his brother.

They drove to the burial site. The ground was darker, moister, where they'd dug it up. Calvin raked the area, inspecting for depressions that might indicate a cave-in. They'd wanted a steel shipping container, but it was too expensive, too hard to have delivered to the quarry unnoticed. Instead, they'd cannibalized a moving truck bought at the same New Jersey auto auction where they picked up the vans. The wood and aluminum frame was durable, up to a point. They knew how heavy earth was.

"So far, so good," Calvin said.

"Let's get back to the garage," Jason said.

He turned for the truck, but Calvin slid to one knee and cocked his head.

"What is it?" Jason said.

Calvin shooshed him, his finger in the air. "I think I hear them," he whispered.

"Impossible."

"Sounds like someone is screaming."

Jason squatted, his ear inches above the dirt. He heard something, but what? The ventilation fan, the creaky whine of the fan blades masquerading as a voice? That was probably what he heard. Or it was birds. The quarry had strange acoustics from the combination of hills, pits, and flatlands. Sound traveled oddly all over the place.

But what if? What if...? Would everything still be wrapped up then?

"It's the fan," Jason said. He needed it to be the fan.

Calvin rubbed his hands on his jeans. "If you say so."

"Come on. We've got to get back."

They drove to the garage and got to work, passing the time until lunch when they would make the ransom demand. The plan was to wait until midday to call Governor Cuomo, to confirm everyone's worst suspicion and give the instructions that would bring the hostages home.

Three hours to go. Jason didn't know if he could make it. He dropped the steam hose and rested his hands on his hips. His head was sore from where Lindsey Robinson hit him with the rock. Above, four turkey vultures circled, the sun silvering their wings.

"You kissed Andy?" Emily said for about the fifth time.

"He started it and that isn't the big takeaway from my story."

The LEDs in the kitchen covered the room in a sterile, almost explicit, yellowness. It was just midnight and Brenda had relaxed considerably from when she'd shown back up, exceeding minor tipsiness, and ranting about the confrontation at the bar.

"Do you think he'll tell his girlfriend?" she said.

"Can we please focus on Jason Schott?"

"Fuck him, truly," Emily said. "Fuck that motherfucker."

*

"Tell me again what you said to those motherfuckers," Angie said.

They were slouched on her couch, coffee mugs in laps. Jason had the sensation of having committed a felony the night before, his popping up out of nowhere a kind of assault.

"I can't remember."

"You remembered in bed."

"I told them to listen to Stern's letter."

What were the odds they were at the same restaurant at the same time? Jason wondered. What were the odds Angie would overhear them talking about the documentary? Now he had to admit his lawyer was right and the cease and desist letter was a waste of time. He couldn't bring himself to hoist his ass off the couch to check in on Bertie because he didn't know what to say to her. What was gained by telling her?

"I'm proud of you," Angie said.

"I hardly did anything." He felt the opposite of pride about the whole altercation, even if it had gotten him energetically laid. It was weird that Angie thought he was standing up for them, when really he'd been flailing to feel not quite so puny. "Want to take a ride with me? I don't think I can face Bertie alone."

"Scared of your mom...not your sexiest quality."

*

"What was it like to see him?" Emily said. "Scary?"

"It was scary seeing him, but I don't know if he was actually scary. Does that make sense? I'm not sure I would have recognized him if Andy hadn't called him Bunny Man."

"Was this before or after you guys made out?"

"Are you saving that bottle of Riesling in the fridge for anything?" Brenda said, debating if it was too late for a drink. She couldn't decide if she wanted a drink or if she only wanted to hold a drink, to smell it, while she got ready to ask Emily the big question. In the cab she kept thinking, we need to pressure them. Get in their faces and mix it up.

"Help yourself."

She poured two glasses.

"Do you still want to interview Calvin?" she said.

*

"Well, that's it, isn't it? Cal's gone forever," Bertie said, and boosted the volume on the TV until the bass rattled the picture frames on the entertainment console. She chewed a bite of her egg salad sandwich and followed it with a crunch of a pickle spear. Juice collected in the corners of her mouth and she dabbed the wetness with a paper napkin.

Jason stood in front of the TV, blocking it. He raised his voice over a commercial for the highest-rated, most long-lasting pickup truck in America.

"Mom, listen, one thing has nothing to do with the other," he said.

She sipped from the straw in her ginger ale, ignoring him. Her scalp was visible through the halo of her brittle hair. Jason turned off the TV. The whine of a nearby lawnmower filtered through the window.

"Just because they're making that movie doesn't mean it will have any effect on Calvin's hearing," he said.

Bertie crumpled her napkin and tossed it on her plate next to the sandwich crusts. "Out of my way, shithead." She shuffled unsteadily by him. "I'll tell you what," she said, "something needs to be done."

*

Emily asked Brenda why seeing Jason Schott changed her mind about the interview. What was different now?

"It's a good idea," Brenda said.

"But it was a bad idea when I said it?"

Brenda shrugged. "It was a good idea then too."

She'd underestimated how living in Brookwood affected Emily. It wasn't until she was at the Bar & Grille that she understood there was no way of escaping your past here. It was bad enough to run into people like Al Tiles without warning, or to kiss men you went to high school with, but the possibility of seeing your abductor every time you left your house was a crazy-making prospect. How could you function under that kind of cloud? And since she couldn't escape the past, the best remaining option was to punch it in the face. That was what interviewing Calvin was about. That was what the documentary was about. It finally made sense to her.

"Why just Calvin? Why not both of them?" Emily said.

"After what happened earlier, there's no way Jason would say yes."

"But you think Calvin would?"

"No," Brenda said.

"Then why bother?"

"They need to know we're not going away."

Emily lay awake for a long time that night. She wasn't thinking about her broken screen door or of being in the same room with Calvin Schott. She was puzzling over a different question: What kind of hunger dwelled in Brenda, and not in her, that enabled her sister to be threatened and say "nope, not even close," and let herself be whisked off to greater danger? It was their central distinction as people.

*

If Bertie wanted something to be done, Jason thought, he was going to have to be the person to do it.

"Did we hurt that boy?" Emily said.

"He fell over us," Brenda said.

"But we were in his way."

"We were minding our own business."

"It's our fault."

"That girl pushed him."

"Sure?"

"Very sure."

Who told Brenda they weren't partly at fault? Emily didn't ask. She trusted her sister. But she was so confused about everything. Was it day or night? She caught herself looking at the walls of the box for a window. Also, were those men still going to drown them? She'd been so sure of it on the bus. She slipped her hand into her pocket and wrapped her fingers around the half straw Brenda gave her to breathe underwater. Being buried was sort of like being drowned—drowned in dirt. If she was wrong about that, what else was she wrong about?

The boy who tripped over them was crying. Emily felt bad for him, but not terribly bad because he was a jerk and smelled like ham.

Mr. Pat was screaming at the ceiling. Could someone up there hear him?

"We should help that boy," Emily said.

"How?" Brenda said.

"Let's make him comfortable."

They followed the sound of crying.

"Hi, boy, here you go," Brenda said. She dropped their beach towel next to him.

"Not like that." Emily kneeled and tucked Doodoo in. "Okay, get some sleep now," she said.

"I'm so thirsty. I think I'm dying of thirst," Brenda said.

They mixed a drink, half juice and half water, gulped it fast and made another, which they brought with them to a mattress.

"I threw up yesterday. In the van. I didn't tell you," Emily said.

Brenda started crying. She ducked her head down into the front of her shirt, gently snuffling.

"I want to go home," she said.

Emily put her arm around Brenda's shoulder and pulled her close.

"Oh, my goodness, Mr. Pat is giving that boy a piggyback," Emily said.

Brenda popped her head out of her shirt. "Where? Show me."

Martin Mendoza sat atop Pat Earl's shoulders, extending his arms. He strained, exerting himself, banging his palms against the metal plate that covered the hole.

"Any luck?" Pat said, grunting, winded.

"It's not moving," Martin said.

Pat put him down. They stood staring up, rethinking it, and then they talked with the girl who pushed the boy, and the girl who Emily thought was dead in the van. They started gathering the mattresses and stacking them up in the corner. Pat came to Brenda and Emily.

"I need you to get up," he said.

"We're resting," Brenda said.

"I don't have time to play games, young ladies."

The girls hopped off. He might not have been wearing pants, but they knew he was in charge.

"Is that boy going to die?" Emily said.

"I don't want to hear that kind of talk."

"But is he?" Brenda said.

"You two mind your business," Pat said.

"We were, but that girl pushed him over us."

Pat and Martin dragged the mattress over to the corner and added it to the pile. The bus driver interlaced his fingers and

     TIME WILL BREAK THE WORLD

made a stirrup Martin stepped into and scurried to the top. He offered his hand and helped Pat up. They started banging their palms on the metal plate.

Brenda whispered in Emily's ear, "Mr. Pat has hairy legs."

"Like a gorilla," Emily said.

TUESDAY, MAY 20, 2014

Jason woke up on edge. Before work, he typed an internet search for the Mashburn sisters individually. He scrolled down pages of links for Brenda, most of them related to her career: the TV stations she'd worked at, videos of her interviews, studio broadcasts, remotes. An image search turned up appearances at industry events, awards dinners, philanthropic galas, various low-res headshots with numerous hairdos. A decade ago, she was engaged to a celebrity chef. She was rumored to have had an interest in adopting a baby, possibly several babies, from post-earthquake Haiti.

Info on Emily was sparser. A LinkedIn page, a website for her audiology practice, a private Facebook page. According to an article in the *Daily Times*, she was one of the organizers of Brookwood High's Class of '92 twenty-year reunion. Last year she ran in the Turkey Trot, the Thanksgiving Day 5k fun run in Village Memorial Park. There was a photo of her jogging beside several other women, autumn trees in the pixilated background, the caption identifying her: "Emily Mashburn, of 484 Hillside Street, breaks from the pack."

Jason typed "Jason Schott" into the search bar and clicked enter but closed his laptop before the results loaded.

He went to work. Dug post holes for the Isaacsons' new back deck by hand because his auger ran out of gas. And now he was driving home, or toward the general vicinity of where he lived. Post-work exhaustion usually centered him, a day of outdoor labor clearing his head, but he left the job feeling sluiced with unease. He punched through the radio presets, his body clammy and sour.

He had no control. That was the whole problem. He couldn't stop the Mashburn sisters from making their movie. He couldn't stop the fallout of their movie from landing on everyone he loved. He couldn't make the parole board spring Cal. He couldn't even make the lame-ass radio play one shitty song he wanted to hear.

What was within his control? Food, of course. He pushed his truck through the early evening traffic on Milford Ave. to Franco's Pizza, ordering three slices and a large fountain root beer to stay, slotting himself into a booth beneath an Italian Serie A soccer game on the TV. His indigestion was almost immediate. He couldn't even control his acid reflux. He chewed ice and burped. He yanked out his phone, to text Angie, but to say what? He searched the internet for the Mashburns again. There must be something he missed, a piece of data he could leverage, a morsel of online shame to discredit them. The same information filled his phone. Brenda's haircut fifteen years ago, ten, five; her standing half-bored on a red carpet next to her chef fiancé lunging at a side of beef with a samurai sword; Emily's audiology practice; her photo in a white lab coat with her arms crossed over her chest; her lightly pigeon-toed gait in the Turkey Trot, the caption unchanged, "Emily Mashburn, of 484 Hillside Street, breaks from the pack."

What occurred to him was idiotic in its simplicity. If he couldn't stop them from making a movie about him, they couldn't stop him from making a movie about them. Privacy didn't exist, he remembered Jon Stern telling him. So, let them see how it felt.

He drove to 484 Hillside with no GPS assistance and idled in front of Emily Mashburn's house, an average-size colonial with dormer windows, a detached garage with a basketball hoop over the door, an oak in the yard whose roots had spread to buckle the sidewalk. Jason didn't know what to think about finding his enemy's home so plain. He'd expected an evil lair, or at the least a tasteless McMansion.

His first video was shaky, like a Bigfoot sighting video, until he steadied his hand holding the phone. He recorded her front door, her mailbox, the car in the driveway. He shouldered open the truck door, his boots silent on the asphalt crossing the street. He recorded the license plate on her car and pointed the camera into the driver's side window. He would have to decide what to do with these videos, what value they had, but if all he did was show them to Bertie, it might appease the old woman. She might give him a tiny vote of confidence that he was doing the "something" she believed needed to be done.

Two boys barreled through the front door, a woman's voice trailing them. Jason straightened up, but stayed. The boys held balloon swords, the kind shaped by a birthday-party clown. They dueled across the brick walkway. The woman's voice sounded again, and she came through the door. She seemed to be chasing the boys down and also urging them forward. She pulled up short when she saw Jason.

In person, Emily Mashburn resembled a hounded version of the woman running the 5k, boxed in by the life that had settled over her. She also resembled Brenda, uncannily so, which was to be expected, but was a little older and healthier looking, or possibly just less haughty. Jason, in his grimy work clothes, realized he probably looked like a bloated version of her abductor, which he was. All that was missing was the pantyhose. What had seemed clever at the pizza shop was now an obvious mistake. There was no moral high ground he could claim with the cell phone video, almost no dignity. This was stalker behavior.

A mosquito landed on his forearm and he smacked it dead. The slap jolted Emily into action. She put herself between her sons and Jason. She ordered the boys back inside the house.

"What are you doing here?" she said.

He had to admit it was a good question. The answer—trying to exert control over the uncontrollable—sounded ludicrous in his head. He could be at home right now, showered, three beers deep, drowsing beside Bertie as she watched *Wheel of Fortune*.

He raised his phone, aimed the camera at Emily. "Would you like to comment on the disruption you're causing? Care to make

    TIME WILL BREAK THE WORLD

a statement on the record? Do you have anything to say in your defense?"

"My defense?" She glanced over her shoulder to make sure the boys were in the house.

"I'm making a documentary too," Jason said.

"I would like you to leave us alone."

He also wanted to be left alone. It was the only thing he wanted.

"I will if you will," he said, but it was clear Emily didn't understand. "My mother is old," he said, trying to explain, but again it didn't convey what he meant. He stuffed his phone in his pocket.

"I'm calling the police," she said.

"I'll see myself out."

He walked off her property, relieved to be going. He turned around when he got to his truck. Emily had her phone out, but she wasn't calling the police. She was recording him. The fucking balls to do that! Jason felt as though he were plummeting from a terrific height within himself. He couldn't hear the internal voice that should have warned him, "Hey, man, haven't you done enough to this woman?" From the toolbox in his truck bed he removed his eighteen-inch pipe wrench and recrossed Hillside. He tilted the heavy wrench overhead and with one swing, decapitated Emily's mailbox. He would never know how much further he would have gone because she ran inside and slammed the door, leaving him alone on the sidewalk.

FRIDAY, AUGUST 3, 1984

The noise rose spectrally from the lightless floor. If it sounded like both laughter and tears, it was because that was what it was—Doodoo Viscuso laughed as he cried. Because nothing had ever hurt like this. The pain was unreal. It almost felt fake, like he was being tortured in a dream. He lay on the floor beneath the beach towel the twins draped over him. The slightest movement produced jolts of sharp agony that overlaid a constant throbbing pain. There was some disruption in the box. He heard them moving about. Their steady back and forth vibrated the floor near him, increasing his suffering.

They were doing it on purpose, these sweaty dildos, for revenge, these pussies who couldn't deal with him at full strength. So goddamn typical, he couldn't say he was surprised. He expected nothing less of them. Everyone except Martin. They had become buddies this summer, which was cool timing since he'd had a falling out with Eddie Earl, Mr. Pat's grandson, and the two flunkies, Kevin and Mitch, right at the end of school, which was just a misunderstanding really. Doodoo and Martin had hung out every day, sitting next to each other on the bus, joking around. Always joking. They might have hung around on weekends too, but Lance worked Saturday and Sunday helping his brother Joe, who drove for Dedicated Bakery, making deliveries to restaurants and delis. In the truck at 5:00 a.m., Joe would let him steal a warm roll out of one of the brown paper bags marked for Neptune Diner or the Willis House, a restaurant so fancy men had to wear jackets to get in. The job was okay, he liked that Joe paid him in cash, but getting up early sucked a fat one, and most mornings Joe was hurtin' for a certain with a hangover that put him in a bad mood. Doodoo would offer up his services to drive the truck, and Joe would tell him to go jerk his hairless pecker, except for the morning he stopped the truck to throw up behind a dumpster. He staggered back and lay down in the back with the bread and told Doodoo if he got pulled over to tell the cop that Joe's appendix was about to burst and he was rushing him to the hospital. The most powerful machine Doodoo ever handled up to that point was a 125cc Honda dirt bike with a choked carb that made a choppy noise at the top of each gear, but he hopped up into the driver's seat and pushed the truck into traffic.

He'd wanted to tell Martin the best part was when he pulled alongside some girls walking down the street and said, "Jump in, I'll give you a ride," and the girls laughed, but Doodoo and Martin were school friends, not out-of-school friends, and on Monday he forgot to tell him. His other friends, guys like Eddie Earl, well, like he said, he'd had a bit of a problem with them and they weren't talking, due to a temporary misunderstanding. The misunderstanding was that Mitch was a yellow rat bastard who told Eddie what Doodoo said about Mr. Pat, that the bus driver's breath smelled like he ate shit sandwiches for lunch *and* dinner. Mitch the Snitch, running to Eddie when he'd said much worse things about Pat Earl. The whole town said worse things about Pat Earl. Eddie said choose your friend, him or me, and Mitch and Kevin chose Eddie.

It was true that when Doodoo still hung with those guys, he used to fuck with Martin, but it was never serious. And since summer school started, Doodoo realized that the things he thought were weird about Martin were cool in a way. Like how he never said anything. The kid didn't run his mouth like everyone else, and definitely didn't snitch. He just drew his fish pictures, and never worried what people said. Eddie Earl should be more like the Fish Fucker and grow a sense of humor.

He didn't understand why everyone was moving around but he wished they would stop because his shoulder hurt so much it was making him sick to his stomach. Why did they trip him anyway? They were all laughing at the kid who shit his pants, not just him. Doodoo was scared that the pain was going to kill him. He tried calling out for Martin, but couldn't raise his voice.

Through his laugh-crying he tried again, using Martin's real name and not one of the joke names like Marcia. He tried again. "Martin," he said. He said it a few times. But his friend must not have heard because he didn't come.

Out of the gate, the first thing he was going to tell them, the very first thing, was that no one called him Doodoo anymore. Some people—his exes, his siblings, his pals, of which there were many—called him Lance. To everyone else he was Mr. Viscuso, and people called him this out of respect. Even when he insisted, like to his favorite teller at Wells Fargo, "Call me Lance, sweetie," most couldn't bring themselves to that level of familiarity. As proof, the staff at Hudson Valley Cancer Center, where he was undergoing a round of chemo to treat acute myeloid leukemia, called him Mister.

Good morning, Mr. Viscuso.

How is our friend feeling today, Mr. Viscuso?

Mr. Viscuso, we're pleased with the progress we're seeing.

After he made it plain to the sisters that he wasn't Doodoo anymore, lest they have some antiquated idea about who they were dealing with, they could get down to business about the bus. On that score, he would tell them that, in general, he didn't have much to say about his life before twenty, other than it had been unfair. There was the kidnapping, which was the reason they were talking. But not only that. Try growing up with eight older brothers and sisters in a three-bedroom house—one bathroom!—and see if that doesn't warp your personality. And because there were so many Viscusos in town, everyone knew him, like teachers and cops he'd never seen somehow knew who he was, and he'd gotten into a ton of scraps when they made presumptions about him based on someone else in the family. The thing he'd wanted most was to get out of Brookwood. It didn't matter where he went, so he enlisted on his eighteenth birthday, only to be turfed from the Marines over some bullshit. And then, if that weren't enough, he lost his right testicle in a motorcycle crash. But he would make it crystal clear to the Mashburns that the accident hadn't impeded him *at all*—four kids and a herd of satisfied women throughout the tri-state area could speak to that—and, from a strictly visual perspective, gave his body a more streamlined appearance.

So, yeah, the bus thing was bad, but it was of a piece with what he knew about life.

Lance was saying this to his girlfriend Teresa, from the passenger seat of her Acura, outside the cancer center. He was telling her about what he planned to say to the sisters, in between taking puffs of a bowl, strictly medicinal to combat the nausea, although the buzz took him back to his younger days. His bald head, covered in a do-rag, was no side effect of the chemo. Genetics stole his hair before his thirtieth birthday. Besides, the cancer was busy taking his size, thirty-plus pounds so far, and his stamina. He had Teresa pull up to the front door, in the fire lane, to shorten the walk from the parking lot.

The important thing, he told her, the thing he wanted the sisters and everyone who watched their movie to understand, was that Lance Viscuso was doing great. Leukemia was a temporary setback to what had been an unbelievable run of success. If they were focusing on a part of his life, it shouldn't be when he was a kid, but when his luck changed, when he finally found his calling.

He held the smoke in his lungs and mentally counted to five before exhaling. He and Teresa went inside, and he checked in. The nurse brought him to the infusion lounge and set him up. An elaborate constellation of tattoos sleeved his arms, and where the IV was inserted into his hand went directly into the portrait of his mother, into her mouth like she was drinking up the medicine.

"Hope you're thirsty today, Ma," he said, chuckling and high.

Lance owned Advanced Asset Recovery and Remarketing. In layman's terms, he was a repo man. Everything he'd ever been told about being a bully, how his anti-social behavior would lead to a sad and lonely adulthood, turned out to be a lie. Here was this job that it seemed he'd been training for his whole life. Success in his field meant being craftier and stronger than others. It was about exerting dominance over the weak. He couldn't believe his job was to steal cars, legally. And that it was making him rich. Business had been good overall, but then a few years ago the Great Recession hit. Even he couldn't believe how busy he was. The economy of the entire world ate shit and he worked in the one industry not only unaffected by the downturn, but suited to go through a boom. That was the name of his boat, *Boom Times*.

He asked Teresa to pass him his tablet, on which he'd downloaded a show about military ships. She said she left it in the car. Did he want her to get it? Well, he couldn't get it himself, right?

The thing about leukemia that he hadn't expected was how boring it was. The waiting to see doctors, the tests, more waiting for test results. The blood work. So much blood work. The time spent at the cancer center was excruciatingly dull. This whole experience was an annoyance rather than a threat.

Teresa returned with the tablet but said that he forgot to charge it.

"Shit," he said. He had at least forty-five minutes of treatment. "Talk to me. Entertain me."

She asked what he wanted to do for dinner. Should they make a nice meal?

A nice meal? As if he could think of food. There was an ulcer in his mouth that hurt worse than the time he lost his right nut.

She asked him where he was doing the interview.

He said he was thinking about doing it on the boat. If he was feeling up to it. Take Brenda and Emily out for some fishing, some boat drinks, make a day of it.

Teresa said it was best if he didn't push himself.

"You're not being very entertaining, now are you?" But—and this he didn't say—she was right. Of course, no time was a good time to get cancer, but his diagnosis was inopportune. He was worried that after this run of success, following his crappy childhood, his luck was once again turning. He needed to put himself in remission. That would prove he stopped the slide. He needed to put himself in remission and get back to work. That was what he needed to do. He needed, he just needed. What he needed to do, he suddenly realized, was get up. He needed to get up out of the chair. Because, *because*, something, *something* was wrong. He looked at Teresa and she receded before him with the rest of the infusion lounge. He felt pulled backward down an ever-narrowing, ever-darkening tunnel. He tried to say something, tell her to get a nurse, but his mouth didn't cooperate and his words were gone. His voice was a groan he couldn't even be sure was coming from him. Teresa hove into view, standing over him, but from a distance too far to be able to help.

Later, in the emergency room, a doctor told Teresa that disseminated intravascular coagulation was not uncommon in patients with acute myeloid leukemia, and it caused the simultaneous ischemic and hemorrhagic strokes. She didn't understand the words he used besides *stroke*, and then *coma*, to describe Lance's condition. She was trying to figure out how to unlock his phone, to call his kids, to let them know where their dad was, to have them come and make the decisions about his treatment that she, thank God, wasn't allowed to make.

We picked the second to last day of summer school in case we hit a snag and needed to regroup and try again the following day. In a perfect world, we wouldn't have had scheduling conflicts with the Olympics. Not for the first time in my life, I looked to the athletes and reminded myself that we all must sacrifice for what we want. I tried to tell myself, "Do you really think Carl Lewis or Joan Benoit or Mary Lou Retton didn't miss out on things they enjoyed to be the best at their sports?" That worked to focus me, to keep me concentrating on the task at hand. Up to a point.

Jay and I stashed the vans at the reservoir the night before. The tension of the previous weeks had plateaued, but I wouldn't say we were serene, or even at peace. We were ready. We were grateful the moment was here. We showed up for our shift that morning knowing we were so close to never putting in another shift. We were done putting in shifts. Munsee Granite could have disappeared down a sinkhole and it wouldn't have mattered. We were leaving it behind. *Citius, Altius, Fortius.* Faster, Higher, Stronger. I used to say it all the time because I loved the Olympics and thought speaking Latin made me sound smart. It was just a cool thing to say. But I never meant it for myself, as if I embodied those qualities. If anything, I spoke the motto how it was intended—as an aspiration. It was what I wanted to become. The kidnapping was my chance to make it real.

It's almost impossible to be as holistically wrong about something as we were about the bus kidnapping. But that was me and Jay for you.

Jason stormed down the stairs and past the living room, to the front door.

"Keep rattling the whole house if you want my damn bridge to fall out," Bertie said.

He mumbled about someone or something.

"What is your problem, Jason George?" she said.

"Just stay put," he said.

That was enough to get her curious and off the couch. Jason had his eye to the peephole.

"Pizza guy running late?" she said.

"I told you to stay put."

"Request denied." She moved the curtain on the sidelight window with her cane handle. "Are those two sluts across the street who I think they are?" she said, squinting.

"How can you even see them? You're blind."

Emily and Brenda Mashburn, and a cameraman, had set up in front of the Schotts' house. They were all talking, relaxed, chatty, giving off a *funny-seeing-you-here* vibe.

"I can't believe this," Jason said. Why were they at his house? What did they want? What the hell was going on?

"Looks pretty damn believable to me."

"Shut up, Roberta."

"You think it's far-fetched that the two bitches making a movie about you came here with a camera?"

Jason peeled his eye from the peephole. "Why does this make you so happy?" He was practically imploring her.

"I like to be right."

Bertie kept watching from around the curtain. "Alright, well, something's about to happen."

Jason opened the front door to see three police cars rolling up to the house, one parking on the street and two behind his truck in the driveway.

"Why are you doing this?" he called out to the Mashburns across the street. He walked down the front steps.

"We need you to stop right there," one of the police officers said, holding up his hand.

"Excuse me. Hey, excuse me," Jason said to Brenda and Emily, who continued to ignore him. They directed the cameraman into position.

"Just stop where you are," the officer said.

Bertie, from the doorway, counted five cops. She saw Jason take another step and a half closer to the street, closer to the officer who had twice instructed him to not come closer.

"Christ, Jason, listen to them," she yelled.

Her serrated voice landed on his ears. He turned to her. "What?"

"The goddamn cops. Listen to them."

He turned back to the officers. "What are you saying?"

"Just stay where you are."

Jason put his hands in his pockets and looked down at his bare feet.

"Hands out of your pockets," the officer said.

Meanwhile, the cameraman rotated off the far curb to the edge of the Schotts' property.

"Can we go inside?" the first officer said to Jason.

"What for?"

"To talk."

"About what?"

"We just want to talk."

"About what?"

"We received a complaint."

"About what?"

"Let's do this inside."

Jason put his hands in his pockets again, and they yelled that he take them out. Maybe it was best to invite the cops in and sideline the Mashburns and their cameraman. But he counted too many police for civil conversation. Once they were inside there was no guarantee they would leave if he asked them to. Once they were inside they could do whatever they wanted, ransack the house, plant evidence, murder him in front of his mother and claim reasonable force because they said he grabbed a knife or hit one of them.

"Let's talk here," he said.

"Where were you yesterday evening?" the officer said to Jason.

Five cops for a broken mailbox? "This is bullshit," he said.

"Can you tell me where you were?"

"What a setup."

"Mr. Schott?"

"Why are they here with a camera?" Jason gestured across the street. "You can't see they're playing you?"

Brenda and Emily held their phones up, taunting him. "Look! Will you just look at what they're doing?"

"Calm down, Mr. Schott," the cop said.

"This is harassment. My mother lives here."

Jason imagined how he must have looked to the police, his hairy triceps jutting from a shapeless T-shirt marked with boob sweat, his jeans unfashionably baggy and frayed at the cuffs, out of which bulged pale feet with long toenails. There was a time when the name Schott would have been enough to squash a legal beef—God only knew how many jams George pried him and Calvin out of before they got into real trouble. The owners of the Munsee Granite Company were a *prominent* family. One of the lesser consequences of the kidnapping was the way it toppled certain notions about respectability in town. Tucked away in the darker part of Jason's brain was the thought that his dad had really died of embarrassment.

He was getting nowhere with the cops and had gotten too worked up to notice them tightening their formation around him.

Bertie limped down the cracked concrete steps into the yard.

"What is it with you people? What's your problem? Why don't you get lost?" she asked, brandishing her cane like a cattle prod. Regardless of how far she'd fallen, she was still Dan Reilly's daughter, and feared the dead man's disapproval were she to allow these pissants to disrespect her family.

"We just want to talk to your son, ma'am. That's all."

"Chatting with him shouldn't give you a devil of a time."

"Excuse me, ma'am?"

"Say what you came to say. He's right here. And when you're done, I want to report those two bitches across the street."

Jason was the only one who saw it. When his mother called them bitches, Brenda raised her hand and extended her middle finger. He couldn't mistake the gesture for anything else and he wasn't sure how he reacted. He must have reacted, however. He never saw which officer held the Taser. He just felt something cut far into him and hold him up from the inside. He thought he said "stop," but possibly just tried to say it—50,000 volts scrambling the signal from his brain to his mouth. He fell over into the grass. The pain continued, and it obliterated his ability to judge the passing of time. It just hurt and hurt and hurt until it didn't anymore. As he regained motor function, the cops were on him with handcuffs and hauled him to his feet, his legs heavy and unready. He was working out what had happened while his mental circuitry came back online, when they moved him to the backseat of one of their cars.

And then they drove him away, leaving Bertie on the lawn. Her neighbors had turned out to watch. The cameraman was on the edge of the property and Brenda and Emily were across the street. She wasn't alone but felt alone. After George died and before Jason came home, she spent years by herself. She enjoyed it at times, the solitude, the privilege of hearing only her own noise. It was another thing, though, when the aloneness stretched on without break, a permanent isolation where her own noise was deafening. The police car carrying her son turned the corner and slipped from her fuzzy sight. She'd expected this day, waited for it, not his leaving but his being taken from her. It had always been just a matter of time. She eased down onto the concrete steps of her house and sat there. She'd gotten more time with him than she ever expected. In a way, that was worse. How long would it be, now that he was gone, before she knuckled under for good?

She began thinking the whole neighborhood was staring at her, a dehydrating husk under a housedress. She couldn't let those sluts and their hired gun gawk at her too. It was their fault Jason had been taken from her.

"Get off your ass, Bertie," she said.

She stabbed the walkway with her cane and flapped her arms at the cameraman, shooing him. She couldn't push herself and risk falling, but she was determined. Brenda and Emily watched her approach, their heads crowned by the sun. They seemed eager to hear her out. Only Bertie had nothing to say. She got close, and closer, and then cracked Brenda in the temple with her cane.

Memorial Day, 1971. That was when I checked my dad into St. Vincent's Hospital. The day before, my mom called and said that something was wrong. She was so nonchalant she could have been talking about literally anything.

I asked her what was wrong. She said my dad wouldn't get up. Wouldn't or couldn't? She didn't know. Could she ask him? Oh, he wasn't talking to her. Could Uncle Fred ask him? She said my dad wasn't talking to anyone. Since when? Since Thursday when he went to bed.

I said I would be right over.

Fred met me at the door, said my dad had finally snapped. Like a wishbone, he shouted and wobbled off on his stumps to the kitchen where he and my mom were playing Gin and drinking vodka. I jogged upstairs to my parents' bedroom. The bed was made, and empty. I went back downstairs. Smoke snaked from Fred's cigar in the ashtray, and the cocktail shaker dripped a puddle of condensation on the table. Neither he nor my mom looked up from their cards.

Unless Dad's turned invisible, he isn't in the bedroom, I said. Of course not, Fred said. My dad was in the second guest room. I started asking why he was in the second guest room but decided to see for myself.

The hall light outlined his shape in the bed. His back was to me and the sheet covered him up to his neck. I said his name. He didn't answer. Didn't answer when I asked if he was okay. He didn't even stir when I turned on the light and came in. His expression was tense, several days' worth of white stubble covering his mouth and cheeks, his eyebrows rowdy on his face, his thin breath whistling in his nose. His burgundy wingtips jutted from the end of the sheet.

He was catatonic or seemed that way. I left him for the kitchen. I helped myself to the contents of the cocktail shaker and demanded to know what was going on. My mom laid down her hand and sighed.

Isn't it self-explanatory? she said.

Like a wishbone, Fred said.

I said I was calling an ambulance and my mom said, Dear Jesus, there's no need to make a scene. She said my dad came home from work early on Thursday. She didn't realize until dinner that he was lying down in the second guest room. She thought it was odd, he never went in that room, but if he wanted to take a nap in there that was his right, he owned the house, didn't he?

That was her rationale for not disturbing him. It was his prerogative. He'd earned a rest, hadn't he, after taking care of the family for decades? Fred grunted and puffed his cigar and stole a peek at the next few cards in the top deck.

I said he might have had a stroke, but Fred said there was nothing the matter with him physically. His mind was shot. I asked Fred what made him so sure. He said he had the bum body and my dad the bum brain. That was how things got divvied. Get him a bed at St. Vincent's. They would know what to do.

In the morning, I packed a bag for my dad. He didn't so much cooperate as he was unable to put up a struggle. It was the first time in my life I realized he was only a couple of inches taller than me, and not the giant I'd always thought he was. He stayed at St. Vincent's for ten days, recovering from extreme exhaustion, a euphemism for God only knew what. The exhaustion, or whatever it was, became semi-permanent, sending him into semi-retirement. He put in appearances at the office no more than three times a week. Still, it was his signature on the checks, and his

　　　　TIME WILL BREAK THE WORLD

business cards continued to read PRESIDENT AND CEO. George was respectful and kept him in the loop about company doings, though I never knew how much my dad's opinions factored into George's decision-making. Then Uncle Fred died in December, right after Calvin's twelfth birthday. The loss took what little fight was left in my dad. He resigned his position, while maintaining his seat on the board of directors. George was now the boss. For the first time in its long history, Munsee Granite Company Inc. was led by someone other than a Reilly.

My dad died in 1978 from a heart attack. I was executrix of his will. He'd arranged to leave most everything outside of the company to my mom but gave me power of attorney. My dad was a meticulously organized man and made the job of going through his personal effects rather easy. In his home office, I found over three decades of tax returns, bank statements, mortgage state-ments, investment statements, insurance policies, the deeds to cars, land, and boats, and the keys to two safe deposit boxes. The contents of his wall safe included three gold watches, a 1911 Colt .38 semiautomatic pistol, and $18,000 in cash.

I also discovered the medical file from his stay at St. Vincent's. Though he was treated for the catchall malady of exhaustion, the record showed that he was admitted for Gross Stress Reaction.

Picture this: On the Thursday before Memorial Day in 1971, Dan Reilly left his office on Fifth Avenue at lunch to get a head start on the long weekend. At home, he tossed his jacket on the coat rack. He climbed the stairs to his bedroom, took off his wrist-watch, counted the cash in his pocket and placed it on the dresser by the window, the stack of bills fluttering in the spring breeze. He sat on the bed, about to take off his shoes, when he heard a noise. He thought Frances was talking to him from another room. What did you say? he said. For a moment, he heard nothing. The noise picked up again. Huh? he said, annoyed now. He went to find out what his wife was saying. The noise would stop, and then start again. He traced it to Fred's room.

Now, picture this: Dan opened the door. Fred was in bed. Frances was on top of him, pounding on his chest. His shirt was unbuttoned and her fists disappeared into a thatch of white chest hair. Dan believed his brother was dying and his wife was attempting to resuscitate him. He didn't rush in and help. Other details he initially missed were coming into focus: Frances's velour pants on the floor, her bulky cotton underwear ringing her left ankle, Fred's angry stumps kicking at the mattress while he bucked his hips. They turned their heads and saw him. Dan's hand was on the doorknob, steadying him. Once he put a name to what he was watching, once he understood that they weren't going to stop on account of him, not out of surprise or guilt or fear, there wasn't anything left to do but—and keep picturing this—softly close the door behind him, to give them privacy. He walked down the hall, to the room farthest from Fred's, the second guest room, and went to bed.

I confronted my mom about what I had learned. She said there were a lot of things I didn't know. I asked her why then, why 1971, why the Thursday before Memorial Day?

She looked at me like I was speaking to her through sound-proof glass, like she was trying to read my lips. It was going on the whole time, she said, and cracked open a can of Tab.

The whole time! Fred moved in in 1944. How did my dad not know? How did *I* not know? I wanted to believe the affair was my mom's revenge for my dad's physical abuse, even if that would be a tidy explanation for a messy arrangement. The thing I can't help but wonder is how our lives would have been different if their relationship was uncovered years earlier, when I was a newlywed, say, before George was entrenched at the company. Perhaps the situation would have been volatile enough to destroy Munsee Granite. Our entire lives would have been different. George and I could have moved to Albany, and he would have joined his family's business. Calvin and Jason would have become different boys. Or maybe not. Maybe they would have become the same

   TIME WILL BREAK THE WORLD

boys they were. One thing I'm certain of is that they would have never had the opportunity to use the quarry, which I'd rightfully deemed an evil place when I was a little girl, as the location of their crime.

THURSDAY, MAY 22, 2014

Emily couldn't get comfortable. The chair in the waiting room at urgent care was scratchy, and the room temperature was slightly milder than northern Greenland in February. She shivered and flipped through an eight-week-old issue of *In Style* magazine, while Brenda was in with the nurse practitioner. Brenda had refused to go to the emergency room or make an appointment with her neurologist, insisting that she barely felt the blow from Roberta Schott's cane. It was like a tap, she'd said. Emily knew she was lying. There was a lump the size of a quail egg right at her hairline. Her injury in Anaheim made her susceptible to future concussions, so when it was Emily's turn to insist on things, she had Brenda stay the night at her house. Then she cleared her schedule for the morning. Brenda made only a passing attempt to complain and then got in the car, which Emily considered proof of the severity of the injury. She blamed herself for not stepping in front of her sister, offering herself up as a human shield. Really, though, who could have imagined the old woman was violent? But, of course the old woman was violent. Look at the sons she raised. What Emily hadn't expected was that Mrs. Schott was still game. The old bitch could still land a blow.

She walked to the water cooler, filled a paper cone, took one sip, and poured the rest into the trash can. There had been a moment last evening, when the police first arrived, that rivaled the most thrilling moments of her life. Watching them climb out of their cars, the unhurried, near-bored way that they stalked across the lawn, knowing that she brought it about, had given her a sense of depraved, electric resourcefulness.

Normally, she would have just bought another mailbox and not escalated the confrontation, but it hadn't taken much to talk herself into thinking that this wasn't a personal vendetta. She was performing a public service.

"I thought he was going to kill me," she'd said with faux meekness to the officer who took her report.

At what cost, though? she now wondered, thumbing through another magazine. Could she ever accept an incarcerated Schott at the expense of an incapacitated sister?

The sister in question came out from the exam room. Brenda squared up her co-pay at the front desk, took a squirt of hand sanitizer from the dispenser, and started for the exit. Emily met her at the door.

"Well?"

"You're not going to believe it."

"What's wrong?" Emily said, her face mushy with dread. "That's it, you need to see your neurologist."

"Calvin's in," Brenda said. Jon Stern had confirmed the interview. She'd just gotten his email.

It wasn't what Emily was thinking about and she didn't know what to say. They had only requested the interview a few days ago, before the mailbox incident. Emily hadn't expected a response so soon, or at all. She chased after Brenda through the parking lot.

"What do you mean he's in?" she said.

"What's so confusing? Did you get hit in the head too?"

"You said he would say no."

"Well, he said yes."

Emily knew Brenda was prone to caginess, so maybe this news about the interview was her way of distracting from her diagnosis.

"What did the doctor really say?"

"Nurse practitioner."

"Whatever."

"She said I'm fine."

"She said those words?"

"Verbatim."

Emily doubted it, but what could she do? She drove them home. Calvin Schott was housed at Coxsackie Correctional

Center, a maximum-security prison, about an hour and a half away. She tried picturing herself sitting across from him but couldn't conjure the image. How would the interview work? When was it? Video, or audio only? Were there topics that were out of bounds? Would the lawyer be there? Brenda, having made the big announcement, was suspiciously tightlipped about the specifics.

"I don't get it. What's in it for him?" Emily said.

"Do you want to interview him? Yes or no?"

Did she? She thought about it and realized it wasn't a lack of details getting in her way. It was Calvin himself. More than wanting him to die in prison, she wanted her judgment of him to stand. She wanted him to prove that he was an animal, the way his brother had when he came at her with a pipe wrench. And yet, when the police tasered Jason, for a second she believed they shot him. From her angle across the street, she saw the officer's hand slide up his thigh and unholster what looked like a gun. She expected to hear a blast echoing down the block. In the moment before she grasped that the police were only subduing him, he became an actual person, a human being gunned down in front of his mother. Emily didn't have room inside herself to hold competing versions of her kidnappers. She saw how dangerous it would be to give Calvin the chance to change her mind about him. So, no, she wasn't sure she wanted to interview him anymore. She wanted to know what Brenda thought, but Brenda was staring out the window, not talking.

Brenda wanted the halos in her vision to go away. She wanted not to throw up in her sister's car. The sun hit the side mirror and she had to find somewhere else to look. She stared at her lap. She didn't need a nurse practitioner to tell her she had another concussion, but the woman did anyway, sternly, as if it were Brenda's fault. She couldn't accept the diagnosis. She didn't have time for another concussion. She would work through it. The Catastrophe Queen had worked sick and injured before. Her

   TIME WILL BREAK THE WORLD

job right now was to defend Emily. She'd taken the first train into town after her sister called in a panic. They'd stood over the dented mailbox lying in the street. In a timorous voice, she told Brenda that unless they did something, this was her future. Calvin would be released, and he and Jason would never stop tormenting her.

"I know," Brenda said.

Neither of them expected Jason to be arrested. Brookwood cops were lazy. All he had to do was deny it. They only wanted him to know they weren't going away either. But he went crazy when Brenda flipped him off. He was so easy to goad. Now his brother agreed to sit down for an interview, like an idiot. Some people couldn't help themselves. Maybe he didn't really want to get out of prison. If so, Brenda would be glad to help him get what he wanted.

Mr. Pat said Martin was old enough to know the truth. They were running out of air, and the roof could cave in. The roof would cave in, it was just a matter of time. The only way they were going to get out alive was if they got themselves out. Clawing, scratching, climbing, whatever it took. They had to fight to get out because no one was coming for them. That was what Mr. Pat told him when he took him aside. He wasn't telling him this just to scare him shitless. He needed his help. They were all going to have to work together, but some people would have more to do, more responsibility to shoulder. They would have to put themselves at greater risk where they might get hurt, and if that seemed unfair, well, he had news for Martin, that was how life worked. Did he understand?

Martin said he understood.

Was he sure he understood? Because the bus driver didn't know what this kid's story was. He'd watched him all summer and, frankly, Mendoza seemed a little checked out, and not just in the distracted or unruly way the rest of the weirdos and rubberheads were. He was here but not here. So Pat asked again if he understood. Did he understand that even if they somehow figured a way out of this box, even if they reached fresh air before the roof collapsed and killed them (Pat wouldn't pull punches, the kid needed to hear it), there was no telling if the gunmen were waiting for them and the first one to pop his head through the hole would get it blasted off? Did he understand what they were up against? Could he look Mr. Pat in the eyes and tell him that he really understood?

"Could you please look into the camera and state your name and age?" Brenda said.

She needed to keep the interview simple. There was no reason to manipulate him or put words in his mouth. Let him hang himself with his own words. The prison interview room smelled spicy with disinfectant, filling her nostrils like smoke. She wondered if Emily was as sensitive to the odor as she was.

"Glad to. That's a good place to start, actually. Doesn't presume we all know each other." He grinned from his side of the metal table.

"Before we start," the lawyer said, "I want to make clear Calvin is participating voluntarily and can stop at any time he wants."

"Yeah, Jon, everyone knows, but thanks for the reminder. Alright, let's do this. My name is Calvin Daniel Schott. I'm fifty-four years young. In civilian years, that is."

"As opposed to?" Brenda said, mildly dizzy. It might have been the disinfectant, but she knew the nurse practitioner at urgent care would have disagreed.

"That's got to be a solid eighty in inmate years."

"How old were you on August 2nd, 1984?" She read from a list of questions she and Emily had written. She hoped she wouldn't have to deviate from them often.

"That's an even better question. I was twenty-four. So, do the math. That means I've been incarcerated longer than I was ever free."

"You were born and raised in Brookwood, New York?" Simple question.

"Correct." Simple answer.

"And your brother, Jason? He grew up in Brookwood too?"

"I'm not comfortable speaking for him."

So much for simple answers.

"I'm confirming that you were raised together."

"We were."

"Did you and Jason have a normal childhood?"

"As opposed to?"

"How would you describe your homelife growing up?"

"Fine."

"Fine?"

"Comfortable."

"In what ways?"

"We were rich. Well, our parents were rich. Jay and I were along for the ride. I'll say this, though, we lived in a really nice home."

(Home is Beverly Rd. in Fairmont, West Virginia. She's the youngest of five. The family name is Rotunda, but that was back in Italy before her great-grandfather immigrated and changed it. Her mother signs her up for dance classes to keep her busy, to give her limitless energy an outlet. At four years old, she possesses a level of kinesthetic intelligence rarely seen in children. She has more than potential, but an endowment. Her dance teacher should know, she also coaches gymnastics at WVU. Her mother, wanting to find the parameters of this unordinary talent, enrolls her in classes at the Aerial Port Gymnastics Center. This is where it starts.)

He brought Martin over to where it started, their confinement, to the corner of the container beneath the hatch they climbed through. The hole was covered with a metal plate. He had the boy get on his shoulders and reach up to see if it was movable. Martin slapped his palms against it but couldn't budge it. Pat put him down and they regrouped. It was the girls' idea, Jodie and Lindsey, to stack the mattresses. They could climb on top of them and reach the ceiling and work together. They could take turns. Pat saw the lump on Lindsey's cheek. It had purpled from the day before. He asked if it hurt, and she said it was nothing.

Martin scrambled up the pile first, floundering on his belly; the old, mildewed mattresses sagged under his weight when he stood. The pile started swaying. The girls leaned against it, holding it into the corner. Pat recruited more children—Thomas Burke, Nelson Garcia, Kaito Watanabe, and the twins—instructing them to put their weight into the mattresses to stabilize the pile. Thomas let out a yelp. A spring poked through the fabric and stuck him in his palm.

Pat climbed up next. He and Martin had a go at the metal plate, separately and together, but the downward pressure sunk them

    TIME WILL BREAK THE WORLD

deeper into the mattresses. They couldn't dislodge the plate. Pat bent his knees and braced his arms against the wall, locking his body stiff, and told Martin to climb him. The kid was all knees and elbows and the bus driver grunted and breathed wet and heavy, clenching his jaw and squeezing his eyes shut. Martin tried the plate again, and again the plate was immovable. If it weren't for the dirt sifting from the corners when he banged on it, he would have thought it was welded to the box. His shoulders were already burning, and his hands and knuckles were scraped. It seemed hotter and stuffier near the ceiling and he remembered once learning about heat rising due to hot air expanding and becoming less dense than cool air. He drove his forearm into the metal plate, sending a sharp bolt of pain from his elbow to his neck. It was like hitting a wall. He wanted to take a break, really he wanted to quit, but he was afraid of failing in front of the others. He grimaced and struck the plate again. A shower of dirt fell thick on his head.

As the shower's hot water pelted Brenda's head that morning, she'd thrown up, so she knew it wasn't the disinfectant alone bothering her. She focused on the yellow legal pad with her questions and found constancy in her familiar scrawl. She checked off the ones she'd asked and moved on to the next.

"Were there any issues with physical abuse or substance abuse in your home?"

"I grew up in the sixties."

"Can you elaborate?"

"Did my parents spank me? Yes. Did they smoke and drink? Duh. Was that child abuse, substance abuse? I don't know. It was a different time."

"I see. Thank you for clarifying."

"Were you two spanked?"

"Let her ask the questions, Calvin," the lawyer said.

"I'm just asking if their parents ever smacked them around."

"Was corporal punishment the only violence you experienced during your childhood?" Brenda said.

"Our father would chain us to a pipe in the crawl space if we didn't make our beds with military corners and that's why we became criminals."

"You misunderstood the question."

"No, I didn't."

"Your mother attacked her," Emily said, speaking up for the first time, her voice loud and a little wild, as if something was clamping down on it and she fought to get it out.

"No shit?" Calvin said.

"Say no more," the lawyer said.

"Thank you, Jon. Your advice is invaluable." He nodded once and was quiet.

"Did you ever have problems with drugs or alcohol?" Brenda said.

"Jay and I were hopeless addicts. We'd seen a drug-induced hallucination that looked like the Virgin Mary with Heather Locklear's face. She told us to do it."

Here came Brenda's headache, a needling pain radiating from the back of her eyeballs. It annoyed her more than it hurt her. So did Calvin, for that matter.

"What would you say your issue was, then?" she said.

"Who said I had an issue?"

Emily beat her to it, overturning her chair she stood up so fast. "You kidnapped twenty people and buried us alive. I would say you had issues."

(The issue is that her parents don't want her to leave. She can keep training in Fairmont, they say. But in 1982 she takes the all-around title at the South African Cup, sweeping the four events, and they give in, knowing that she has outgrown her home. She leaves for Texas to train under the Romanian coach, Károlyi, who talks like Dracula and who'd molded the last great, Nadia, before he defected. "Just don't let him bite your neck," her dad says at the airport. She lives with the Spiller family, reliable surrogates but no substitutes. The morning practice starts before dawn,

   TIME WILL BREAK THE WORLD

then a quick recess at home for lunch and to hear Mrs. Spiller recap the latest installment of *Days of our Lives* ("*Neil* is really the father of Liz's baby!"), and then back in the gym for the afternoon practice, to the repetition, the pain, the gravelly coach bellowing praise and disappointment in equal measures; though why does it feel like the encouragement is so much harder to secure, why do the mistakes and lapses in attention happen without even trying? She believes in herself, but is belief enough? Is she good enough? Can she really do it?)

"You can do it, Marty!" Lindsey said, her swollen cheek aglow in the lantern light. Pat Earl agreed that the kid needed all the encouragement in the world, but encouragement wasn't going to move the metal plate. He strained to keep in his half-bent pose with Martin on his back, his heart pounding. The yelling around him gave him a splitting headache. If they could just shut up for a few minutes. He concentrated on not falling over with the kid wriggling on top of him.

Then the wriggling stopped. Martin slid down, wheezing a little. Pat asked what was wrong. The kid hopped off the mattresses and walked to the folding table with the food, his back to them, his shape barely visible in the darkness. He just stood there. He stood in front of the table. Then he began gathering up the provisions in his arms and transferring them in a semiorganized mound to the floor. He upturned the table and inspected the legs and the hinges that opened and closed them. Pat was impatient to get back to work. This was what he feared, the kid spacing out, quitting on him, play-ing with food and fooling around with the table.

What the hell did he think he was doing?

"I just thought of something," Martin said.

"I just thought of something," Calvin said, and slapped the table—*Blam!*—with the palm of his hand, as if it was the bright-est idea of his life. "Arrogance. How's *that* for an issue? What's the new catchword everyone's using—entitlement? My brother and I were arrogant and entitled. We thought we deserved to be total badasses, doing whatever we wanted, whenever we wanted. We expected to impose our will on the world."

(Gymnastics isn't direct competition, like swimming or tennis, where you can impose your will on your opponent. There are judges, there is politics. Technique counts, attire counts. She isn't a known entity within the sport. There are other girls who want what she wants, who already have national rankings and championships. A first place finish at the McDonald's American Cup changes that for her. She arrives as a sub and gets her spot when Dianne Durham goes down with a strained hip. She sets the record for the vault. Her coach chuckles when he calls it the greatest shock of 1983. Now people know who she is and what she is about.)

Pat Earl still didn't know what this kid was about. He seemed to work hard one minute and was totally spaced out the next. "Come on, Mendoza, we talked about this, we don't have time." Martin was on his hands and knees, looking at the hardware that screwed the hinges into the particle board. If they laid the tabletop flat on the mattresses, it would give them a firm surface to stand on. If they tore the legs off, they could use them as levers to jimmy under the metal plate and pry it loose. Pat had a change of heart. Maybe the kid was on to something.

They stood on the upside-down table, pushing and pulling on the legs until the particle board splintered around the hinges. Once the legs were free, they laid the table across the top mattress. Mr. Pat climbed up again and the pile wobbled. The kids pressed their weight against the mattresses to steady them. Brenda and Emily sensed their effort would affect the outcome, that their determination was directly proportional to their chances of escaping. If they just tried hard enough... They leaned into the pile until their legs quaked under them, the thin tendons in their necks sticking out. There was magic in their effort and if everyone gave as much as they gave, they would make it out. They knew this in their hearts without saying it.

    TIME WILL BREAK THE WORLD

"It goes without saying, but no one gets everything they want," Brenda said. For instance, she wanted a dark, noiseless room that smelled of nothing, but that was unlikely. "Why did you think you were special?"

"Can we just stop here for a second? I can't believe you do this for a living. What kind of questions are these? Seriously, what does any of this matter?"

"Mr. Schott, people know what you and your brother did, but they don't know about you. I'm trying to contrast who you were in 1984 with who you are now. Is that okay with you?"

Calvin raised his eyebrows, thinking about it.

"We weren't just frustrated because we couldn't do what we wanted," he said. "It felt like a huge injustice."

"Would you agree that one of your issues was that you and Jason were delusional?"

"That's a strong word."

"Is it accurate?"

"Let's say we just loved the sound of our own bullshit."

"Sounds like you still do," Emily chimed in, and Brenda waited to see how Calvin would react.

"It's more of a love-hate relationship at this point," he said.

"I'd like to move from issues to motives," Brenda said. Just keep moving forward, she thought, and it would be over soon.

"Our motivation was money. Everyone knows that."

"If you needed money, why didn't you ask your parents for it? Didn't you grow up wealthy?" She flipped through her notes. She thought he'd said it earlier but couldn't remember. It might have been a fact she just knew.

"It was their money. Not ours. They were very clear about that. We had a little trust we inherited from our great-uncle. Sweet old guy. We started a business with it, but things didn't go the way we planned."

(She plans to make the team. The top four finishers make the team. But win? Well, she does, first place at the Olympic trials. Vidal

Sassoon is tapped to be the official hairstylist of the women's team. During the men's finals, he gives her a trim. After, young girls race to the chair and grab clippings of her hair off the floor.)

Martin grabbed dirt off the floor and rubbed it between his hands to dry his sweaty palms. He didn't want to lose his grip on the table leg. Mr. Pat lifted both arms and the top of his head against the metal plate, pushing on it, while Martin drove a table leg underneath it. The leg found no purchase around the edges. He tried shimmying it into the corner. It scraped and grated, and Martin noticed more dirt falling. He called out to the bus driver that he thought something was happening. Starting to happen. Maybe. It was hard to tell. "Push it again, Mr. Pat," Martin said, and Pat muttered, "You're killing me." He drew a deep breath and heaved himself upward. Martin timed it so that he jabbed the table leg right when Mr. Pat threw himself at the metal plate. And this time, the plate separated from the box just enough for the leg to wedge into the gap. For a minute they could only stare at it sticking out of the ceiling. Martin was more surprised than anyone else. He never really thought it would work out.

"What do you mean your business didn't work out? What business?" Brenda said.

"I'm done talking to the celebrity," Calvin said. "The other one can ask me questions."

Brenda thought it was best for Emily to stay out of it. She would be an additional person to manage, another voice piercing Brenda's already hampered focus. She couldn't find the notes she was looking for and she wanted to take a break. She pushed aside her legal pad and, despite knowing it was going to cause a problem, thought to herself, fine, let Emily go for it. She was the reason they were all here.

"Tell me about your trust fund?" Emily said.

"Why?"

"It means you had money. It means you didn't need to kidnap us."

"We lost it."

"How?" Emily said.

"Better not get into that," the lawyer said.

"Did I tell you Bertie and George charged us rent? Did you know that? We worked at the quarry that they owned so we could pay them rent at the house they owned. That made us, what, indentured servants, or sharecroppers? Now do you see why we couldn't ask them for money?"

"I'd like to know more about this trust. You say you lost it?" Emily said.

"On the advice of my counsel, I respectfully decline to comment."

"Is it a secret?"

"Johnny Boy here feels it's best to leave my relationship with the Godfather of Land Fraud in the past."

"Calvin," the lawyer said.

"The godfather of...?" Emily said.

"Oops," Calvin said, and slapped his palm on the table again—*Blam!*

"This is not a line of questioning I'm comfortable having you answer," the lawyer said.

"What he means is that the parole board needs to be one hundred percent convinced that I know my crime was two hundred percent my fault," Calvin said.

"And you feel like it was? Or wasn't? I can't tell from your answer," Emily said.

"Life is complicated."

"What does that mean?"

Brenda watched the interview slip out of control. Calvin Schott was running the show and Emily didn't realize it. Brenda needed to rein it back in, but the problem was that she was having a tough time parsing his answers. It was more than his being a secretive, deflective asshole. She struggled to understand what he was saying. She looked at Emily to see if he was making sense to her. She really wanted to take a break, ten minutes and a glass of water, but there was some concern on her part that she wouldn't be able to restart. The only way to end the interview was to finish it, and they weren't finished yet.

"On the advice of my lawyer, I'm afraid not."

(She is not afraid of the competition. She is undefeated in '84. She is sixteen. Four feet, nine inches and ninety-five pounds. A size 3 shoe. Her dreams don't seem like dreams because she has been dreaming them for eleven years. No, they are goals. She has set her sights on the world.)

Everyone cheered at the sight of the table leg sticking out of the ceiling. Pat offered his hand and Martin shook it and then Pat fell to his knees, onto the layer of dirt that had accumulated on the table. They climbed down and drank water. Lindsey Robinson befriended Martin by the cooler. She told him he did an awesome job. Martin didn't understand what she was so excited about. They were still trapped. He found himself repeating Mr. Pat's words to her, that they were in a race against death. There was nothing to celebrate. They needed to get back to work.

Which they did, Pat and Martin, Lindsey and Jodie. They were the oldest and tallest and they took turns levering the table leg— glacially, incrementally, painstakingly moving the metal plate to the side. The leg, hollow metal, was soon bent out of shape, kinks and crimps running its length. They replaced it with another leg and they were just as hard on that one. It went on like this. Pat and Martin, Lindsey and Jodie, destroyed table legs, while Brenda and Emily and Thomas Burke and Kaito Watanabe and Nelson Garcia made sure they had a steady platform to work on.

And then, nobody was sure how long after: sunlight.

He deserved to never see sunlight again, Emily thought. Jesus! Their kidnapper was spewing volcanic, explosive bullshit. She'd sat there deferring to Brenda, out of more than just respect for her profession, but it had gone on too long. Just listen to him.

"We were rationalizing when we said getting the money

would make us happy. But we were lying to ourselves because we weren't happy even before we met Lonzo."

"Calvin," the lawyer said.

Emily anticipated Brenda would ask the obvious follow-up, but she sat with her hands in her lap. "Lonzo?" Emily said, again having to interject.

"Lonzo gave us the story we told ourselves: we're in this shitty job, stuck at our parents' house, with no way out. And the reason there was no way out was because Jay and I had been ripped off. It was all his fault. Anything we did after that could be traced back to him. Lonzo Feldman was the original sin."

"What do you expect me to do if you don't listen to me?" the lawyer said.

Calvin almost made sense if you ignored the part where he nearly murdered twenty people, two of whom were in the room with him. His level of detachment was unreal. Emily was wrong to think meeting him would trigger feelings of humanity. He wasn't evil, but he didn't elicit her sympathy. He was stupid. That was all there was to say about him. How had he and his brother come so close to pulling off their crime?

Still, Lonzo? There was a reason why Calvin kept bringing him up. Maybe threaded through his meandering, self-pitying, nonsense was a truth about the kidnapping that would be beneficial to the documentary and their own understanding of it.

Emily waited once more on Brenda, still deferring to her. And then, as if Brenda hadn't heard anything to this point, she said, "So, what do you think motivated you to break the law?"

Emily couldn't pretend it was a tactic, to ask a question a second or third time to provoke a different answer. She saw that Brenda was shivering lightly, as though feverish. Her sister wasn't blowing the interview, but struggling through it. What Emily had suspected was true: Brenda was lying when she said she'd never felt better.

(She's never felt better, stronger, and yet, a fragment of her articular cartilage—which knows nothing of her goals—tears free and lodges in her knee joint. Six weeks before Los Angeles, at a gymnastics seminar in Louisville, she is sitting cross-legged on a mat, signing an autograph, and when she gets up, she can't straighten her right leg.

"Something terrible has happened," she tells her mother. She can't face the larger implications. She will be too old in '88. She will never be as good as she is right now. This is her one shot. Her parents initiate a nationwide hunt for a specialist. She meets them in Richmond, at her appointment with Dr. Gaspari.

"Will I be ready for the Olympics?" she asks.

"Which Olympics?" the doctor says.

She is hysterical.)

Hysterical laughter rose from Pat Earl's chest—no, deeper, it came from the bottom of his stomach, from his bowels. He watched daylight break into the container in a line the width of a sheet of loose-leaf paper, dirt particles swirling in it. The children had never heard him laugh. They, too, were drawn to the light and gaped at it, everyone but Doodoo who lay damaged on the floor. Andy came from the opposite corner, where he'd been feigning sleep, and fell in next to Kaito and asked what day it was, which got a big laugh though he wasn't joking. Pat reached up to see if he could worm his hand through the gap, but his meaty fingers got stuck. He asked the girls if theirs could fit. It was tight and Jodie worried about getting her hand caught. Could they push the plate out of the way? "No chance." He told them to try again, this time while he maneuvered the table leg back and forth. Did it move? "Maybe," Lindsey said. "A little," Jodie said. "Again," the bus driver said. They worked at it for several minutes and he tested it and his fingers slipped past the metal plate, then his whole hand. Martin watched and listened for the shotgun blast, followed by Mr. Pat flinching back a gory stub. When his arm emerged intact, Martin thought the gunmen were waiting for a juicier target, like a face that they could cover the ground with.

"This is ground we've covered, so if you're out of questions, I think we should wrap it up," the lawyer said.

He was giving them an out, Emily thought, and they should take it. She should end the interview, thank Calvin Schott for his time, though he didn't deserve thanks for anything in his tiny, disgusting life, and take Brenda to the hospital. But she found herself saying, "You said the reason you kidnapped us was for money."

"It's an established fact," the lawyer said.

"But Mr. Schott and his brother never demanded ransom."

"Of course we did," Calvin said.

(Of course, she leaves the hospital on crutches the same day as the arthroscopic surgery. Of course, a day later she pedals the stationary bike at the gym. Of course, she packs three months of physical therapy into three weeks. She and her coach tell no one about the injury. If people know about it, the rumors start, confidence fades, and judges underscore you. You find yourself peering up at the leaderboard and you can't see your name.)

Pat Earl peered up into a beam of daylight, but he couldn't see the surroundings up there above the hole. He felt the air, though. Humid, stagnant, dirt-filled summer air, and yet it smelled of outside. It smelled like life. It reminded him he was still alive. Pat called the children one by one onto the tabletop and let them breathe, lifting the smaller ones so they could raise their faces and inhale, in case they forgot what it felt like.

"You forgot to ask for ransom," Emily said.

"Check your sources. We didn't forget. Jay called the governor, but his office thought we were pranking them. They'd gotten dozens of calls from people claiming to be the kidnappers."

"Governor?" Brenda said, holding the legal pad somewhat in front of her face, as if it were a shield. Shielding her from the intrusive ceiling light, but also a point upon which to rest her eyes, which felt heavy. Talking would help keep them open but she couldn't think of anything to say.

"I'm of course referring to the honorable space governor of the Andromeda Galaxy... Mario Cuomo, you idiot."

"So, you did nothing?" Emily said.

"You know, if you think about it, we should've known you just can't get the governor of New York on the phone."

(The pay phone in the hall is off-limits and her dorm room in Webb Tower on the campus of USC doesn't even have one. At night she lies in the dark, atop her made bed, hearing helicopters over the Olympic village, their propellers beating the sky. She stares at the ceiling and projects upon it her routines, visualizing her program, each event done perfectly: Floor exercise, where again and again she executes a double back layout somersault with a full twist, her feet touching the mat for the briefest instant before springing into a front flip. On the uneven bars, she has a maneuver named for her, the Retton Salto. A handstand on the high bar, and then she swoops down and belly-beats the low bar—*Blam!* And then she just swings back up, letting go, into a front somersault. The beam, just four inches across—here she hits the double back dismount so hard, so solid, she shakes Pauley Pavilion.)

Jennifer Strauss shook her head in the beam of light, letting it wash over her. Pat put her down. He'd so lost his bearings, his sense of passing time, and his eyes were so accustomed to the darkness that he couldn't tell the sunlight was waning, that it was evening, not long from dusk. He again shoved his hand through the hole and groped around. It didn't seem that the metal plate had been buried in dirt but covered with heavy objects. They felt like rocks, large, jagged rocks. He gathered Martin and Lindsey and Jodie and sized them up, determining Martin was skinniest. He said if they could move the plate over a few more inches, they could boost Martin through the opening, possibly get his torso out of the container and see if he could shove off whatever held the plate down. The kids nodded, even Martin, who was now convinced, who had never been surer of anything in his thirteen years, that he would be the one blown away, that when Mr. Pat told him earlier that some of them would risk more danger, he was preparing him—Martin Mendoza—to die. What else should he have expected?*

"What did you expect if you didn't ask for ransom?" Emily said.

"If you'll let me talk, I could tell you that we called the police later."

"Brookwood police?"

"The one and only Officer Tiles. We said it would take five million dollars to end it."

"Five million?"

"It was a nice round number." And again he slammed his palm on the table—*Blam!*

("Blam!" she says under her breath, mentally sticking yet another landing, and then finally she slides under the thin sheet.)

They slid the metal plate over by inches, the sun setting while they worked. When it looked like they could squeeze Martin through the opening, they hoisted him up. He hoped the gunmen got him from behind so he never saw it coming.

Brenda no longer saw what questions were coming. She listened to Emily ask them, and listened to Calvin answer them, and hoped the sound of their voices could vault her out of this fatigue.

(It is the vault that she loves best, though. Loves to soar. And before she can fall asleep, she visualizes standing with the gold around her neck, the national anthem playing, her parents cheering along with the entire massive crowd, knowing the vault is responsible for putting her up there.)

Martin knew that if he didn't want the responsibility of going up there, now was the time to speak. He looked at Mr. Pat, and then to Lindsey and Jodie. He was afraid, but he accepted his fate. They lifted him up. He felt the evening air on his wet hair, wet face. He swiveled his head looking for the kidnappers but saw just dirt in the narrow light. He yelled down that there was no one watching them.

"It's clear you and your brother weren't watching us."

"Is that a question?"

"I'm asking what you ended up doing?"

"After my brother talked to Al Tiles?"

"Yes."

"We went home and watched the Olympics."

"You're not serious?"

"American women had never medaled in individual gymnastics. That was fifty-six years, from 1928 in Amsterdam."

Emily exploded out of her chair. "We were buried in a moving truck and you were more concerned about Mary Lou Retton?"

"You sound like Jay. I'll tell you what I told him. I'd missed the men's all-around and I wasn't missing this."

(The men's team takes the gold, and she feels the vicarious glow, sees how it transforms them. They have written the first five words of their future obituaries: Former Olympic gold medal winner... She wants that for the women. And yet, an inauspicious start for them. A drop-to-the-knees dismount, a near-fall off the beam. Don't forget the Romanian judge Rotorescu is jobbing them on each routine, doling out scores to the Americans half a point lower than the other three judges. Coach Peters files four complaints, official protests. It's one thing to be beaten by a better opponent, another to be robbed. Their score drags them 1.75 points into second place.)

After Martin fought to drag the second of four granite slabs out of place, he tried lifting the plate up, but it was still too heavy. He rolled off the remaining slabs, his hands abraded and swollen, and, with Mr. Pat and the girls' help, moved the plate across the dirt, out of the way. He reached his hand down to start pulling the kids aboveground. The youngest were first: Andy Kraven, Jonathan Medina, Kaito Watanabe, Jennifer Bartoli. Martin warned them to stay small and quiet, out of the way. The gunmen could be anywhere, he said, which was true, even if the area looked deserted. It was what he believed. It was unthinkable that they had been abandoned.

"How could you abandon us in that container?" Emily said.

"Abandon? Look lady, I'm not your deadbeat dad."

"Why did you agree to this interview if you're not going to take it seriously?"

The lawyer jotted something on a sheet of paper and passed it to Calvin.

"My illustrious attorney has advised me to—what was the legal term you used, Jon, something in Latin?—oh, right, stopping jerking everyone off. And I'm nothing if not a sensible client. From here on out, I'll be a perfect little boy."

(She's perfect—10.00—on the vault and Julie McNamara is perfect—10.00—on the uneven bars, the first ever 10s by American women in the Olympics. They do what they can to claw back points. It's not enough. The final score is posted. Romania: 392.20, USA: 391.20, China: 388.60. Thirty-six years since the women's team medaled, London, 1948, the first post-WWII games. She knows she should be light and ebullient in celebration. Still, she is unsatisfied. She is not finished.)

Martin wasn't finished helping the kids up, but his arms shook, his muscles exhausted. He didn't know how much longer he could hold out. They kept coming: Sarah Ramsarup, Jennifer Strauss, Robert Avery, Christopher Armbrust, the Mashburn twins. All of them clung to him, threw their arms around him, tried to attach themselves to him like he was a stationary object, a boulder or tree. They were hungry and thirsty and repulsively dirty. "How many more?" he asked.

"A few," Pat said. "We're close."

Were they close to the end? Close at all? Brenda couldn't take it another minute. She made every effort to think of the one question that would end the interview, a question so outrageous, so out of bounds, the lawyer would put a stop to further questions. It should have been easy to think of, but she came up blank. She was too tired to think. She heard the drone of voices—Emily's, Calvin's, periodically the lawyer's—and she thought it would go on forever. She thought this concrete room was not unlike the moving van, but much, much brighter. She felt trapped by the walls and their voices and the impossibly bright lights.

(She heads into the brightest lights of her career, the individual all-around, with a slender .15-point lead over Szabo. She is tougher than the Romanian national champion she informs the media, but she might be talking for her own benefit, to convince herself. She enters Pauley Pavilion wearing the American flag leotard. Károlyi, at the games in an unofficial capacity, lurks in the photographers' pit. He bellows her name. She pumps her fists in the air.

He taught her to never watch her opponents. She can't control their performances. Don't give them any attention, he told her. She can't help but watch. On the beam, Szabo floats through one, two, three, four back handsprings, into a double back somersault dismount. The floor exercise is choreographed to "The Battle Hymn of the Republic," as if taunting the host nation in front of the world. She watches Szabo put up a predictably solid 9.90 on the uneven bars and finish in the lead with a final score of 79.125. She discovers that not even the silver medal is guaranteed this late in the competition.)

Their safety wasn't guaranteed, not at this late stage, even with only Pat Earl, Jodie Hoffman, and Doodoo Viscuso in the box. They almost forgot Doodoo. He was just coming to, after having finally fallen asleep, and he tilted his head and saw the pile of mattresses and Jodie standing on them. "What?" he said, meaning what were they doing, what was going on. His hoarse voice startled them. The bus driver asked if he could stand up. He said he knew the boy was hurt bad and he would do what he could to go easy on him but first he had to stand up. He also had to be quiet. He had to be tough, had to be a man, had to handle the pain in silence, because if he kept weeping and whimpering the gunmen were going to find out that they were escaping. Did Lance want that? What did he think the gunmen would do to them if they were caught?

"What did you think when you heard we were rescued?" Emily said.

"You weren't rescued, you bolted. Take a little credit for yourself."

This was the first time he said "you," referring to Brenda and Emily as his victims and not dancing around it with vague terms. Emily caught it right away, and she sat up in her chair, her body tensing. He was admitting that she and her sister were in the group of people he stole. It was difficult to tell if Brenda noticed the change in his phrasing. She'd stopped shielding her face with the legal pad, pretending to search her notes. She didn't look bad, but she sat there a spectator, not a participant.

"How did you find out we escaped?" Emily said.

"We were watching history being made—"

"Please stop talking about the Olympics."

"I'm answering your question. All of a sudden, the news breaks in and says you were out."

"You heard it on the news?"

"Everyone heard it on the news. I bet that's how your parents found out."

"Then what?"

"The world ended. I went from believing I was a few hours away from being a millionaire, to having the cops call the house."

"Looking for you?"

"They didn't know who did it. George owned Munsee Granite. It was his property. They called him down to the quarry to talk about it."

(Károlyi calls her over and he can't stop talking. He has her by the shoulders. "You need a ten, Mary Lou. Listen to me. Now or never, this is it, I want to see you now, see what you can do. You need a ten. You can control it. I know you can control it. It's now or never, you can do this.")

Mr. Pat told him it was now or never. He had to stand up and control himself. Doodoo got to his feet, tears just soaking his dirty face, but the only sound he made was his choppy breathing. Pat and Jodie lifted him up where, with his right arm pinned to his chest and his left arm reaching up, he met the face of Martin Mendoza. Doodoo was happy it was his friend taking him this last part. Martin pulled him up and they lay on the ground beside the hole, breathing hard, looking at each other.

"Ew," Doodoo said, "the Fish Faggot just tried to kiss me."

"Our own mother wouldn't even kiss us goodbye."

"She knew it was you."

"She didn't know shit. It was a lucky guess."

"But she was right."

"She just assumed the worst about us."

"But she was right. What am I missing?"

"She knew jackshit about what happened. You think she could hold off on jumping to conclusions for maybe five minutes?"

"Where did you go?"

"We camped out in Pheasant Hill Park for a few days. That was actually nice. We used to camp in our backyard when we were kids. It was kind of like that, except with more worrying about the manhunt."

"Why did you go there?"

"There weren't too many places we could go, you know, on account of the manhunt. The park was closed. There was a public works project, something about dredging eighty lakes."

(Eighty feet. The mat is eighty feet long. Eighty feet separates her and the stationary leather horse, which is five feet long, one foot wide, three and a half feet high. The springboard is in front of the horse. The trick is speed. There is physics involved, but she doesn't know about physics. She knows that the faster you run, the higher you're going to go. When she runs, she looks as though someone has stolen from her and she is chasing them down to take back what is hers.

She chalks her hands, rubs her palms together. There is the green light, the TV announcer says. She raises her right arm

     TIME WILL BREAK THE WORLD

over her head. And then she flies, her short hair bouncing as she tears up the mat. A half turn off the springboard onto the horse, she pushes herself into the air—the flashing cameras like strobe lights—and goes into the full-twisting layout double Tsuk, named for Mitsuo Tsukahara. Her feet hit the mat—*Blam!*—and they don't move. She is rooted in place. There is an almost imperceptible instance of silence between her sticking the landing and the awestruck eruption of the crowd, a scant delay between action and reaction, as though it takes them a moment to reconcile what they have just witnessed.)

It took them a moment to realize they were all aboveground. Pat brought the kids in close for a head count and then said to stay together. They ran crouched down in a group, away from the hole, following his lantern light. He didn't know where they were, but he found a dirt road. It had to lead somewhere. They ran, nineteen students and the bus driver, but it wasn't really running. They shuffled along like a gang of zombies. But he said to keep running, because to them it just meant to move. Move so you don't get caught.

"And then we were caught. The police swarmed us at the park, while we were stoking the campfire. They'd traced the moving van back to the auto auction. We'd paid cash and used aliases, but it didn't matter. The woman who filled out the title work identified us from photos. I always suspected our dad gave the cops our pictures, even though he swore until the day he died that he didn't. Maybe he was telling truth. He bankrolled our lawyers so I can't be too mad at him. Anyway, that was all she wrote. No money, no New Orleans, no Mexico, no happily ever after."

Emily decided to give him one last chance. "Do you have any regrets?" she asked.

"A man without regret isn't worth a crap."

"You know you've never apologized."

"We don't even know each other."

"I've sat in on your prior hearings. You've never said sorry, never showed remorse."

"My actions were a mistake. I've said that."

"That's not an apology."

"If I say sorry, what do I get?"

"What do you mean?"

"Will you forgive me?"

"You're incredible. You just don't fucking get it."

"Take it easy, princess."

("You did it, princess," her coach says when she runs into his arms.

The judges take their time. She waits. She waits. It's too much time, time enough for them to take it away from her. She waits.

Then the score hits the board. One. Zero. Point. Zero. Zero. Ten.

Gold.)

The gold blur of Mr. Pat's lantern bobbed ahead of the group. Martin hung near the back to make sure no one fell behind. He was completely drained. Lindsey was next to him and she whispered that what he had done was awesome. She called him Marty. She asked, whispering still, if he really tried to kiss Lance. The look on his face. Even in the dark, Lindsey saw his horror. She said she was kidding. It was only a joke, Marty. And she leaned over and kissed him, caught the corner of his mouth with hers. The look on his face. Horror still, but overlaid with something brighter.

They all ran behind the bus driver down the dirt road. "Hey, Pig Face," Emily said. She and Brenda ran hugging. "Together, we are safe." "Don't call me your name," Brenda said. "But yeah, we are. Can you believe it?"

"Can you believe this asshole?" Emily said to Brenda. That was it. That was enough. They were done here. It was time to go home. But by then, Brenda was sliding out of her chair without a sound onto the floor. Calvin pushed his chair back and moved to the far wall, going to his knees and putting his hands on his head, and said, "They're going to blame me for this." The lawyer ran to the door and banged on it. "Help! We need help!"

The floor was cool against Brenda's cheek. It didn't occur to her that she didn't belong down there.

(It never occurs to her not to do the second vault. It won't affect the outcome, the gold is hers, but her coach says, "Let's honor yourself. Do it for everybody who loves you. Do it one more time."

"I'm going to stick it," she says.

Another ten.)

Jason unpacked Styrofoam containers of cheeseburgers from Neptune Diner onto the dining room table and gave the house a final inspection. From his anxious eyes, everything looked in order. The WELCOME HOME banner smiled over the couch in the living room, the mirror surface of each letter glinting with afternoon light. Mylar balloons bumped against the ceiling, trailing ribbons. There were glass bowls of chips and dip on the coffee table, beer cooling in the fridge, mugs frosting in the freezer, and AC/DC rocking out through a portable speaker Angie brought over. Bertie was a stenotic bundle in her armchair, the TV remote clutched in one hand, a paper cup of Gallo Chablis in the other.

"What do you think? Pretty fancy?" he said.

"As long as I'm not the one cleaning it up," she said, and snorted.

She sipped the wine and gazed at the television. That she was her usual annoyed and annoying self was a comfort to Jason. Over time they'd reached a cruising altitude common to long-term relationships, but now they had to adapt to the new disruption in their lives. He didn't think he was exaggerating when he felt the atmosphere in the house today was altered—not better or worse, just different.

He scooped a handful of chips into his mouth.

"Who's Melvin?" she said.

"What?" he said, chewing.

"Who is Melvin?" Pleasure ignited her face.

"Are you stroking out on me? What are you talking about?"

"The cake on the counter. It says, 'Welcome Home, Melvin!'"

"Angie, can I see you in the kitchen?" he said.

Icing rosettes lined the circumference of the cake, and sure enough, there on the surface, beneath an American flag, in red cursive letters, was the typo Bertie had spotted.

"Illiterate Italians," he said, and raised a butter knife inches above the cake.

"You're going to make a mess," Angie said, and opened a beer for him and one for herself.

Calvin was upstairs. When he didn't come down for breakfast, they let him sleep in, but no one had seen him since he shut the door to his room last night after they picked him up from Coxsackie Correctional Center. His absence gave them time to set up the party, but here it was, three o'clock, and he had yet to join them.

"Do you want to go get him?" Angie said.

Jason sighed and drank half the beer in one go. He let the butter knife hover over the cake.

"Leave it," she said.

"I can hear you whispering in there," Bertie yelled. "There will be no secrets in my house."

"Shut it, Roberta," Angie said.

"Make yourself useful and pour me a refill."

The upstairs shower rushed to life, the water chugging through the pipes overhead.

"The guest of honor is getting ready," Jason said.

"How was he when you got him?"

Hard to say. By the time Calvin was processed and they were driving home, the sun had set, and his first view of the outside world was limited to electric light. He'd scrutinized the inside of Jason's car. The eight-year-old sedan was from another universe, alien technology. Jason wanted to use the ride to size Cal up and offer him a partnership in the handyman business, although since his arrest, his work had, in a word, sucked. He'd lost several steady jobs and was taking gigs up county for less money. The good news, if you could call it that, was that the police dropped the resisting arrest charge. Emily Mashburn-Bauer threatened a civil lawsuit, but the summons never came.

Instead of talking, Calvin examined the radio. It seemed to Jason that he wasn't leaving the horrors of life imprisonment for new opportunities, but that he was emerging from a bomb shelter into the wasteland of a world he only dimly remembered. In the backseat, Bertie hummed and tapped her cane against his headrest. She'd been skeptical that Calvin was getting out, even as they were driving to get him. Jason studied the traffic ahead of him and decided to leave his brother alone.

At the house, Cal stood in the doorway, dumbfounded, taking it all in. "You don't need an invitation," Bertie said. Jason showed him to his room, the guest room that never saw a guest. Jason had fixed the faulty light switch, and Angie bought new sheets for the bed and a potted plant for the window. They held back from further personalization, opting to let Calvin put his touches on the room. Jason asked if he wanted a beer, and Bertie asked if he wanted to watch TV. Cal just thanked them and closed the bedroom door.

"He was quiet," Jason told Angie.

The shower reduced to a trickle, then nothing.

"He's glad to be home, though, right?"

Jason shrugged and finished his beer.

"What is taking so damn long with my wine?" Bertie yelled.

Angie heaved the jug out of the fridge and left the kitchen. Jason frowned at the cake. *Melvin.*

They clapped when Calvin finally made his entrance. He was wearing the clothes Jason had bought him. His legs were shiny and pale sticking out of the baggy shorts. He didn't have a belt and kept hiking the waist up. His thin hair was damp from the shower, combed straight back. Prison-issued glasses in cheap plastic frames magnified his eyes, giving him a slightly terrified expression.

"Let's eat," he said, and hugged each of them, starting with Bertie.

That was the extent of his affection, or interest in conversation.

He devoured two burgers with his head down, elbows out, the frosted mug in front of him untouched, the glass going from opaque to transparent as it warmed. Cal wasn't acting without manners but making himself unavailable, going into isolation. It was so unlike him, Jason thought, until he realized that when he pictured his brother, a much younger person sprang to mind. All his hopes for Cal relied on him having preserved an underpinning of that former self.

They brought out the cake and Calvin was a sport about it, never mentioning the wrong name. He just asked about the American flag.

"I told the guy at the bakery you were coming home, and he assumed you were in the military. I didn't want to get into it," Jason said.

Then there was coffee and they were back in the living room, where Angie corralled them on the couch for a photo, Calvin in the middle, the WELCOME HOME banner above their heads. She took several pictures and even got Bertie to smile.

"How does it feel to be home?" Angie said.

"That's a good question. I'm going to go think about it," Calvin said, and pushed himself off the couch and went upstairs to his room.

Bertie leaned into the space he'd occupied. "Hey, you, come here to me," she said, crooking her finger at Jason, her face flushed with cheap wine, a smudge of ketchup in the corner of her mouth. "Listen up, it's you and me."

"You have to give him a chance, Mom."

"It's you and me. That's the way it's always been. Got it?"

Jason didn't have access to what his mother was really feeling. He guessed that she, like all of them, was groping for a sense of the familiar, the normal, something from the past to carry with them into this new arrangement and to hold like a talisman against the unknown. "Got it," he said, and wiped the ketchup away with his thumb.

SUNDAY, AUGUST 19, 1984

There was the parade route down Brookwood Boulevard into Village Memorial Park; and past the ballfields and picnic area there was the stage; and on the stage there was the podium and three rows of folding chairs; and near the stage there were the media—not just local but national print, radio, and television—who convened at the park hours ahead of the twelve noon start of Kids Day; and there was Mayor Brad MacDonald, grandmaster, wearing a blue and gold sash, leading the parade into the park, holding his wife's hand and raising it above their heads; and behind them, there was the Brookwood High School marching band, coming to formation in front of the stage, their unbreathable polyester uniforms like individual saunas on their bodies; and there was, behind the band, the Brookwood Fire Department in their Class A dress uniforms, hanging off the side of their polished engines, queasy from the hotdog and beer breakfast served at the station house; and there was the Brookwood Police Department, comfortable in their air-conditioned patrol cars; and there was the Chamber of Commerce float, the VFW float, the local troops of the Boy and Girl Scouts of America float, and the Brookwood Youth Athletics Association float, where Eddie Earl, Pat's grandson, captain of the Indians, fronted his team while hefting the Little League summer travel league championship trophy; and there, filling the chairs on stage, were the children, the passengers of Bus #8, Burnt Velveeta, and their driver Pat Earl; and there was Chief of Police Devine, and Principal Ferguson, and School Superintendent Tomasetti; and there was, blanketing the grass of Village Memorial Park, not only the entire Brookwood community, not only large sections of the neighboring towns and villages, but people who had traveled from out of state, whose lives had been briefly but indelibly touched by the story of the kidnapped students.

Mayor MacDonald stepped to the podium and welcomed everyone to Kids Day. He thanked them for coming. He spoke about why they were here and what they were celebrating. Their town had been tested, had encountered a trial unlike anything in its history, a truly one-of-a-kind ordeal and, confirming what he'd always known in his heart about this place he called home, they came out the other side better for it, their relationships strengthened, their spirit enriched. He didn't wish to take up too much of their time because the day wasn't about him, but before he handed over the microphone, he thanked them again and said he wanted to introduce a very special guest, someone who had taken a personal interest in the trouble they had so bravely faced. He asked them to put their hands together in a rousing Brookwood welcome for Vice President of the United States George Bush.

The marching band broke into their rendition of "Hail, Columbia," and the crowd exploded into a rousing greeting, and there he was, tall and lanky in a light-grey suit, waving at the crowd from the stage and shaking hands with the mayor, then shaking hands with the children and Pat Earl. He found the podium and leaned toward the microphone.

"I am honored to be standing next to these courageous young men and women who represent the best of what it means to be an American. Being an American is about facing challenges, not running from them, of pulling together and working as a team. I can tell you that Barbara and I were just taken aback by your resilience and..."

Officer Al Tiles stood next to the stage, sweating out the ungodly mishmash of chemicals he'd ingested the previous night. It wasn't his fault he'd backslid on his sobriety. He couldn't leave the house without someone buying him a drink and asking him to regale them with the saga of his heroism. After all, it was Tiles who found the bus at Butler Reservoir and then answered the phone at the station, coming voice to voice with Jason Schott and the ransom demand. As a civil servant, he felt he owed it to the public to give them what they wanted. One drink turned into several, a dozen, and then he always reunited with his old friend Benny Benzedrine. He swore to dry out again once the hoopla died down, definitely tomorrow. Probably tomorrow. Today was for partying, and he had good reason—a formal commendation presented by Chief Devine in front of the most important people in town.

But what was the deal with the vice president upstaging everyone? He didn't care about taking a backseat himself because he wasn't in it for the glory, but this was Kids Day, not Bush Day. Those kids had been through absolute hell and they deserved better than this reptilian politician drawing attention away from them. Like he said, he didn't care about how it affected him, he didn't become a cop for laurels, but the kids, the kids deserved better.

He palmed sweat off his face and shuffled his feet, the sun beating down on his patent leather shoes, making his toes feel on fire. He hoped Bush finished soon. He assumed he was getting the Medal of Honor, not because it was the highest citation available but because it was what he earned.

"...and what it all comes down to is this: your courage shows us what we are capable of when we set aside our differences and work toward a common good..."

The Medal of Honor was the kind of award that changed an officer's career trajectory, opening doors for him, not that Tiles was looking for greener pastures. But still, a little recognition would be nice for his sister to see, to show her what he'd made of himself. She was out there in the crowd.

"...so finally I want to say, God bless you and God bless America."

Thank God, it's over, Tiles thought. Chief Devine moved stiffly through his prepared remarks and Tiles finally heard his name. He bounded up the stairs and his right foot was on the stage when he heard the chief say, "On behalf of the Brookwood Police Department I'm honored to present Officer Alphonse Tiles with a Meritorious Police Duty Medal for a highly creditable, unusual police accomplishment."

An MPD? Not the Medal of Honor? Tiles felt like jumping off the stage, onto the marching band, diving headfirst into the tuba. Who had found the bus and kickstarted the whole investigation? Who had kept the kidnapper talking on the phone, keeping him calm so he didn't hurt the kids? Al Tiles, that's who. He forced himself across the stage, the eyes of the community were upon him. He figured he could clear things up in his speech. But the chief didn't let him anywhere near the podium, meeting him halfway, and pinning the medal on his chest.

While they saluted each other, Tiles whispered, "An MPD? That's all? Disgraceful."

"You smell like pickle and onion vomit, Shingles. Get your ass off the stage," Devine said through gritted teeth.

"Yes, sir," Tiles said, and departed.

The mayor returned and it was time to award the children with plaques. Doodoo Viscuso claimed his with his left hand, his right arm in a post-op sling. Martin Mendoza received a special commendation for courageous conduct, which he accepted wearing one of his father's work shirts. The collar was too big and the knot on his tie crooked. The crowd cheered, the cameras whirred, and Martin, at a loss what to do, put his hand over his heart, as if reciting the Pledge of Allegiance. Lindsey Robinson said, "Nice job, Marty," when he sat down. The swelling in her face was gone, the faded bruise concealed behind makeup. Pat Earl received a Key to the Town and a gift certificate good for one year of free haircuts at Nick's Barbershop.

Afterward, the band closed the ceremony with Van Halen's "Jump." Pat Earl and the kids gathered for photographs with the mayor and the police chief, and an aide from the Reagan-Bush campaign arranged a photo op with the vice president, who then climbed into the back of a black sedan driven by the Secret Service and rolled out of their lives.

Brenda and Emily found their parents and they fanned out with the rest of the town for the afternoon festivities, the food tents, the carnival games. Liz and Phil Mashburn had to temper their urge to never let the girls out of their sight again with their wish to let them be the children they always were. Since they'd escaped from the quarry, Brenda and Emily hadn't once spoken of what happened. They praised the nice nurses and doctors they met at the hospital, and they gushed over the beautiful reporter who interviewed them. But whenever their parents asked about the bus, or what took place in the buried moving van, they refused to answer. Liz and Phil couldn't get a word from either of them. Maybe the girls had repressed the memory, they thought, blocked it out, and that was probably for the best. But then one afternoon Liz overheard them talking about Pat Earl's hairy legs and the boy who tripped over them. They talked about it in a dreamy sort of way, and Liz couldn't tell if they were making it up. Brenda and Emily were always close, but now they were inseparable. If one left a room, the other followed. They shared a bedroom but now they slept in the same bed. Liz would find them in the morning entwined on the narrow mattress, or curled up on the floor, the windows thrown wide open. When she and Phil would check on them in the middle of the night, light pooled on the carpet outside the door because they wouldn't sleep in the dark. They heard the girls talking, but could never make out what they were saying.

Brenda and Emily had little interest in the plaques, passing them off to their parents as they ran for the jumping castle. One of the perks was that the kids from the school bus didn't have to wait in line, and they were ushered right to the front. Phil recognized two boys in the castle from the stage. They were wildly play fighting, screaming out, "Your time has come, Switchblade," and, "Never, Stingray, never."

Phil warned his daughters to be careful, to stay away from them, but Brenda said, "They're our friends, Dad," and she and Emily joined the melee.

They were double-timing it away from Temperate Territory. They passed Tropic Zone and Central Garden and came to the sea lion exhibit minutes ahead of the 1:30 feeding.

"Are you ready to watch the sea lions eat lunch?" Emily asked her sons while scanning the crowd for Brenda, who'd gone ahead to get them a spot. A crowd had already gathered on the stone steps around the pool. On a platform beside a rock formation jutting from the water, stood two zookeepers with buckets of herring hanging from their belts.

"I want to stay with the snow monkeys," Ryder said. "I want to live with them."

"Do you think they like peanut butter and jelly sandwiches? Is that what sea lions eat?"

"Snow monkeys," Sonny said, echoing his brother.

Emily lingered behind the crowd. She looked to her left and right. Why did they come to Central Park Zoo on the weekend when it was just teeming with people? Because Brenda invited them. Their meeting here was an unspoken reconciliation of sorts. They wouldn't spend the day addressing grievances because there was no need for a public clearing of the air, but it was the first time they saw each other all summer. The invitation itself was a gesture.

She pulled out her phone to text her sister but saw Brenda's slender arm waving wildly over her head.

"There's Aunt Brenda, let's go."

She had secured a coveted location. The boys could press their faces right up against the glass tank and practically kiss the sea lions swimming underwater.

"You don't know what I had to do to get this spot," she said.

"Was it of a sexual or violent nature?" Emily said.

"Both. I raped a marine biologist."

Emily laughed despite herself. Brenda looked great today, her voice clear and slightly musical, large gold earrings swaying when she talked, her white V-neck T-shirt revealing her tan chest and collarbones. Besides, there was no point in asking how she felt. Per Brenda, her post-concussion syndrome symptoms had ebbed, not that she would admit it if it weren't true. And Emily was forced to leave it at that. In the days after the interview with Calvin Schott, long, exasperating days, Emily attempted to take care of Brenda and to understand how she could have walked into that prison knowing she was so impaired and keep it a secret. In both instances her efforts were rebuffed, and she thought maybe they had finally found the limits of their sisterhood. The one unbridgeable imposition was not asking too much of the other, or being a burden, but going it alone, saying your concern was not valid and your help was neither needed nor wanted. Which was how Brenda preferred it when it came to her injury and recovery. Emily tried to involve their mother, but all Liz said was, "You're different people, Em."

Julio, the head zookeeper, introduced the two sea lions. Lulu and Raquel each weighed in at a willowy 280 pounds. Ryder and Sonny cackled when the zookeepers began tossing out the herring. The sea lions clamored out of the water onto the rocks and performed dog tricks. They sat, they rolled over, they spoke. They dove back into the pool and raced around the platform, high-fiving Julio at each pass.

"I've got something for you," Brenda said. She was holding a DVD in a paper sleeve.

Emily took the disc as if it were a bloody knife, holding it by the corner between two fingers. She slid it into her bag with a nod.

After the feeding they bought lunch at Dancing Crane Café and ate at an outside table.

"Hot dogs? French fries?" Brenda said to her nephews. "I

thought you were going to chow down on a big, fat, juicy herring."

The boys recoiled in disgust. "No, that's what you eat," Ryder said.

"Are you calling me a sea lion?"

The boys cracked up.

Between bites, Emily quickly slathered their faces with sunblock. She put the tube back in her bag and her hand reemerged with the DVD. She turned it over a couple of times, as if seeking additional information. "What is it like?"

"It's a professional piece of documentary filmmaking."

"Sounds awful."

Emily knew there would be no premier, no screenings at film festivals, no A.O. Scott or Manohla Dargis review in the *New York Times*. Brenda got word from her bosses that *They've Taken Our Children!*, clocking in at twenty-four minutes, would eventually stream on an online news service for paid subscribers.

"You did a good job," Brenda said, and stole a fry from Sonny, who was distracted by a pigeon walking under the table.

"Thanks," Emily said, though she felt like screaming, "So what?" She put the disc away and sipped from her bottle of water. "I wish they served wine here."

"I have a bottle of sparkling at home. It's a bit of a walk but we could cut through the park."

Emily couldn't remember the last time she'd seen the inside of Brenda's apartment. Did she still live in the doorman building, in the sunny one bedroom? She was positive the boys had never visited. It was still early and they had covered all the exhibits worth seeing. But what really tipped the scales for Emily was that Brenda was asking. Another gesture. "Sure. Why not?"

"Day drinking with the kids. You've got to love it," Brenda said.

That night, after she got home, after her sons had breakdowns from exhaustion and were finally fed, bathed, and put to bed, after she and Roger turned on an episode of *Dateline* where a white husband reported his white wife missing on a canoeing trip—only for the police to discover he murdered her for insurance—during which Roger fell asleep by the second commercial, Emily popped the DVD into the player. She hadn't intended to watch it, at least not right then. When they couldn't even edit a short video in time for the parole board, she'd convinced herself she could go the rest of her life without seeing a final product. Not that it would have mattered. Calvin put on a master class in allocution at the hearing. A command performance. One for the ages. That plus the letter of recommendation from the state senator, along with nearly thirty years' time served, did the trick. Tonight, he was as free as she was.

Before she pressed play, she understood she would be disappointed, and not because Calvin Schott was paroled. She just knew the movie couldn't live up to the perfect concept that had lived in her head before she started making it. All she could do was judge it by how far or close it came to her original idea. Or maybe there was a simpler way to assess it. It was completed, and that was adequate. She'd started it and seen it to its end, just like she had with her crusade to keep Calvin in prison, that larger project which occupied so many years of her life.

Earlier, at Brenda's, the boys were huddled on the leather pouf, watching a video on their tablet, and Sonny climbed off and shuffled over to the couch. He rested his hands on Brenda's lap and said, "I have to pee. Where's the bathroom?"

"I think it's down the hall," Emily started to answer, but her son looked at her as if she were interrupting an intimate conversation.

Brenda took him by the hand and walked him to the toilet.

When they returned, she was telling him, "I call her Pig Face and she calls me Pig Face."

"We're not allowed to say bad names," Sonny said.

"It's not a bad name the way we say it. It's a joke because we have the same face. Don't you think we look alike?"

"You're funny," Sonny said, and rejoined his brother on the

pouf, where he whispered to Ryder, "That lady thinks she looks like Mommy."

Hearing her son, Emily was caught off guard. Brenda was the person she considered herself closest to in her life and her children barely understood they were family. She wasn't sure how this had happened. Had she allowed it through inattention, or simply taken for granted that their bond was a permanent and static object known to everyone? They refilled their wine glasses and clinked them together and drank, and Brenda continued her story about a new project at work.

Now, Emily went to the kitchen for a glass of seltzer and settled in on the couch. She checked to see if Roger was still dozing and, finally, she pressed play.

It wasn't lost on me that the four of us together, not fighting, was rarer than a white peacock. We were watching the gymnastics. The phone rang and I assumed it was a friend from the club calling about our American girl who had just won gold, but it was Chief Devine for George. George listened for a while. Sometimes he said Jesus. He said he was on his way. Then he hung up.

You're not going to believe this, he said.

I waited for him to leave. Then: What did you two worthless shit-for-brains do this time? What have you done to this family?

I knew it was them. I don't know how I knew. I just knew. The same way I knew the quarry was evil. I told them to get out. I said grab your things and get in your car and go. They thought I was kicking them out, but I was telling them to run. Get out of town, out of the country, get out and don't look back. I couldn't save them this time.

They didn't fight. They didn't complain. Jason turned off the television. They went to their rooms. They were up there a while and then they came down and said, Goodbye, Mom.

Once they were caught, I was treated as if I dug the hole myself. The police interviewed me and George, skeptical that so much scheming went on under our roof and we didn't know about it. I don't want to talk about Jason's plea, Calvin's trial, the guilty verdict, the sentencing, the lawsuits, the closing of Munsee Granite, losing our big house and moving to a small house, George's deteriorating health and death. I won't parade my suffering. Think of all the families involved in this. You think they don't have bruises? Try to imagine the damage my sons did and you would still be off by a mile.

Years ago, after George died but before Jason came home, a woman engaged me over a pile of yellow onions at Save Mart. She was one of the mothers. One of my boys punched her daughter, she said. She said that she used to hate me as much as them, but not anymore. She'd forgiven me because she knew I was a victim too.

What am I supposed to do with your forgiveness? I told her. I said I didn't want it.

I thought that if I went back far enough, to a time when Uncle Fred still walked on both legs, and really combed through the story of how we got here, my family that is, I could reach a conclusion in which Calvin and Jason sprung unique into this world, uninformed of where they came from. But that woman near the onions at Save Mart got it right the first time when she blamed me. I blamed myself. This is the natural reaction of a mother. You need to take responsibility, to be the one accountable. It isn't a choice. If not you, then who? You look at your sons on their way out the door, believing it could be the last time you ever see them, and you say to yourself, This is my fault. You learned ages ago that you couldn't protect them from the world. You tried, but you didn't have the resources. No one did. So, fine, you couldn't stop the world from happening to them, but you could shoulder their share of the guilt, couldn't you, to make it lighter for them? You could transfer the blame to yourself and make it yours, even if it wasn't. Because if you couldn't do that much, if it wasn't your fault and never would be, if you couldn't follow a plumb line from their failure straight to your own heart, then what was the point of your silly little life?

What was the point of my silly little life?

ABOUT THE AUTHOR

Aaron Jacobs is the author of the novel The Abundant Life. Other writing of his has appeared in Tin House, Alaska Quarterly Review, The Main Street Rag, and elsewhere. He lives in Brooklyn and the Catskills with his wife and dog.

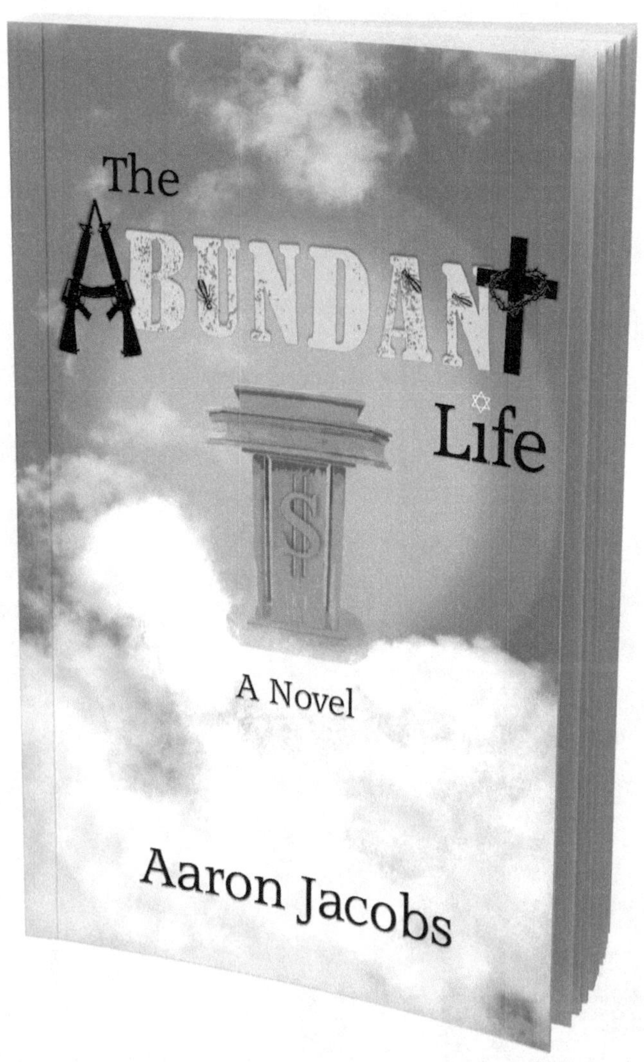
The
ABUNDANT
Life
A Novel
Aaron Jacobs

www.ingramcontent.com/pod-product-compliance
Lightning Source LLC
Chambersburg PA
CBHW021040310726
48969CB00006B/1738